NOW YOU KNOW

NORA VALTERS

For my grandma, Eileen

CONTENTS

PROLOGUE

F riday, 22 November.

Lauren Cohen, I see you.

There you are, in your perfect little life. Oblivious to anyone other than yourself. Oblivious to my feelings. Oblivious to me. Oblivious to the pain you've caused. Insulated from the real world, with layer upon padded layer that you've wrapped around your-self. Well, I'm going to unpeel them one by one. Strip you back until there's nothing left.

That bubble you're in is about to burst. And I'll be watching it all. I can't wait to see your downfall. It'll set me free. And to think you thought you'd got away with it. Ha! As if. I don't let things slide. I don't forgive and forget. No, I hold grudges. Why should you get away with it? Why should you happily carry on as if nothing happened? I'm out for revenge. With you taken care of, I can move on.

I've got it all worked out, you see. You're going to suffer, just like I did. Everything you inflicted on me is coming back to bite you, to gnaw you, to chew you up and spit you out. I'm a dog with a bone, unwilling to stop until it's finished – until *you're* finished.

Now, you'll know how it feels. Now, you'll know what you did. Now, you'll know who I am. And now you'll know just what I'm capable of.

Let the games begin.

1

"No. No, no, no, noooo." I swipe my finger back and forth along my laptop's mouse touchpad and frantically click the mouse buttons. "Aargh!" I slap the keyboard.

Madeline looks at me from behind the desk in her office and over her compact mirror, mid nose-powder, and raises a questioning eyebrow.

"The screen's gone blue," I exclaim.

My pitch presentation, the one I've been working on for the past three weeks, and the one that was looking spectacular with a couple of small tweaks left to make, has disappeared into the void to be replaced with a fear-inducing blank screen. My heart attempts to leap out of my chest, and my body temperature gauge flicks to 'furnace'.

A high-pitched squeal erupts from my laptop, as if it's being slowly tortured to death.

"What the hell is that noise, Lauren?" Madeline says, dropping her make-up and grimacing. She presses her palms into her ears.

I stab the power button. The screen goes from bright,

angry blue to a dead black, and the noise painfully peters out. "It's well and truly died."

Madeline sighs. "Well, you can't have much more left to do to the deck?"

I glare at my laptop as if it might magically restart, and then shake my head. "No, it was almost done. But the pitch is in three hours."

"I presume you saved it in the cloud?" Madeline eyes me.

I swallow. My answer is the difference between being in my boss' good books or jumping straight to the top of her out-of-favour list. And that's not a place anyone wants to be. I've spent the last four years working to stay on Madeline's good side. Saving to the cloud and not on personal desktops is company policy. Occasionally we all forget, but thankfully, this time I remembered, and she presumed correctly.

"Of course," I say.

Madeline gestures her pristinely manicured hand at her second laptop. "Use mine to access it."

She swivels her chair to face her first laptop and nudges her immaculately blow-dried hair off a shoulder. It's still black and thick, cut in a kind of Goldie Hawn shag, with the long fringe and layers perfectly framing her face, and belies her fifty-odd years.

No one else in the agency has two laptops, but Madeline Whittaker is not only the managing director but also the founder, setting up MBW with her now-retired husband, Bill, twenty years previously and building it up to the full-service marketing agency that it is today – the largest in Manchester.

Madeline can't abide unplugging and replugging in a laptop every time she leaves work and needs to take her laptop home, so she has two. One for the office, one for travelling. She's also the only one to have a private office, the rest of us working in the open-plan area outside her door.

I put my disgraced laptop on the coffee table, stand from the sofa and walk to her desk. In the few steps, I can feel the sweat behind my knees making my tights damp. I gently lift up my elbows to air my hot armpits. The last thing I need is to head into the pitch meeting smelling of BO. I take a long breath in through my nose.

It's going to be brilliant, I tell myself. *YOU'RE going to be brilliant.*

It's the first time Madeline has let me lead such a critical pitch for the agency. If we were to win it, we'd have business in every department: PR, which I head up, as well as content, advertising, web design, video design, email marketing, planning, and social media. It's the real deal – a major national supermarket chain. And Madeline knows as well as I do that I'm nailing it. Up until this technical glitch, the entire process has gone smoothly. And the pitch team crushed it in the presentation rehearsal yesterday.

I know she wanted me to put the finishing touches to the presentation in her office so it looks to all outside that she actually had some input. In truth, I've done the entire thing with Madeline's contribution being to request – sorry, *demand* – the agency's logo to be bigger on the first slide.

I pick up her second laptop. Madeline ignores me, looking at something on her screen. Her calmness makes my emotional, stressy outburst a few moments ago look ridiculous. I sit back on the sofa that faces her desk and open the laptop, powering it on.

"You need to put in your password," I say as nonchalantly as I can manage considering the pitch is mere hours away and it's the contract of a lifetime. I move to stand again, but Madeline holds up a palm to stop me.

"It's Whittaker123," she says, still not looking at me. "With a capital W."

I type in the password, and her laptop whirs to life. I log in to the cloud and click until I get to the New Business folder, find the name of the supermarket chain and navigate to my 'Lauren' folder within it. I scroll through all the numerous iterations of the PowerPoint presentation, looking for the one labelled 'Final Final FINAL'. I can't see it. A spike of fear lands squarely between my shoulder blades.

Calm down. It's there. It has to be there. I'm just stressed and not looking properly. I scan through the contents of the folder once again.

But it's not there.

"Oh, shit," I blurt.

This gets Madeline's attention. She finally looks at me. "Is there a problem?"

"The final version of the presentation isn't there."

"What do you mean… 'isn't there'?"

I hear the tinge of iciness in Madeline's tone and know I need to handle this delicately. I gulp back the anxiety that threatens to engulf me to evenly project my voice. "The final presentation isn't in the cloud anymore. It's gone."

Madeline purses her lips. "Oh, for goodness' sake. Call Rob. It'll be somewhere. You've probably accidentally saved it or moved it to the wrong folder." She looks away from me, as if problem solved.

But my panic spills over. "But what if he can't find it, the pitch is in three hours!" I bring my hand to my mouth.

"Lauren, Rob is excellent. I had a tech issue a few

weeks ago, and he solved it in minutes. He was a great hire. Imani recommended him, you know."

I smile tightly. Imani is so high up in Madeline's good books that she's practically a saint. She's my most junior team member. Smart, sharp, and stunning. But also very, very lazy with absolutely zero interest in applying herself. She's Madeline's daughter's best friend. And that's how she got the job.

I take my mobile off the table and dial Rob's number. I have the IT guy's mobile phone saved in my contacts, as everyone in the agency does, for emergency issues. I've never had to call him before, only ever emailed. My technical issues have never been urgent.

Rob answers with a less-than-confident hello.

"Hi, it's Lauren. I have an emergency. My laptop has died, and my extremely important pitch presentation isn't in the cloud where it should be. Madeline told me to call you because we need the presentation in a few hours' time." I name-drop the MD. It's bound to make things happen quicker.

There are a few moments of silence before Rob replies. "I'm working from home today. Can you come here? I'll text you the address. I'm about a thirty-minute drive from the office."

"Sure. I'm on my way," I say.

"Don't forget your laptop," Rob replies, with a strange *haw haw*.

It takes me a while to realise he's cracked a joke. An awkward, unfunny joke that I'm in no mood to humour. "Err, yeah. I'll see you in thirty." I hang up before he can say anything else, grab my laptop and practically sprint from Madeline's room, saying, "I'll be back shortly," to her as I leave.

I get to my desk in the open-plan office. My coat's hanging on the back of my chair, and I whip it off and put it on. As I wrap my scarf around my neck, Imani also stands and puts on her coat. It's 11 a.m. on a Friday. No one else in the PR department moves. It's too early for lunch, and Imani rarely goes out without a more senior member of staff to meetings.

"Where you off to?" I say as casually as possible as curiosity overcomes me.

"To get my nails done," she replies brazenly. "I've got a hot date later. Need to prep."

Cleo, my account manager, glances up at me, and I can sense the other three on my team listening to this conversation with indignation. Even the intern cocks an ear. Not one of us would dare to take off in the middle of a workday for a nail appointment. Not even me, and I'm the head of this department.

"Imani, you don't have this afternoon booked off as holiday," I reply.

I can feel my usually steady temper fraying. It's like I'm on a race-against-the-clock game show and can hear the tick counting down every second before the pitch meeting at 2 p.m. It's pounding in my ears, and the last thing I need is a headache. I need to be on form.

She snorts. "Holiday, pah." She pushes in her chair and gathers up her handbag.

I snap, "Imani, you are not leaving this office until 5.30 p.m. Your working hours are exactly the same as everybody else on this team."

She sighs dramatically, flicking her long, braided hair over one shoulder. "I just told you, I have a *date*."

"And I just told you, you aren't leaving this office until 5.30 p.m."

Imani tilts her head and screws up her lips. We stare at each other. The ticking booms in my ears. I don't have time for this. Sternly, I say, "Sit your arse back down."

Cleo whistles. Imani huffs, then yanks out her chair

and sits on it, giving me an unimpressed smirk and pulling off her jacket. "You're always pissing on my life," she mumbles under her breath, but I have no time to reprimand her.

"Off somewhere?" Cleo asks me as I scoop up my handbag and stuff my laptop and charger into the top of it.

"Yes. I have to go see the IT guy quickly," I reply. "I'll be back shortly," I say pointedly at Imani, who completely ignores me.

I dash for my car, which is parked in allocated parking next to the office building – a sign of MBW's success: a city-centre office with attached car park. I see Rob has texted me his address. I plug it into Google Maps and curse at every set of traffic lights that turn red and at anyone going slowly or taking ages to turn. I attempt to focus on my bit of the presentation, mentally running through the order of the slides and what I'll say, but I can't concentrate, and it flitters away.

After a thirty-minute drive, the app tells me my destination is on the left and that I have arrived. I look left to see a farmhouse and outbuildings surrounded by quite a bit of land. Not what I was expecting. I make a note to ask Rob about this place at the next work function. Not now, though. There's no time for polite chit-chat.

I pull into the driveway, parking behind a few industrial-sized containers and heavy equipment. It's a grey, overcast late November day, and I thank my lucky stars it's not raining. I got up an hour earlier this morning to blow-dry my shoulder-length blond hair and carefully apply make-up to look and feel my best for the new biz meeting.

There are a few buildings, and I read Rob's message again:

*Come round the back of the main farmhouse building. Back
door is always open.*

I pick my way through the damp gravel and knock
on the door, pushing it open. "Rob?"

"In here," comes the reply.

I step into the cosy kitchen and then through into a
large room with a fire crackling in the hearth. The room
is filled with tech hardware: screens, laptops, desktop
towers, boxes with flashing lights and speakers. It's a
complete contrast to the exposed brick walls and
cottagey feel of the building. Rob sits at a long desk with
his back to me, staring at something indistinguishable
on the screen in front of him.

I clear my throat, but Rob doesn't turn or even
acknowledge my presence. I try a second time. His
concentration breaks, and he swivels his chair around to
look at me. He says nothing. I realise I've never really
paid him much attention before, even though he's been
working at MBW for nearly a year now.

He's almost exactly how I would picture an IT
support professional, and I chastise myself for such
stereotypical thinking. He's slim, mid-height, probably
in his mid- to late-twenties with balding, fluffy, mousy-
coloured hair and a tufty, sparse beard with the chin
hairs growing a touch too long, curling under and
sticking out in odd directions. He has a wide forehead,
which tapers to a prominent V-shaped jaw. His facial
features are all slightly too petite, and his small, round
eyes are a little too far apart.

He wears impossibly unfashionable rectangular
metal-rimmed glasses that don't suit his face shape, a
grey jumper, baggy mid-blue jeans, grey socks with
some ancient dark-green Adidas Gazelles and a black

plastic digital watch that reminds me of something I had as a child.

"Lauren *Cohen*, right?" he says, then leans forward to look at something on another screen. "PR group account director, right?"

"Yes, that's me." I smile, but this is taking too long. "Here's my laptop. It died earlier – blue screen, weird noise. But more important is finding my presentation that's gone missing from the cloud."

"Mmm hmm," he replies, with zero urgency. He takes the laptop and puts it on the desk without opening it.

"I need the presentation for a meeting at 2 p.m. today," I say.

He hands me a pad and a pen. "Can you write down the name of the presentation and the folder it was in? And I'll take a look."

I scribble the information and hand both back to him.

Then he gives me a yellow Post-it note and the same pen. "And can you write your laptop password on here, please."

I do as he says. He takes the Post-it note from me and sticks it to the top of my laptop. He places my laptop next to two others, each with Post-it notes on top. Broken machines from other MBW employees, I assume. He spins so his back is to me and starts tapping on his keyboard. His screen is black with white text.

My patience evaporates after a few seconds, and I pace. Rob hasn't offered me a drink or suggested that I sit down on the ancient-looking sofa in one corner of the room. I wonder if I should sit anyway and whether the lumpy sofa cushions will swallow me up, when my phone rings.

It's my brother, Toby. "Just going outside to take this," I say to Rob, but he doesn't react.

I head back through the kitchen and stand outside the back door, welcoming the cool air on my flustered face.

"Hey," I answer.

"Hey, sis. You okay? You sound stressed."

"I've got a pitch meeting in a couple of hours, and I haven't finished the presentation, and my laptop died, and it's missing from the cloud."

"Oh," Toby replies.

Everything I just said probably went right over Toby's head. He's fifteen years younger than me at twenty-three. We share the same father, who divorced my mother when I was seven. Even though I'm thirty-eight, we're really close. He works in a fancy gin bar in town and has never stepped foot in an office.

He continues, "I'm sure you'll smash it."

"Thanks. What's up with you?"

He sighs, and I know a whinge is coming. I'm his more experienced, worldly-wise, agony-aunt older sister.

"It's Jenna," he says.

As soon as he mentions his girlfriend's name, I realise I'm not in the mood right now to dish out relationship advice.

"What's she done now?" I say tersely.

But Toby doesn't pick up on my impatient tone and ploughs on. "She's doing my head in. I can't do anything right. She has a go at me for literally everything. Urgh. I don't know what to do. Nothing I say is right…"

While Toby's talking, I hear Rob shout my name from inside.

I've heard this moan from Toby before. It's pretty

much all I've heard for the past two years he's been with Jenna.

Impatiently I blurt, "Just dump her already. Jeez, Tobe, this has been going on *forrreverrr*. You're clearly not happy, so get rid of her."

Toby is silent, not used to me being quite so direct.

I continue, "Look, gotta go. Speak later. Love you." I hang up before he can reply and dash back into the farmhouse.

Rob is standing, drinking green juice from a huge flask. He beckons me to him, sits in his chair and points to his screen. I lean over his shoulder to see my folder in the New Business drive.

"I've found your presentation."

"Yes!" I hug him from behind and stand up to do a little happy dance. "OMG, Rob, I could kiss you!"

He swivels his chair to look at me seriously. "I don't think my girlfriend would like that."

I'm not sure what I'm more shocked by: that he actually thought I'd kiss him, or that he has a girlfriend. "Oh, I, er... it's just an expression. Sorry."

He looks at me for a beat too long. Awkward.

"Could you open it?" I ask.

He swivels back around and clicks on the file.

The first slide pops up with the too-small-for-Madeline MBW logo, and my breakfast churns in my gut. "That's the old version. Before the designer made it look amazing. Are you sure that's the final, final, *final* one?"

"Absolutely certain. I recovered the file, and that's the only one in the cloud."

Don't freak out, Lauren. This is fixable. It has to be.

The ticking clock chimes in my ear, and I look at my watch. My heart booms. Only two hours to go before the pitch, and I don't have a finished presentation, and I'm in the middle-of-nowhere countryside. I need to get back to the office to sort this mess out. "Did you fix my laptop? Maybe it's on there?"

"Alas, no. That'll take a little longer. Looks like you've picked up a virus. Easy enough to do. You probably clicked on a link in a junk email."

I rack my brains but can't think of anything and shake my head. "I definitely haven't clicked on anything."

Rob shrugs, as if to say, 'everyone says that when they've clicked on something'. "I'll look at the laptop this afternoon and bring it in on Monday for you."

"Okay, great," I reply and turn towards the door. "Oh, no, wait." I turn back to Rob. "I'm not in the office on Monday."

"I can bring it in on Tuesday, then."

"Sorry, but I need it on Sunday."

Rob looks unimpressed.

I rally my emotions. The last thing I need today is for them to blast out from the depths like a geyser. I tell him the truth. Honesty is the best policy, after all. "It's my mum's funeral on Monday, and I need to print out some photos that I saved on the desktop."

Rob holds my gaze long enough to make me squirm a little and says, "Where do you live? I'm coming into town on Sunday, so can drop it over."

"Oh, thank you so much. In Chorlton, so on your way in from here. I'll text you my address. Gotta go. Thank you again, Rob."

He smiles, blinks twice and then turns his back on me. I let myself out, run to my car and race back to the office but get stuck in traffic, and the journey takes closer to an hour. I try not to let it ruffle me, glancing at my engagement ring and forcing myself to think of good things and the upcoming wedding, but it's no use. The stop-start frustration of bumper-to-bumper vehicles makes me shout "Come on!" and "Get out the way!" and "Why is EVERYONE on the road today?" about a million times.

When I arrive – traffic-stressed and running on adrenaline, the exact opposite of how I like to be before a major meeting: composed and laser-focused – the receptionist tells me Madeline and the rest of the pitch team have already headed over to the coffee shop opposite to talk through the presentation and that Madeline wants me to go straight there.

But I can't go straight there because *I don't have a fecking presentation.*

I run to my desk, clock that Imani is still there, and ask the intern if I can use her laptop. She diligently brings it over and, without taking off my coat or my handbag, I open the latest version that Rob recovered. I rapidly make all the tweaks to this presentation that I was making earlier to the sexily designed one. I bash the keys and swear every few seconds.

"All okay?" Cleo asks, knowing full well I'm not okay. I never usually get this frazzled.

"No. Pitch is in less than an hour, and the presentation is gone. Having to amend an old one."

"It'll be fine, Lauren. It's not titty now, is it?" She smiles.

This is a story I tell all my team before pitches and has become a bit of a legend to calm everyone's nerves and to remind us to prepare well in advance. My first-ever pitch was a traumatic experience that I vowed never to repeat and never to let any of my team members repeat. I'd been at my first PR job at a high-profile agency for three weeks when I was told I was attending a pitch, we were leaving in five minutes, that I had some slides to present that I'd never seen before, but it would all be fine.

It wasn't fine. I got massive stage fright, rambled some incoherent nonsense and then incorrectly pronounced the product 'titty-kah' instead of 'tea-teak-ah'. It was mortifying. For the first time in a long time, the memory gives me the shivers, and my nerves squirm like they did on that day.

"Where there's a will, there's a way," I reply to Cleo in a reassuring tone, as much to reassure myself as anyone else. This is NOT going to be a titty disaster. I need to get it together.

I make the final amend, press save on the Power-Point, close it down and give the intern back her laptop. I attempt to ignore the ache in my bladder and bypass the toilets on the way to the coffee shop, but it's no use. I dash in and wee as fast as I can and blot my armpits with toilet paper. I pat some powder on my shiny face in front of the mirror, rearrange my outfit, try not to care that I'm looking slightly disheveled and not the polished PR professional I was this morning, and hurry to the coffee shop.

Madeline is lording it over the pitch team, large coffee in hand, and raises her chin at me. The four others shift chairs to make space for me, but Madeline sips her drink.

"Well?" she demands.

"Technical difficulties. Rob found the old presentation, but the designed version is gone. It looks basic, but all the content is there, and it'll have to do."

She glares at me for a long time, and the pitch team collectively hold their breath. Then she nods to her second travelling laptop, which is on the table. "Open it and we'll go through it."

"Right."

As I open the file, one of the pitch team goes to the counter to get me a coffee. By the time he's come back, the presentation is ready. I pick up the cup. My hand trembles. I put it down again. I never get this nervous before pitches, but the dead laptop/lost file rigmarole has turned me inside out, as if timed perfectly to exert maximum pressure and cause the most carnage.

I take a deep breath. I've got this. Forget the virus on my laptop and how it got there, I have a presentation.

"Let's go through this, then," I say over the chatter around the table, and all go quiet to look at me.

I quickly run through the slides, remind each person of their part and give a debrief about the supermarket chain, the people we'll be pitching to, and remind everyone of the pitch brief and the contract should we win it. When I'm done, there's a palpable buzz about the table.

"We've nailed the brief and, yes, the presentation could look better, but we know our stuff. We're going to win this business," I say.

The creative director slaps the table, and I get a couple of whoops. I grin, smooth my flyaway hair, which is now looking more limp than sleek blow-out, and peek at Madeline. She's smiling, like a matriarch surveying her talented brood.

I look at my watch and stand. "Let's flag a couple of taxis over to their office. I've got the address."

As we're leaving the coffee shop, Madeline positions herself to ensure she's not in the same taxi as me. And I know, even though the lost presentation wasn't my fault, that I've fallen out of favour.

2

After a what-should've-been-a-disaster-but-actually-turned-out-awesome pitch on Friday afternoon, I allowed myself Friday evening to destress by binge-watching a steamy period drama on Netflix.

On Saturday I sacked off my morning exercise class to catch up on some sleep and chill out on the sofa, daydreaming about the wedding, googling idyllic honeymoon destinations, scouring Pinterest for wedding dress inspo and researching home décor ideas to update our bathroom.

But I wake early on Sunday knowing I've got tons to do ahead of tomorrow.

I write out a to-do list and set about tidying the house and doing a thorough deep clean. It's not too bad; I like to keep on top of it. I enjoy cleaning, finding it relaxing and satisfying. Sometimes I'll listen to an audiobook or music. But often I just like quiet. My best mate calls me Monica from *Friends*, and I'm quite proud of that comparison.

When I first moved in with my fiancé, I worried he'd

be a nightmare to live with. Messy and with an aversion to cleanliness. I thought, I love him, I'm just going to have to put up with it. But – to my delight and the jealous grumblings of my mates with untidy partners – I couldn't have been more wrong.

It turned out I fell in love with a fellow clean freak. Hurrah. Akshay and I have been known to draw straws as to who gets to clean the bathroom – the winner cheerfully donning their rubber gloves, the loser having to wait for the next time.

Gosh, I've missed him like crazy these past two months that he's been in New York for work, but he's back today. And I can barely contain my excitement, twittering around the house like a chirpy bird.

As I'm unloading the dishwasher, wiping every item on a tea towel just to make sure it's definitely dry and to avoid any annoying smears on the glassware, my phone pings. My insides go all fuzzy when I open WhatsApp and see it's Akshay.

Just landed. Waiting for luggage. Should be home in an hour or so. Can't wait to see you xxx

I reply:

See you soon. CANNOT wait to see you too.

I rush upstairs and slip on my new sexy underwear, purchased especially for this occasion, my luxe, cosy-but-sexy loungewear that hugs my average-sized figure in all the right places, and some super-soft cashmere socks. I dry my still-damp hair from my earlier shower and apply a touch of make-up and a spritz of perfume. I slick on some lip gloss.

My phone pings again. But this time it's not Akshay. It's a message from Toby.

I've finally done it. I took your advice and dumped Jenna.

I tap out a message to my brother.

How are you feeling about it?

Happy. Should've done it ages ago.

Good. Must mean it's for the best.

I experience a flash of joy at this news. Jenna is a sweet girl, not exactly the sharpest tool in the shed, but she and Toby never quite gelled in my mind – their two-year relationship always riddled with tumultuous drama rather than coupled-up, googly-eyed bliss.

I think of the time about a year ago when the four of us went out on a double date. Akshay and I had fun keeping up with the 'kids' and let them choose the bars and restaurant we went to. Jenna and I ended up syncing our comfort breaks and were stood in the queue for the toilets when Jenna, very drunk at this point, and I, not so drunk but still pretty far gone, ended up having a rambling heart-to-heart, which didn't end very well.

Jenna: I don't think you like me. I don't think you've ever liked me.

Me: Noooooo, I like you.

Jenna: You're just saying that.

Me: Am not.

Jenna: Are. I don't think you think I'm good enough for your brother. You think he can do better.

Me: *Whaaat*, nonsense.

Jenna (shouting): Stop lying!

Me: ...

Jenna: You'd be happier if he was dating someone else. I know it. But we're happy and I'm not going ANYWHERE.

Me: Okay... (Pointing at an empty cubicle) Your turn.

This conversation was forgotten by the time we'd left the toilets and returned to our men to then – at Toby's insistence – go clubbing until 2 a.m. I have a feeling Jenna doesn't even remember it. But I do. And she was right. Although it's not that I didn't think she was good enough, it's more that Toby never seemed completely smitten with her. And that's what bothered me.

Although I didn't mean to so bluntly tell him to dump Jenna on Friday, I'm pleased it's worked out for him.

I see Toby's typing, and a second later another message pops up:

She didn't take it well. At. All.

I frown and tap out a reply.

How come?

We were at hers, and she TOTALLY freaked out. I mean, she threw a proper tantrum. She punched her bedroom wall and actually put her fist through it. Her flatmate had to come in to calm things down.

Wow. Who knew Jenna has such a violent streak?!

It was insane.

What did you do?

*I left Cammy to it. She was doing a good job of consoling J
and told me to go home.*

Have you spoken to Jenna since?

Nope. Hopefully won't have to again.

I send him the thumbs-up emoji just as the doorbell chimes. I jump up and fly down the stairs, taking a deep breath and partly unzipping my hoodie to show off a big dollop of cleavage. I fix my most alluring pout on my face and – as sultry as possible – open the door.

"Hello, sexy," I say in a way I hope is as seductive as Marilyn Monroe.

But it's not Akshay. Of course not, I realise in my excited haste, he has a key.

It's the IT guy.

Rob has my laptop under an arm, and his eyes almost pop out of his head at my blatant 'come to bed' performance.

I blush hard. I completely forgot he was coming over today. He probably thinks I've made a massive effort for him. *Cringe.* "Oh, er, hi. Sorry, thought you were my fiancé."

He recovers himself, tears his gaze from my boobs and finds his voice. "I've got your laptop working. Can I come in and show you?"

"Sure, come in."

Rob steps into the house, and I close the door behind him, fumbling to do up my zip as quickly as possible. I edge around him in the hallway and lead him through to the lounge at the back of the house, walking as stiffly as possible so as not to draw attention to my bum in these knitted joggers that skim and accentuate it. I bought this loungewear set to only ever wear in the house and only ever in front of Akshay. I gesture to the dining table, and Rob heads there to set up my laptop.

"Do you want a drink? Cup of tea?" I ask, hoping he'll say no and this will be a brief visit. I want him gone before Akshay arrives.

"Glass of water, please," Rob replies while pulling out a chair, but he doesn't sit on it. He powers up my laptop.

I head into the kitchen and pour him a glass of water. When I return, he's taken off his coat and put it over the back of the chair next to the one he's pulled out. His scarf is also neatly folded and hung over the top, and his gloves are on top of that.

Dammit, he looks like he's here for an extended visit. He gazes purposely around the room and out the window with interest, as if taking in every detail.

"Here you are," I say and place his glass on a coaster next to the laptop.

"Thanks." He indicates to my garden. "Your fence panel is down."

"Yes. Been down a while. Need to get it fixed. Haven't had a chance recently."

"I know someone who can come and fix it. He works on the farm. Do you want his number?"

"Oh, thank you, but no, it's fine. My dad will come and do it with my fiancé at some point. My dad's a massive DIY fan. Honestly, he'd be really put out if I got someone else in to do it."

I laugh, but Rob doesn't. He gestures for me to sit in the pulled-out chair. Cursing under my breath, I oblige. He leans over me to place a finger on the mouse touch-pad. The yellow Post-it note with my writing is stuck under the keyboard. He glances at it and types in my password.

His proximity to me is a smidgen too close, his

armpit pretty much over my shoulder, torso almost touching my arm and elbow nearly knocking my boob. I tilt in the opposite direction to regain my personal space, but he's oblivious. This must be a move he does with everyone.

Not looking at me, his eyes fixed on the screen, he says, "So, I basically had to download everything off your desktop onto a hard drive, then restore factory settings and reinstall everything. A few things might have moved about, and you'll need to download non-work-related apps like Spotify again, but there's no data loss." He uses the mouse cursor to point things out on my desktop.

"Oh my goodness, that's great news. Thanks so much, Rob. I was so worried that I'd lost important files and documents. Phew."

He pauses what he's doing and takes a long inhale through his nose. "What perfume are you wearing?" he asks.

I'm a little taken aback, but he's asked so innocently, as if asking me where the dining table is from (Ikea, of course).

"It's Daisy by Marc Jacobs," I reply.

He nods and then hovers the cursor over a folder labelled 'Lauren's Desktop' and says, "Your, ahem, personal folder is now in here."

He stumbles over the word 'personal', as it's against company policy to use our work laptops for personal use. But everyone does. My own personal laptop is ancient, and I can't actually remember the last time I turned it on.

"So all my documents are definitely fine? All my photos?" I ask.

"Yes."

"And it's working again as usual?"

"Yes. In fact, it should all work a lot quicker as I got rid of some redundant programs that were clogging up the memory."

"Wonderful," I reply and attempt to shift my seat back to hint that it's time for Rob to leave, but he's still lingering behind me. I feel hemmed in by his presence.

Rob has done me a massive favour and an excellent job, and I don't want to sound ungrateful, but... Akshay will be home any minute. And that is pretty much all I can think about.

Trying not to sound impatient, I ask, "Is there something else?"

"Yes." He clicks a few things and then indicates a box. "Can you put in a new password."

He makes a point of turning his back on me while I type it in like some servers do at restaurants when you tap in your bank card's pin code to their handheld card machines. He turns back when he hears I've stopped typing.

"All done," I say.

"Perfect." He peels off the Post-it note and screws it up in his hand and puts the squashed paper on the dining table. "Please bin that."

"Yes, of course," I reply with a hint of sarcasm. "Thought you were going to ask me to eat it or flush it down the toilet or burn it dramatically in an ashtray. Or maybe tell me that it's about to self-destruct." I laugh at my joke, but Rob is baffled. "Like in spy movies. No?"

He clearly has no idea what I'm referring to and says, "To ensure you don't download any more viruses, you need to make sure you don't click on any links in suspicious emails—"

But his voice trails off as the front door opens, and I hear Akshay's cheery, "Hey."

"Don't click links in dodgy emails. Got it," I quickly say to Rob. "Is that all?"

"Yes."

"Amazing. Thank you so, so much for dropping it over on a Sunday. I owe you big time. I'll show you out."

I stand and Rob backs away. He picks up his coat, gloves and scarf, and I usher him from the lounge into the hallway, where Akshay is rolling his suitcase in through the front door.

Akshay looks up. "Oh, hi."

"Akshay, this is Rob from the IT department at work. Rob, this is Akshay."

A curious energy crackles between them. For a moment I think they might know each other, but it's not that. Akshay looks directly at Rob, attempting to make eye contact, to suss him out, but Rob stares intensely at the floor and looks everywhere but at Akshay. It makes Rob look guilty. Of what? I don't know.

Akshay's hand twitches to shake Rob's, but he holds it back. My fiancé must sense Rob's severe discomfort at this situation and realises a handshake might tip the poor guy over the edge.

Rob's hands are firmly planted by his sides, and he almost looks as if he's cowering from Akshay. Which is odd. My fiancé is agreeable, personable, and not in any way intimidating.

I didn't realise quite how shy Rob is and have an urge to protect him. To explain Rob's presence to Akshay and help ease Rob's obviously crippling social anxiety at the same time, I continue brightly, "My laptop got a virus on Friday, and Rob fixed it. I need it for tomorrow."

"Right." Akshay smiles his big warm smile.

Rob nods and squeezes past Akshay, who takes up

most of the hallway, by turning sideways and sliding his back along the wall. He hurriedly dashes out the front door, still clutching his coat, gloves, and scarf. Akshay watches him go and then closes the front door.

He turns back to me and frowns. "Not the welcome I was expecting, that's for sure."

3

I run towards Akshay and practically leap onto him. He's about an inch taller than me with a lean, athletic build and just about holds up my less-than-petite frame.

"Oh, my love," I say as I pepper him with little kisses, "it's been sooooo long. I've missed you so much. That's the longest time we've ever been apart. Don't ever go away for that long again, promise?"

He chuckles but gently extricates himself from me, a hint of frown still lingering across his brow.

"Gosh, I'm shattered after that long flight. I need to sit down." He makes sure my feet touch down and then wanders into the lounge and sinks onto the sofa.

I follow him, not able to keep my hands off him, touching his back, arms, neck. As if my hands need to remind themselves of every little bit of his form. And my eyes are locked on him, greedily taking in every little detail once again: his thick black hair with barely any grey is gelled up and over, as usual, but I know that when its freshly washed, it's floppy and enviably silky.

He has clear, smooth brown skin on his long slim

face with a slight double chin. His long nose is a touch wonky at the tip, bending to the left. It's set off by his heart-shaped mouth with a lower lip that is marginally thicker on the right side. I find this little zigzag of his face endearing, but it's his deep brown eyes that get me every time. I fully believe they're the definition of 'smouldering'.

I kneel on the sofa next to him, beaming from ear to ear and pawing at him like a kitten kneading its mother. I swear I'd purr if I could. This man renewed my faith in men. I called it off with my first fiancé. I just knew in my gut he wasn't the one even though everything seemed perfect on the surface. It was painful at the time, but thank goodness I did it because more than ten years later I met the love of my life.

I fancied Akshay the moment I set eyes on his Hinge online dating profile, and we had an instant connection, messaging for a couple of weeks before having a Zoom date and then meeting in person. And the rest, as they say, is history.

"Do you know how long it is until the wedding?" I ask.

Akshay looks to the ceiling, calculating, but I can't wait.

"Eight months and three days," I squeal excitedly, his presence making me giddy.

"Wow, that's precise."

"I have a countdown app. It also tells you how long to go in heartbeats."

"Hmm," he replies, unimpressed.

"Hmm?" I tickle him. "Aren't you excited?"

He yawns and looks away from me.

"Akshay, what's the matter? Come on, out with it."

"Okay, fine. You're all dolled up, and I come in to another man in the house. That was... well... weird."

Akshay and I have never once doubted one another. We have had full-on trust since day one. I grin at him.

"Babe, number one – if I were having an affair, do you think I'd have the man in the house when you were due home? And two, do you honestly think I'd be having an affair with the geeky IT guy?"

I laugh and snuggle into him, and his frostiness melts.

I continue, "You are the most handsomest, sexiest, kindest, funniest, most awesomest man in the whole wide world. I haven't seen you in two long months, and all this"—I slowly unzip my cashmere hoodie to reveal my new sexy bra—"is for you, you idiot."

Akshay's face transforms; his frown dissolves to be replaced with a lusty grin and a twinkle in his eyes. One of my favourite looks of his.

He kisses me and trails a slow fingertip from behind my ear, down my neck and to between my cleavage. "Suddenly I don't feel so tired anymore."

I hold him away. "Oh yes, I forgot. You're shattered. I don't want to tire you out any more..." I fake-turn away from him, but he takes the bait.

"Come here, you." He spins me onto my back on the sofa and edges on top, nuzzling my neck.

AFTER SOME MIND-BLOWING SEX, we cuddle until the sun goes down, and my stomach gurgles.

"I'll fix us some dinner," Akshay says. "And then we need to sort everything out for tomorrow."

I nod. My mother's funeral is finally upon us. When mum died, Akshay was away, but we spent hours on the phone, me grieving and him being my support, my rock. No matter the time in New York, he listened to me babble about my childhood and happy memories of

Mum and asked questions that showed he was paying attention. His unconditional, unwavering emotional support made me love him even more. And it bodes well for our marriage – for better or for worse, we'll get through anything together.

As Akshay clatters pans and bustles around the kitchen – his favourite domain in the house – I go to the dining table and tap a key on my laptop to wake it up. The screensaver disappears to reveal my desktop. I find the folder with all the photos of my mum that I'd spent hours finding in old albums, scanning and saving.

It had been traumatic going to her apartment after she died to find the box of albums and the few USB sticks that she'd organised. And I haven't gone back. I'll sort it out after the funeral, when I'm ready. She put all her affairs in order before she passed, talking me through the details – I inherited my organisational tendencies from her, that much is clear. She left every-thing to me, her only child, so there's no rush to do anything, thank goodness.

"Saag paneer sound good to you?" Akshay calls from the kitchen area.

The dining room, lounge area, and kitchen are open plan with a sliding glass door out to our small garden. Akshay and I purchased this semi-detached house shortly after he asked me to marry him six months ago. It's our dream first house. I sold my city-centre apart-ment, and Akshay sold his small terrace house to afford it. As soon as we walked inside at the first viewing, we both knew: it was home. Our home. We have plans to upsize, of course, when we have the money and when we've outgrown it by filling the place with children, but for now these four walls are a safe, comfortable, wonderful place to live.

"Sounds delicious," I reply. "I've seriously missed your cooking."

I hear him rummaging in cupboards.

"Have we got any ghee?"

"Yup. In the usual place," I reply. Akshay, for all his incredible qualities, is not so great when it comes to looking for things in obvious places.

"Ah yeah, here we go."

I stocked up on Thursday with all his favourite ingredients to cook with, as well as his favourite orange juice and coffee beans. I've pretty much been living on pasta and tomato sauce for two months, too shattered and overcome with sadness to make myself anything more demanding.

I print out all my favourite photos of Mum and all the photos she'd made me promise to have out at her funeral. Photos of my uncles and aunts, my grandparents, her best friends, me as a baby and her in happier times with my father, Keith, in his seventies flares. And lots of hilarious pictures over the years of her and her twin sister, Joyce, in matching outfits. Including more recently when, much to everyone's surprise, they wore the same dress to their sixtieth birthday party just for a laugh.

After pressing print on the last few photos, I pop into the small front room, which we use as an office slash dumping ground, as we don't have a garage. The printer is busy whirring away, and I thank the tech gods that it has decided to work today. Although I know Akshay would be able to coax it back to life; he's a lot savvier with gadgets than me.

I head back to the dining table, kissing Akshay on the cheek as I pass through the kitchen and pinching his pert bum.

"Cheeky," he says as he chops onions as fast as a professional chef.

I print out my reading and go through it again on the screen. My heart hitches, and I fret for the umpteenth time that I'll clam up with grief and won't be able to get my words out.

For you, Mum, I whisper, *I'll do it for you.*

I spent a few hours writing and rewriting this speech, wanting it to tell my mum's story in just the right way – with the appropriate humour, as she was known for her sense of humour and funny stories, but with the right amount of respect for the occasion too. It was hard. With every sentence, fresh grief speared my soul. But I'm happy with it now.

Tears come to my eyes as I look again at a photo of Mum and her twin sister. Judy and Joyce. When Mum had been diagnosed with breast cancer five years earlier, she'd been determined to live her life to the fullest and had made many trips to Portugal in between chemo treatments to stay with Joyce and her husband at their holiday home. But near the end, she'd been in the hospital. She was about to be moved to a hospice when she passed, with me holding one hand and Auntie Joyce holding the other.

Her last words to us before she slipped away: "I've had so much fun."

The memory pushes up a great sob, and before I know it, I'm bawling. Great floods spill from my eyes and stream down my face.

Akshay is at my side in an instant, his comforting arms tightly wrap around me. He pulls me up from the chair so he can hug me, and I cry into his shoulder. He soothingly rubs my back. But this small gesture reminds me of Mum rubbing my back as a child, night after night, when I was convinced a monster lived under my bed.

"She was the best mum," I sob.

"I know, Lauren. I only knew her briefly, but she was a very special woman and so welcoming of me."

"I just wish she could've made it to our wedding." I sob harder.

"She'll be there in spirit, my love."

Something in the kitchen sizzles and spits.

"It's the rice boiling over," Akshay continues but makes no move to leave me.

I pull away from his embrace. "Go and deal with it. I'll be okay."

He gives me a look as if to say, are you sure, it's only rice.

I continue with a weak smile, "And besides, I'm desperate to eat some of your incredible cooking after two months. Go."

He smiles, kisses my forehead, and goes to rescue his rice.

I wipe my eyes and find a tissue to blow my nose. I head back into the front room to find the Blu Tack and grab the printouts, checking all are there. I spread them out on the dining table.

"I was thinking we could stick these up around the walls and leave a few on the coffee table," I say.

"Sounds like a perfect idea."

Akshay turns on the extractor fan above the hob and starts noisily frying the onions, ginger, and garlic. I head to the window, pull up the blind and open it a crack to let the smell out and take a long, calming breath of cool air.

I walk to the kitchen and watch Akshay cooking for a while, fidgeting and huffing, until he turns to me and says, "Do you want to sort out my laundry?"

"OMG, I thought you'd never ask!"

He laughs. "I thought that might cheer you up a bit. Everything in my suitcase needs a wash. I'll take my suit to the dry cleaners later in the week."

I clap my hands and head into the hallway where Akshay's luggage is. I love doing laundry – especially an entire suitcase full after a trip away. I find it strangely therapeutic sorting the contents of the linen basket into piles and can happily stand watching clothes spinning around in the washing machine drum for minutes at a time.

I settle Akshay's suitcase on the floor, unlock it with the same pin code as I use for my suitcase lock, unzip it and start organising into whites, colours, darks on the hallway floor, putting aside his suit jacket and trousers that are neatly folded on top.

As I pull out a white shirt, I notice a splodge of something just under the collar at the front. I sniff at it, but it has no scent. It looks like make-up, a smear of foundation or concealer. But it can't be that. He's probably dropped his dinner down him or splashed himself with sauce from a sloppy sandwich.

I decide to do the white pile first, gather it up and take it through to the washing machine. I spritz the stain with stain remover and give it a good massage. In a stain-versus-Lauren contest, it's very rare that the stain wins.

After I start the washing machine, I wander back through to the kitchen.

"First load on," I say.

"Thank you, my wonderful laundry fairy." Akshay kisses me on the cheek and then asks Alexa to play some music. He loves to cook with a soundtrack.

I begin to set the table at the end not covered with printouts while he sings to 'Mr Brightside' by The

Killers. A mobile phone rings. It's not a ringtone I recognise. I see Akshay's phone on the coffee table, and grab it. But it's silent. Oh no, has Rob left his here by mistake? Or dropped it when he dashed past Akshay? I listen for the ring and track it to the hallway and pinpoint it to Akshay's hand luggage. I pick up the bag and take it through to the kitchen, holding it in front of Akshay.

"Babe, your bag's ringing."

He waves the bag away. "It's nothing. It's my second phone."

"Second phone?" I repeat. This is the first I've heard about a second phone.

"Yeah. Work gave me another one with a US SIM card in it. Some of my US colleagues can't get their head around calling my UK number."

"Do you want me to see who it is, in case it's urgent? Otherwise why would anyone call you on a Sunday?"

"Honestly, the working hours are insane over there. They work every day, no matter if it's the weekend. It'll be nothing."

This response surprises me. Akshay is the epitome of hard-working – another reason we get on, both of us career-driven and conscientious – and it's not like him to ignore a work call. He probably feels he needs to be watchful of me after my little wobble. So, ever helpful and not wanting him to get into trouble with his work, I fish the phone out of the side pocket and look at the screen. Maya.

"Are you sure you don't want to answer it? It's Maya."

"No," Akshay replies a little too fast for my liking.

It sparks my interest. "Who's Maya?"

"A New York office colleague who I was working with on the project. It'll be some stupid question about some minor part of the contract. She can wait until Tuesday."

And with that he turns back to making his curry, humming to himself.

Maya. Beautiful name for a beautiful woman? I wonder. Akshay has some serious moral principles, and there's absolutely no way he would cheat on me, or cheat on anyone. But I'm curious. I sit on the sofa, pick up my phone and search Maya, New York, and the name of his management consultant firm. She immediately pops up under the people section of the firm's website. Yep. She's a beauty. Of Indian heritage like Akshay and a similar age to us.

The smallest ding of jealousy sounds between my ears, but, as the smell of my fiancé's incredible cooking wafts from the kitchen, I know he'd never do anything to hurt me. He's the man I plan to marry, and he's the man I plan to have babies with. I never felt ready to start a family until I met Akshay.

It all feels so, so right.

4

The following morning, I stare out the window into the garden. The Manchester mist soaks everything with a fine rain that flies in from all directions. The bleak, grey sky reflects my mood. The funeral is to be held at the same church where Mum and Dad married, the one Mum still frequented every now and then for Sunday service and community events.

It's not for a couple of hours, but I'm all ready to go in my black dress, black heels and black jacket. A heavy, hollow ball of grief swirls in the pit of my stomach, and I have a stabbing pain right in the centre of my chest, which hurts every time I breathe in.

Akshay potters in the kitchen, cleaning up after our breakfast. He likes to keep it spick and span in there, primed and ready to cook the next meal.

It reminds me of Mum. She loved to cook, too. A memory comes to me then of when Mum first bought me a McDonald's. I'd never been a fussy eater as a child, wolfing down whatever food Mum or Auntie Joyce or Grandma put in front of me. Grandma used to tell me I had hollow legs and that's where all the food went, as I polished off third helpings of her delicious veggie pie.

But that changed when Dad remarried. I had a short-lived rebellious phase at twelve that soon passed. But for a while I acted out, did a number of things I'm not proud of, and stubbornly refused to eat anything Mum made, telling her I'd rather starve. And I did. I got visibly thinner. I fainted during PE at school.

Then one night Mum came home from work with a paper bag full of – previously forbidden – fast food and said, "I guess you won't be wanting to eat this then, either." Of course, I ate. And we talked. And Mum listened. I got a lot off my chest about Dad's new wife – my new stepmum. And at that moment I thought my mother was the kindest person I'd ever know. She would rather I eat junk than starve. The next evening, and every time after, I ate whatever she made for me.

Oh, Mum, I miss you. I rally myself. I was distraught when she passed, and I need to hold it together for the first part of the funeral, to greet relatives and to give the reading. Then I can let rip. I've got waterproof mascara on, but I doubt that'll help. And three packets of tissues in my handbag. Will that be enough? I go through to the utility area and fish out another packet from the drawers next to the washing machine and drop it in my bag.

As I do, I see my phone flashing. It's on silent. I don't want to speak to anyone right now. I gave all the guests specific instructions and directions so no one would need to bother me. Directing Great-Uncle Bob from Blackpool is the last thing I can handle right now.

My curiosity wins out, and I look at the screen. Finn. The senior account director on my team and in charge with me out of the office for the day. He's unflappable and reliable, and I know he wouldn't call me on the day of my mum's funeral without a very good reason.

I answer, "Finn? Everything okay?"

"Lauren, I'm so sorry to bother you today, but it's Imani. She hasn't shown up for work. I've tried calling her, and she's not answering. I'm sure it's nothing, but I'm slightly worried in case she's been in a car accident or something. She's not on the work-from-home rota for today, so should be here by now."

I hear exactly what Finn is actually saying: Imani is no doubt perfectly fine but hasn't bothered to rock up for work yet – even though it's nearing 11 a.m. on a Monday. She's come in late before, but never later than 9.45 a.m. It's obvious she's taking the piss because I'm not in the office today.

"I'll try her, Finn. Don't worry. I'll have another chat with her later in the week about her timekeeping."

"Sure. I hope it goes well today. See you tomorrow."

We say bye and hang up. I scroll through my contacts and dial Imani's mobile as I walk back through into the kitchen. Akshay sees me and taps his watch. It's nearly time to leave. I nod and walk back to the sliding glass door to stare at the garden again.

It rings and rings, and I ponder what choice words I'm about to use. Finally, a groggy voice answers.

"Yeah?" Imani says.

"Imani, it's Lauren. Are you okay?"

"Yeah," she replies. "Fine."

"Why aren't you in work?"

"What time is it?"

I hear a rustle and a man's voice, and then Imani says, "Shit, is that the time? Had a wild weekend, you know. Overslept." There's a groan, and I can hear Imani glugging some water – or what I hope is water. "Hang on," she says slightly brighter. "I think I'm working from home today."

"No. You're not. I checked that with Finn."

"Oh."

"You need to get into the office ASAP."

"Urgh," she replies.

"Imani, this is unacceptable. Everyone else manages to get up and into work for 9 a.m. Your contracted hours are nine until five thirty. This is not the first time I've had to remind you of your timekeeping."

Imani fake-coughs. "I'm sick."

"Mmm hmm."

"Yeah"—*cough*—"think"—*cough*—"I've got the flu." *Cough, cough.* "Really bad."

"We both know that's a lie."

"Fine," she snaps and then mumbles to the other person in her bed – I imagine her doing an unsuccessful job of placing her phone against her chest to muffle the sound, because I hear loud and clear. "It's just my stupid boss ruining my life again."

"Imani!"

"Yeah. All right. I'm getting ready now." She sighs, then hangs up.

I stare open-mouthed at my phone. Imani has been allowed to take liberties since she joined because she's Madeline's favourite and has a level of protection from the MD, but not anymore. I didn't want to hire her in the first place a year ago. Madeline overruled my preferred candidate to offer the job to Imani. She's smart and charming when she wants to be – winning over many journalists and influencers – but is unbelievably lazy. And rude.

Akshay puts his arms gently around my waist and rests his chin on my shoulder. "Time to go, sweetheart. Ready?"

I inhale deeply and turn. Sod Imani; screw work. Today is all about saying goodbye to my wonderful mother. Everything else is unimportant and can wait.

"HE'S A GOOD'UN, that one, isn't he?" Diane, my dad's second wife, says, nodding towards Akshay.

He's busy bringing out all the Marks & Spencer nibbles, plates, and napkins and laying them on the dining room table. He told me very firmly that he'd organise all the refreshments and that I was to mingle with my family and take all the time I needed to speak to relatives and friends of my mum.

Akshay is from a large family, and he's in his element, loving big gatherings. I once got him to write a family tree out for me so I could remember who was who and all the names of all his cousins and extended relatives. Although I now know everyone in his immediate family, I still refer to that family tree before we attend larger events.

"He certainly is," I reply with a smile towards my fiancé, who is now taking hot drink orders.

"No wonder Judy adored him," Diane says.

"She did." I feel the familiar grief-hitch in my chest but tamp it down. "He was devastated that he was in New York when she passed away and didn't get to say goodbye in person."

Diane sympathetically pats my hand, and I smile weakly at her. My stepmum is a petite, neat, smiley woman with a sociable, likeable and jovial character. We've always got on fine. She's never tried to mother me, and I've never tried to be her daughter. I'd describe us as friendly. Not friends, not close but a perfectly amicable relationship.

After meeting and greeting all the guests at the

church before the funeral, delivering my teary speech, crying a river while sat in the pew, conversing with everyone outside the church and hearing "What a lovely service" about a hundred times, I feel a peculiar kind of exhausted. Wide awake and functioning but a zombie on the inside.

We drove in convoy back to our house, and the guests are still piling through the front door after finding parking in nearby roads. The congregation fitted nicely into the church, but is stuffed into my open-plan living area and back garden with a queue for the downstairs loo forming in the hallway. My auntie Joyce has taken charge of opening the front door and greeting guests, and seems to be thoroughly enjoying chatting to everyone.

For a breather before doing the rounds, I stand with my immediate family: my dad, Keith; my stepmum, Diane; and half-brother, Toby. My mum and dad remained friends after their amicable divorce and, although it tore at my seven-year-old heart for them to split, they were both much happier without the other.

So, five years later when Keith announced he was marrying Diane, Mum was delighted. And when Toby came along three years after that, she was doubly delighted – she loved children – and often babysat for Toby. By that point I was fifteen so helped her to care for my baby bro, although at the time I was desperately jealous of all the attention suddenly lavished on him from every corner. Judy and Diane got on well, so all happy families, really.

Dad looks longingly out the window at the smokers in the garden. He quit when he turned fifty and replaced that habit with beer, as his protruding belly and ruddy cheeks would testify. He sighs and looks back to us, scratching at his closely cropped, balding grey hair with his ex-smoker's always-busy fingers. He knits his bushy eyebrows together over his blue eyes, which look so much like mine.

"Akshay's a great chap with a well-paying, secure and respectable job," Dad adds, and we all know where this is going.

I glance at Toby and hope he won't react. My brother is super chill and usually any kind of criticism bounces off his laid-back exterior shell. Although, I know he's a sensitive soul deep down, and every one of Dad's digs wounds him deeply.

Toby smooths his palm over his impeccably styled curly blond hair that's long on top and short at the sides and straightens his black tie into the collar of his black shirt. He oozes style. He has a street urchin look about him with carved-out cheekbones and dimples, brooding blue eyes and a chiselled jaw. But his face is slightly asymmetrical, and he has a crooked tooth, which is a good thing, as otherwise he'd be simply too beautiful to look at. That quirkiness adds to his attractiveness.

He has tattoos on his forearms, on show as he rolled up his shirtsleeves when we arrived back at my house, a pinky ring, a chain necklace and an earring in the top of his ear. He's effortlessly cool, but with a warm, genuine and unpretentious smile. I've been to his bar and watched his female – and male – customers swoon when he serves them.

Today is clearly not a day that Toby is letting things slide. He rolls his eyes. "I have a well-paying, secure and respectable job, Dad."

"A bartender is not a respectable job," Dad replies.

"Just leave it, Keith," Diane warns.

"I'm not just a bartender, I'm a mixologist," Toby says with pride.

"A what now?" Dad says.

"I create most of the new cocktails on the menu. If it weren't for me, that place wouldn't be doing half as well as it is."

Dad tuts. "Anyone can pour vodka and then orange juice into a glass."

"Cocktails are a bit more elaborate than that these days, Dad," I say, thinking of the smoking concoction I always order at Toby's bar.

"And I'm a drinkstagrammer with a big following," Toby says.

"A drink what?" Dad replies.

"Cocktail culture is huge on Instagram," I pipe up in support of Toby.

But Dad isn't having it. He shakes his head. "You should've stayed at university. You dropped out of a law course to sling drinks." He tuts, still not accepting Toby's decision to leave higher education a few months ago.

"It wasn't for me," Toby states.

"You didn't even give it a chance!" Dad blusters.

"Enough," Diane says.

"I've entered the mixologist of the year competition. I'm pretty fucking good at it."

"You could've been a pretty fucking good lawyer. But I guess we'll never know now."

Toby sighs. Unexpectedly he blurts, "Nothing I do is ever good enough for you, is it?"

His face colours, and his eyes rim with water. I know it's the emotion of the day that's riled him up. He loved my mum, called her Auntie Judy.

But Dad doesn't reply to Toby's question and ploughs on. "Lauren managed to get through university and land on her feet in a decent career with decent prospects."

I cringe. This is the only bone of contention between

my brother and me. Toby's belief that Dad favours me. I don't believe it, and it's rarely brought up. But Toby is clearly on one today, and Dad isn't helping matters.

Toby's nostrils flare. "I have prospects! I plan to open my own bar, my own chain of bars, one day."

Dad harrumphs.

My brother continues, "Why are you always comparing me to Lauren? We're different people on different paths. I know she's your favourite and can do no wrong—"

Dad opens his mouth to reply, but Diane cuts them both off.

"Would you two stop playing silly buggers, for goodness' sake," she commands, and this time they listen to her.

Dad points out the sliding glass door into my garden and changes the subject. "Do you want me to come and fix that fence panel at the weekend? Must've been a nasty gust of wind took that down. Don't remember the weather being that bad our way. Can see right through to the garages at the back there. No good, no good at all."

"I'm going to help Akshay. Can I get anyone a drink?" Toby says in a conciliatory tone.

He gets on well with Akshay, bonding over their mutual disgust of celery and especially drinks with celery, namely the Bloody Mary. They can talk for hours about fine wine and expensive spirits, Akshay being partial to whiskey.

I'm about to request a milky cup of tea with a naughty spoonful of sugar, and book Dad's DIY skills, when a far-too-bubbly-for-a-funeral voice behind me stops me short.

"Oh, hey! There you are."

Toby freezes. I slowly turn. And wince.

Before me is Jenna. She looks stunning with a thrown-together vibe, but I know, from what Toby has told me, that it's taken her hours to get ready. She's wearing black. Not because it's a funeral but because she always wears black and not in a goth way. She looks super cool.

Her arms, hands, and fingers are heavily tattooed, and she drips with gold jewellery. Her ears are adorned with so many different-sized hoops and piercings that she tinkles when she talks or laughs. She has a nose piercing and wears numerous rings, bangles and neck-laces, and a chunky gold watch that must weigh her arm down.

Her light-green round eyes sparkle in her round face, which is almost chubby and doesn't quite match her slim figure. She's wearing a ton of make-up, as usual, and I suspect she looks like a completely different person with none on. Today she's gone for a '90s vibe with brown overlined lips and nude matte lipstick. Her thick, bushy eyebrows match her dark chunky roots, the rest of her bob-length hair being dyed dark blonde and perfectly tousled. She's very fresh, very now. And I understand why Toby *was* with her. They looked perfect together.

A quick scan of my family's puzzled faces confirms they are thinking the same as me: Toby and Jenna are no longer together, *so what is she doing here?*

Dad takes charge of the situation. "Ah, Jenna, love, what a surprise."

Toby's now-ex girlfriend bounces closer to our little group and squeezes herself next to Toby. He purses his lips, unimpressed, but Jenna doesn't notice.

"I met Judy a couple of times and wanted to pay my respects. She was such a wonderful woman. I'm so sorry for your loss, Lauren. I slipped in at the back of the church – oh my goodness, did I bawl at such a moving service – and followed everyone over in a taxi but got talking in the garden to a couple of your second – or maybe third, they weren't entirely sure – cousins, Lauren."

She gives a little chuckle, then continues, "They recognised me from my YouTube channel. So I asked them to make sure they click Like. It's all about the likes! Like, like, like, I said. They asked me for a selfie with them, and the lighting was *perrrrfect*. So I got them to take a few of just me. I'll post a muted funeral look later. Although, of course I won't say 'funeral' – gosh, how sad – maybe 'subdued' or 'low-key'. Yeah, that's it. A *low-key* look for *low-key* occasions."

She holds up a nearly empty glass of white wine. "This is my third drink. Akshay made sure we were topped up." Then, beaming up at Toby, she adds, "I wanted to make sure this one was okay. He really loved his auntie Judy, didn't you, boo."

I glance at Toby. He imperceptibly shakes his head and widens his eyes at me. It's enough to tell me that he definitely didn't invite Jenna and definitely doesn't want her here.

Jenna is oblivious though. She continues to babble without pausing for breath. "Your cousin was so sweet, Lauren, saying she'd watched a few of my full-face make-up tutorials. My lilac eyes one and the all-drugstore-brands one. That's a clear favourite. Everyone loves a bargain."

She makes a point of studying my face. "I could've come round earlier and done your make-up, Lauren. You could definitely take a bold lip, and I have lots of tricks to shape and fill out those overplucked eyebrows. So many women of *your age* plucked their brows into oblivion when they were *my age*. Of course, not fashionable in the slightest anymore…"

She continues, but I switch off. I find Jenna exhausting to be around at the best of times, but right now I'm spent. I can't help it, but my face actually scrunches at her incessant voice as if bracing for a full-on migraine to hit in T minus a few seconds.

Toby must sense I'm overwhelmed and says, "Come on, Jenna. Let's get a drink."

He steers her away towards the kitchen and at no point does her mouth pause; she just switches topic to talk to Toby.

"I thought they'd split up," Diane says when the pair are out of earshot.

"Same," I reply.

I watch as they stand in the kitchen, Toby leans against the counter as Jenna knocks back the last sip of white in her glass, grabs a bottle of red on the counter and fills her glass to the brim. Although I can't hear what they're saying, the conversation is clearly strained, with Toby crossing his arms and Jenna fronting up to him.

Oh no, please don't let them have a massive row at my mum's funeral reception. Please, *please* don't let her punch her fist through one of my walls. Toby has told me that Jenna is prone to throwing things when she doesn't get her own way. I look at my wine glass in her hand and will it not to end up on the floor. Toby raises his hands in a placating gesture, and Jenna backs down.

One of my mum's best friends from work catches my eye, and I excuse myself from Dad and Diane and head over to speak to her. I bounce from group to group, person to person around my living area and decide to head into the garden to speak to the few smokers who are congregated out there.

As I'm chatting to my great-uncle Bob about his journey down from Blackpool and the junction at which he got lost, Akshay places a gentle hand on my elbow and presses a cup of tea into my hand. I'm so grateful I could almost weep. My mouth is dry from talking, and I don't think my body has had a chance to replenish from my floods of tears earlier.

My great-uncle excuses himself to talk to another relative and light up a cigarette, and I turn to Akshay. "Thank you so much for sorting all the food and drinks, babe, and for bringing me this." I take a sip of tea and smile. "I've been craving a brew since we got back."

"I thought as much. I would've made one sooner, but the kettle's been boiling non-stop. Your family and Judy's friends are a thirsty bunch."

I kiss his cheek. I like how he does that: speaks about Mum as if she's still here with us, not shying away from mentioning her now she's gone.

He takes my hand. "You're cold. Let's get back inside."

I do feel shivery. I've felt shivery all day and assume it's the grief. As if I have a hole in my heart where Mum's presence has been bored out and a chill wind is blowing right through me.

I follow my fiancé back inside, and he leads me to the dining table, picks up a bowl of crisps and offers it to me. I see Joyce's trifle in the middle of the table. Mum and Joyce always make – made? – the best trifle, from their mother's, and my grandmother's, recipe. I have that recipe, and it'll be my turn to make it for the next family gathering – the twins always took it in turns, and that duty has now passed to me. It'll be this Christmas, only a month away. My first without Mum.

My stomach grumbles, and I'm grateful for my body distracting me from that awful thought. I grab a crisp.

But before I can eat it, the sound of a mug slammed on the kitchen counter startles me.

The room goes quiet as all the other guests hear the same noise and turn to look – has someone dropped a cup? There are often a few crockery casualties at parties; who's the culprit?

But the noise is accompanied by a raised voice. *That voice.*

"I'm here to comfort you, Toby. I'm always here for you," Jenna says, the pitch of her voice rising a level or two and carrying across the room.

I look at her, as does everyone else nearby.

"I don't need you here to comfort me. I don't want you anywhere near me," Toby replies, his voice rising too.

"You don't mean that," Jenna screeches.

"We're over, Jenna," he shouts back.

Her fists bunch, and she punches Toby's chest – not so that it would hurt him, she's too drunk for that, but rather pathetic little thumps. He doesn't even flinch. Witnessing couples arguing in public always makes me feel uncomfortable at the best of times, but this can't be happening today of all days, and not in my kitchen. I've seen enough.

I hurry over to them, grab them both by an arm and drag them away from all the guests and towards the back of the kitchen.

"Guys, this is not the time or place to be having a lovers' tiff," I say in a firm, but quiet, tone.

"Sorry, sis," Toby replies, matching my volume level.

But Jenna is having none of it. She yanks her arm out of my hand, points at me and seethes. "You. This is all your fault. You never liked me, even though I made so much effort with you, offering to do your make-up and take you shopping to modernise your wardrobe. I did everything to make you like me. But no! You weren't having any of it."

"Jenna, enough," I say, suddenly absolutely shattered, my energy levels hitting a wall.

I glance towards all the guests. Akshay is stood at the end of the kitchen, protectively shielding us and blocking anyone from coming closer.

Jenna screeches, "You told him to dump me, didn't you?"

"That's enough, Jenna. Get out of here," Toby says and leads Jenna through the kitchen door into the hallway and towards the front door.

I'm rooted to the spot, trembling, but just as I hear the front door open, Jenna shouts in a drunken slur, "You ruined our relationship, Lauren. I'm going to ruin you!"

The door slams, and Toby comes back through to the kitchen. He reaches me just as Akshay does. Akshay wraps his arms around me, and the dam breaks for the second time today.

"She's gone, sis. Forever. What a bitch," Toby says.

I nod but can't manage to say anything. I weep into Akshay's shoulder.

I hear my brother say, in his charming, lovable voice, "All over, folks. Sorry about that. Just a little relationship trouble. We're here for Judy." There's a pause as I guess he finds his mug from earlier and says: "To Judy!"

A chorus of voices echo him: "To Judy!"

And I mumble the same into Akshay's tear-sodden shirt.

5

A few hours later, after waving off the last guests, Akshay makes me my favourite for dinner, homemade lasagne, salad and chips, while I tidy up and give everywhere a thorough clean. As a treat, we get the trays out and eat in front of the telly. We usually always have dinner at the dining table, but it's been a long day, and neither of us feel like sitting up.

When we're done and the dishwasher is loaded and the kitchen wiped down, we sprawl on the sofa. I put my feet up and curl into him. He switches over to some show about million-pound mega yachts. It's his dream to own a sailboat one day.

I half-watch, still digesting dinner and the events of the day. I pick up my phone and message Kemi on WhatsApp. She's been my best friend since secondary school when we were eleven. She would've been here today but lives in Bristol with her wife and three adopted kids and is a secondary school teacher so couldn't get the time off.

Service and reception went well. Toby's ex-girlf rocked up and caused a scene but was soon forgotten, and we all had a good time remembering Mum. Everyone gone now, so Akshay and I chilling on sofa with large glass of vino.

Kemi replies:

Glad to hear it, hon. Rest in peace, wonderful Judy. Do you remember when she picked us up at 3 a.m. from that party in that random field when we were 16? And you stuck your head out the car window cos you felt queasy while I talked her ear off about goodness-knows-what drunken nonsense? What a legend.

What a night! What a legend. She loved to remind me of that every now and then.

And that time I came round, but you were out, and Judy fed me dinner anyway.

Haha. She always enjoyed cooking for you.

And her trifle, yummmm.

Mine has a lot to live up to!

Sure does… can I be the first to try it?

Yup. And how's you? How's Gillian? The kids?

G's turn to do bedtime. Trevor is nine going on ninety, Darryl has got a girlfriend – he's five, FFS, and Sindy has just learned how to ride her tricycle, which is suuuuper cute.

Awwww! Pls send me a pic of Sindy on her tricycle.

When Kemi doesn't reply immediately, I put my phone down and watch Akshay engrossed in a superyacht tour at the Monaco Yacht Show. I can almost see his numbers-orientated mind working out how long it'll take him to save for a yacht on his current salary.

A moment later my phone pings. I pick it up, excited to see a cute pic of Kemi's adorable daughter. But instead it's a text message from a number that isn't in my contacts list.

Hey, sexy, thinking about you and feeling horny. What you wearing? Wanna see what I'm wearing?

Urgh. Annoying. A wrong number. I want Sindy on her trike! I delete it and hold my phone, waiting for Kemi's message, and watch the telly.

"Blimey, that yacht's deck is longer than our garden," Akshay says.

"I still reckon we should put a hot tub out there," I reply.

We've had this discussion before. Our garden is quite overlooked, and Akshay is not so keen on all the neighbours seeing him in his swimmers.

"Hmm," he replies.

And I get the distinct impression that he's wavering and coming round to my idea. I'll just need to work on him a little longer.

My phone dings. Sindy! But it's a second text from the same wrong number with a photo this time.

It's a penis.

I sit upright and blurt, "Oh my god!"

"What?" Akshay asks but doesn't take his eyes off the Russian oligarch's yacht on the telly.

"Someone's got a wrong number and is sending me dick pics. Look!"

I shove the phone in front of Akshay's face, and he glances down. "What the hell, Lauren!" He slaps my hand away. "Gross."

"I know. I nearly vommed up my lasagne. Should I reply?"

"And say what?"

"'What a beautiful cock'," I tease, but Akshay doesn't look impressed. "'Wrong number', of course."

My phone pings again with another text from dick-pic guy. I'm reluctant to look and squint my eyes and turn my head away in case it's another full-frontal nude. But there's no photo attached this time, thank goodness.

I read the message out loud to Akshay, "'Well... what do you think? Show me something, and I'll make it grow.' Eeewww."

"This guy has got all the lines."

Another message comes through:

Well... I wanna see you, sexy. Don't keep me hanging...

"We're keeping him hanging, babe." I crack up laughing, and it feels like a sweet relief after the sombre day. Akshay laughs with me and tickles my ribs.

I catch my breath and tap out a reply:

Wrong number.

"How mortifying to be sexting the wrong person," I say.

A text pops up. I expect it to be a cagey apology.

Ha ha. Acting coy. I like it ;-) Have you had your special delivery yet?

"Oh gawd. He doesn't believe me. Thinks I'm

pretending and being a tease." I show Akshay the latest message.

"Special delivery?" Akshay asks. "What's that?"

"Some sexual euphemism the youth are using these days that we've never heard of?"

Akshay brings his hand to his chin in a gesture of 'thinking'.

"Maybe it means ejaculation?" I suggest with a cheeky smirk.

The doorbell goes, and we both jump and stare at each other wide-eyed. Then laugh at our edginess.

"I'll go," Akshay says, recovering himself from our fit of giggles.

He heads towards the front door as I check my phone. No more texts.

I hear the front door open and close, and Akshay comes back into the lounge with a parcel about the size of a shoebox.

He hands it to me. "It's for you."

"Ooooh, yay."

I love getting a parcel as much as the next person. I take it from him as he sits back on the sofa and eyes me, no longer interested in the pros and cons of superyacht helipads being debated on the telly.

"Are you expecting something?"

I mentally review my recent online shopping sprees, but nothing springs to mind. "I don't think so. Who delivered it?"

"It was left on the doorstep, and the van was driving off when I opened the door. Some courier."

"Is this the 'special delivery'?" I joke and use air quotes for emphasis.

But Akshay's tone turns serious. "I doubt it's related in any way to those random texts."

"True."

I rip open the plastic packaging to get at the box inside. It's white with a logo in pink writing: Trudy's. Not a brand I recognise. I ease off the lid and pull back the tissue paper.

"Yikes," I say as I lift out a small hanger with a slinky red babydoll, matching suspenders, and teeny knickers.

For the briefest moment I think Akshay has sent me lingerie. But red and frilly is really not his style. And would he send me saucy underwear on the day of Mum's funeral? Definitely not. His forehead furrows, and I know for certain he's got nothing to do with it.

I put the lingerie in the lid and pull out a smaller box with a clear plastic window in the front. It's not immediately obvious what it is, but as I look closer, I realise.

"It's a sex toy!" I drop it and push the box off my knee. "Some woman has given a guy the wrong phone number and address. Probably to get rid of him at a bar or something."

Akshay grimaces while carefully rummaging in the box to avoid touching the sex toy, and pulls out the delivery slip. "It's addressed to you."

"What? It can't be." I grab the slip and read my full name and address.

"Did you buy these things? For... us?" Akshay asks in a tone loaded with self-pity. As if he's no longer fulfilling my needs, as if our sex life needs spicing up. It doesn't. Not yet, anyway. We're still in the honeymoon phase. Maybe after ten years of marriage we might need something to heat things up, but definitely not right now.

"No. Of course not. This is a seriously bizarre mistake."

"It is." Akshay goes quiet for a minute, staring into space with his lips pursed. Then he turns to face me.

"Give me your phone. I'm going to call that number and get to the bottom of this."

I pass Akshay my phone, and he taps on the screen and then puts the phone on speaker mode and holds it between us. We listen to the dial tone, and I half expect it to ring off.

But it stops, and a gruff male voice says, "Hello, beautiful."

"Who is this? You keep messaging my fiancée's phone—"

But whoever it is hangs up before Akshay can finish. He gawps at me, insinuating I'm not telling him something.

"Why are you looking at me like that?" I say, the injustice flaring.

"Who was that, Lauren?"

"I've got no idea."

"Is there something you're not telling me?"

His accusation that I'm keeping secrets from him makes my hackles rise. "Are you *kidding* me? I'm not hiding anything from you."

My phone pings with another text message, and Akshay looks at it. He spends some time over it, and I hope it's Kemi's photo of Sindy, as Akshay adores the little girl. But he flings the phone at me, and I know it's not a chubby-cheeked three-year-old. He stands and paces back and forth. He grabs the remote and switches off the yacht show, slamming it back on the table.

I pick up my phone and read the message. It's dick-pic guy again.

Lauren, does Akshay know about us? Has he found the letters?

My gut twists, and the breath knocks out of me as if a giant hand is squeezing my lungs.

Akshay stops pacing. He faces me, clenching his fists and grinding his jaw. "What's going on, Lauren? Whoever this is knows our names. Knows my name. Are you having an affair?"

I gape at him for a moment, processing this. I never in a million years thought I'd hear that question from my rock, my one and only. And I never thought I'd have to give a reply. It comes out through gritted teeth. "Of course I'm not having an affair."

Akshay points at my phone. "What letters is he referring to?"

I shrug and hold up my hands. "How should I know? There are no letters."

He looks at me for a beat too long and then shakes his head.

I stand too. "I'm innocent in all this, Akshay. I thought this was a mistake, a funny mistake, but someone must be doing this to me, to us."

He *pffts* loudly and rolls his eyes in exasperation as if I've said the most stupid thing ever. "Why?"

"For a joke, maybe? Who knows. It's a cruel joke if it is, but that's the only thing I can think of."

"Who would do this as a joke?"

I cross my arms and stare daggers at him. Drawing out every word to make my point, I say, "I. Don't. Know." And it's true. I've got no idea who'd do this to us.

Akshay considers me and softens. He rubs his hands over his face and then massages his earlobes. An action he only ever does to de-stress, something his father taught him when he was a child.

"I love you," he says. "I don't believe you'd cheat on me. Just like I'd never cheat on you. We're a team, a unit. We'll find out who did this. But it's late now. Let's go to bed."

He steps towards me and opens his arms in compromise.

I hug him back. "I love you, too. We'll work this out. Together."

But there's a lingering tension in his muscles, and I know there's a part of him that still doubts me.

6

The next morning, Akshay is already up and out of bed when my eyes open.

It was a strained, restless night. He'd got into bed before me, and by the time I'd taken off my make-up, washed my face and brushed my teeth, he was lying with his back to me. I'd attempted to snuggle up to him, in the hopes that he'd roll over so I could rest my head in the perfect crook between his chin and shoulder, but he didn't budge. I was pretty sure he was pretending to be asleep, and the snub annoyed me.

The rest of the night was spent positioning our bodies as far away from each other as the king-size bed allowed. It was obvious that Akshay was still suspicious of me even though he'd said otherwise.

"Morning," I say cheerily as I enter the kitchen and see Akshay making himself a coffee.

"Morning," he replies. "Want a coffee?"

"Yes, please."

He gets another cup out of the cupboard and spoons in the coffee. Instant for us on weekday mornings.

Akshay likes to spend longer over his coffee on the weekends, grinding the beans first. He's dressed in his navy work suit, and my insides squirm. He always looks so handsome in business attire – he has a knack for finding well-tailored suits – with his hair gelled and face freshly shaved.

I move to give him a kiss and morning hug, but he moves at the same time to get the milk out of the fridge, and we awkwardly bump into each other's shoulders.

"Excuse me," he says formally, and the moment is broken.

I decide to address the elephant in the room. "This morning, I'm going to find out who is behind those texts and the delivery. And they'll get a piece of my mind. A joke gone way too far. Totally inappropriate."

"Hmm." Akshay pulls out his portable coffee cup, pours his drink from his mug into it, and screws on the lid. "I'm heading off, got a lot to do today."

He gives me a perfunctory kiss on the cheek, and then he's gone.

I stand for a few moments, irritated that he's clearly still questioning my honesty, then grab a banana and eat it while checking my phone.

No more texts from the sick joker, but a reply from Kemi on WhatsApp with a gorgeous picture of Sindy on her tiny tricycle in Kemi's lounge. I gaze at the cuteness overload for a few moments, then tap out a quick appreciative reply.

I reread the dirty texts, deleting the dick pic before I have to look at it for too long. Who sent these messages? Why? The easiest way to find out is the most direct route... by asking. Screw it. I call the number that sent the texts.

The dead tone blares back at me, as if the number

doesn't exist anymore. I hang up and type a message, 'Who is this?' and press send on the text, but I get an error message that it wasn't delivered. Is the number now out of service? Scenes from movies and TV shows when this kind of thing happens play out in my head. Was it a burner phone? Used once and then binned? Why would anyone do that?

I ponder this as I drive to work distractedly, park in my allocated space as if on autopilot and head to the back door of the office. As usual, I'm the first person there and find my work keys to open up. I walk through the empty open-plan office to the PR department's area, which is round a corner and slightly tucked away.

I set up my laptop. I only turned it off this morning to bring it to work, not daring to touch it after Rob had powered it up on Sunday. Just in case. But it seems fine, loads up in much the same way as before and whirs to life. "Thank you, Rob," I mutter out loud. The last thing I need today is my laptop dying spectacularly again. I need to catch up on all the work I missed yesterday and on Friday when I had my head in pitch mode.

I open my emails first, switch off my out-of-office autoresponder and set about going through all the emails from yesterday, when movement catches my eye. I look up, expecting to see Finn, who also likes to get in early to get a head start on work for the day.

But it's not Finn, it's Imani.

I glance at the time on my laptop: 8.17 a.m. I don't think Imani has ever been in the office this early. She gives me a thin smile and sits. Her desk is perpendicular to mine, so I see her profile. As usual, the make-up on her perfect heart-shaped face with enviable cheekbones and full lips is flawless, with fluttery fake lashes and glowy skin. Her hair is completely different to last week.

She has a collection of very expensive wigs and also has
weaves and blow-outs, so every week is something
different. She proudly tells everyone that she spends
most Saturdays at a fancy hair salon in Alderley Edge.

Today, her hair is a sleek black bob with fringe – a bit
Mia Wallace from *Pulp Fiction* – the complete opposite of
the long braids she had last week. But she always wears
the same diamond stud earrings, diamond ring, and
spangly diamond Patek Philippe watch. Her nails are
acrylic and ridiculously long, so long I wonder how she
does the most basic stuff. They are a different colour to
last week, so she must've found time over the weekend
to go to a nail salon after she didn't make her in-the-
middle-of-the-workday Friday appointment. She wears
a silky lilac shirt, dark-blue skinny jeans that emphasise
her incredible curvy figure, and patent black high-
heeled boots. Money oozes off her, and the word that
always pops into my mind when I see her, no matter
what she's wearing or what hair she has, is 'glossy'.

She puts her phone on the desk. It almost exclusively
resides in her palm, and she goes everywhere with it,
including to the water dispenser in the kitchen or to the
bathroom. She pulls her laptop from her Balenciaga
neon-green handbag, and I debate whether to say something about our conversation yesterday morning.
Perhaps she's turned a corner, and this is her making an
effort to show me she does care about her job. She
knows I'm always in early. I decide to give her another
chance. And see how she performs this week.

I open my mouth to say a conciliatory good morning
to Imani, but the front door opens, and I hear the receptionist's voice cheerily talking to another member of
staff about the postman she fancies.

Finn arrives, wrapped up warm, as he walks the

twenty minutes from his apartment into work. As usual, he doesn't even look flushed from the exercise and is impeccably dressed with an English gentlemen vibe, including black round glasses, a bow tie, a flat cap, and a lot of tweed. I imagine his bow tie collection is on a par with Imani's wig collection. His immaculate attire matches his entirely unflappable personality and straight-backed slim build. Our affectionate team in-joke is 'Nothing Flusters Finn'.

A second later, Cleo arrives. After a round of 'mornings' and removing coats and turning on laptops, Cleo approaches me.

"Can I have a word?" she says quietly and discreetly nods her head in the direction of the meeting room nearest to us.

"Sure," I reply.

Cleo wanders towards the meeting room, and I stand to follow. If Imani is glossy, then Cleo is 'hard'. When I first interviewed her for the account manager job almost two years ago, I had an image in my head of what she'd look like. With a name like Clementine Flickinger, I was expecting posh, Cheshire-set, slightly entitled – especially when she told me on email to call her by her slightly pretentious nickname Cleo.

But when she arrived at the interview, she was none of those things.

She had sharply defined features, with a slightly hooked nose and tattooed eyebrows that were just a little too dark and a little too angular. She was obviously fake-tanned, with simple but heavy make-up, winged eyeliner, and a vivid magenta lipstick. Her poker-straight waist-length hair was dyed a dark-red mahogany, her figure slim with razor-sharp collarbones peeking out the top of her round-neck blouse. Her background wasn't obvious from her looks, and if she'd grown up with money, she didn't ooze it like Imani. It also wasn't obvious when she spoke. She was charming, had an infectious laugh and an impressive CV. I hired her and – for the most part – she didn't disappoint.

But, as I look at her now, I see that she's not looking quite as pulled together as usual. Her trademark winged eyeliner is uneven, and her magenta lippy, which she wears no matter what, is slightly smudged. She has big bags under her brown eyes as if she hasn't slept in days. And as I look, really look, she's perhaps thinner than before. For the first time, I worry she has an eating disorder.

She closes the door to the meeting room once we're both in and faces me. Inwardly I brace myself. What's coming? She's leaving in a few days, so she can't be resigning. Maybe she wants some time off for an interview.

"I'm really sorry to say this…" she starts and then pauses, looking at me apologetically.

Oh crap, has she screwed up with a client? Am I needed to step in and pick up the pieces? But I've taken her off most clients now, phased her out before she leaves. So it can't be that.

She takes a deep breath and continues, "It looks like your car has been keyed."

I'm momentarily speechless. This isn't what I was expecting to come out of her mouth. "What?" I eventually manage.

"I parked in my space, which is a few down from yours, and noticed it on your passenger side. I didn't know if you'd seen it or not, so thought I'd better tell you."

"How annoying. No, I didn't notice it this morning." My car is parked on the street, our house doesn't have off-road parking, and the driver-side door was nearest the pavement. "Some car must've driven too close and scraped it. I'll have to get it resprayed or something. Thanks for letting me know."

I make a move to leave the room, feeling as if Cleo's gone a bit OTT with asking me to come into the meeting room to tell me. But Cleo doesn't move.

"Um, well, it's not that," she says and taps the pin code into her phone, then opens the photo app.

She hands me her phone. I look at the photo and gasp.

"I'm sorry…" she adds.

In big letters on my passenger-side door is scratched 'BITCH'.

That is no mistake. That damage is not from a car driving too close or cyclist losing their balance and falling on it. Whoever etched that did it deliberately, knowing full well what they were doing.

"Did you notice what other cars were in the car park?" I ask, handing back the phone.

"Only yours and Imani's."

Imani's custom metallic-pink Range Rover, a gift from her ludicrously wealthy ex-footballer daddy for her twentieth birthday, is hard to miss. And Cleo knows my car from numerous trips together to client meetings and events. It's a Mini three-door hatchback. Not as bling as the Range Rover or as boy-racery as Cleo's VW Golf, but a nice car that'll cost me to fix.

Cleo continues, "Who do you think did it?"

I consider this for a moment. Immediately the group of boys on bikes who cruise our area come to mind. They've been known to vandalise a few fences, heckle people, litter, and cause low-level trouble. "It's probably some stupid kids who hang around where I live."

"Little shits," Cleo says, almost spontaneously, and

the way she says it makes me laugh, as if she's had plenty of first-hand experience dealing with little shits.

I notice that the tension between us since she handed her notice in seems to have completely lifted.

"Yep, right little shits," I reply and roll my eyes. "I'll message the neighbourhood WhatsApp group and see if anyone saw anything. Probably someone knows who their mothers are, and they'll be in for it."

Cleo smiles. "I know a good garage if you want the details."

"Thanks, but I'll be fine. We take our cars to Akshay's relative's place."

She nods, and I say, "Shall we?" and gesture towards the door.

Back at my desk, I check my phone. No messages. Mentally I add 'get car fixed' to my life admin to-do list, right under 'find out who sent the dirty texts, lingerie and sex toy'. I wanted to give whoever it was a chance to message me first and say 'ha ha, joke!' or whatever before I laid into them. But I've not heard from anyone. So phase two is to reach out first. But I'm completely stumped as to who would do it. Which means phase two is stalling.

I sigh and go back to checking my emails. My full team is in now, and I see my senior account executive, Mikey, and my senior account manager, Deb, briefing our intern, Tara, on a task. I take out my notebook and jot a note to remind me to book a quick catch-up with Tara to see how she's getting on. We have a conveyor belt of interns at MBW, Madeline negotiating some kind of deal with the local college, but I like to take the time to talk to each one of them and give them the opportunity to ask me questions about PR.

I never had that as a student – my college career

advisor told everyone, including me, who liked English that they should be an English teacher. It was as if no other jobs existed. But I love my job. Yes, it's high stress, but I get to work with some fun clients with big budgets to do cool things. And, after all these years, I have an established, enviable contact book full of celebrities, DJs, journalists, influencers, and artists – which makes my job that much easier.

I open WhatsApp on my desktop. It's distracting and means I can't help but read personal messages at work, but some clients and media contacts insist on using it to contact us rather than by phone or email. So it's a necessity.

Almost immediately a notification pops up to say I have a message from Toby. It's early for him to be online. After the funeral he was heading to a shift at his gin bar, which doesn't finish until the early hours. He's never usually awake before midday.

A thought springs into my mind. Did Toby send the texts and lingerie? Hell no. I scratch that idea out instantly. Why would he? That's a creepy thing for a brother to send a sister, and he's definitely not the practical joke type.

I read his message:

Sis. Big news. Know you're at work, so messaging. Been up all night thinking this through and just going to say it. I think I'm gay.

I type back a reply in rapid time to try to catch him before he puts his phone down:

OMG! Tell me more! Immediately!

I see Toby's still online, and the ticks turn blue. Then I see he's typing a reply.

Things with Jenna were awful at the end. I just stopped fancying her. And I thought it was because we'd fallen out of love, you know, but actually I think I just don't fancy women. Not really. And last night a customer at the bar – a man – asked me out, and I said yes! Because I really, really, REALLY fancied him. And everything kinda clicked.

Wow, that's cool. If you're happy, then I'm happy, lil bro.

Ha, yeah, I'm happy.

I could tell he and Jenna were just not right towards the end. So this makes sense. And feels right. Toby sends another message:

But I'm a bit confused. Maybe I'm bi? I don't know.

When's the date? That might help you to make sense of it all.

Next week. Am ridiculously excited about it.

It is VERY exciting. Look, I'd better go. But let's chat later.

Sure thing. Sis – you're the only person I've told. Don't tell anyone, ok? Especially not Dad. I'll tell the parents in my own way, in my own time.

Of course. I have zero plans to steal your thunder.

Lol. Love ya x

Love you more xxx

I click out of WhatsApp with a big grin on my face. But it drops when someone taps my shoulder. I spin my chair around and find Imani stood behind me, phone in one hand, notebook in the other, with a seriously unimpressed pout on her lips.

7

"We've got that meeting in the boardroom with CozMoz Paints in five minutes. It's just you and me, remember, because Deb's got that fashion-event thing," Imani says.

As if on cue, Deb flies past us, shouting, "Byeeeee!"

"Gosh, is that the time already?" My morning has flown by, and it's now ten to ten, and I've done pretty much bollocks all. "We'd best get set up, then."

I unplug my laptop and follow Imani towards the boardroom. It's an unspoken rule that we use my laptop for presentations, as it's more powerful than her older model. The more senior people at the agency get the better machines, and not even the MD's favourite could get round that.

As we near the door, I say, "You added those final coverage figures to the presentation, right?"

"Huh?"

"Deb asked you last week to add the final figures to the coverage slide."

"Oh, yeah."

"So?"

"So what?"

I try to keep my voice impassive in the face of Imani's total lack of interest in actually doing anything anyone asks her. "Have you added them?"

She shrugs. "Oh, no. Forgot."

She really is infuriating. Does anyone enjoy working with people who unashamedly do as little work as possible? But I keep my cool. I give her my laptop. "Here, open the presentation up and add them in now. Then link it to the big screen. I'll go and wait in reception for the client and stall them a bit. Okay?"

"Okay. Is it unlocked?" She indicates the laptop.

"Yes, I was just using it."

She sits herself down at the big boardroom table and begins fiddling on my laptop, tapping keys with her ridiculously long fingernails. I head towards the reception area and check my watch. Almost ten. This client is usually always on time.

I pass the time with the receptionist for a few minutes, asking about her favourite subject: the postman. The front door opens. But it's not the CozMoz Paints team, it's Madeline.

"Hi, Lauren. How did it go yesterday? Well, I hope?" she asks, with just the right amount of concern in her tone that says: I care, but not that much.

"As well as can be expected," I reply and ignore the now-familiar urge to bawl at the thought of my mum no longer being here. I regroup and quickly change the subject. "CozMoz are coming in for their annual review any time now. Should hear whether they'll renew at this meeting. I'm feeling positive."

"That wasn't in my diary," Madeline says accusatorily.

"Oh, I, err, didn't think you'd want to come."

In truth, I don't particularly want her there. They are

a lovely client, but Madeline always tries to sell to them: a bigger PR retainer fee, a new website, some email marketing, or how about some eye-wateringly expensive billboard advertising? Although I know her presence signifies to clients that they are important – *the MD has deigned to grace us with her presence!* And it's a universal truth that all clients like to feel important.

She raises an eyebrow at me.

I quickly say, "But you're more than welcome to attend. We've had a great year. Some really strong coverage results."

"Lorna," she says to the receptionist, who also acts as a kind of PA to Madeline, "check my diary."

Lorna dutifully clicks on her laptop behind the reception desk and looks up. "All clear until 2 p.m."

"Great. I'll be in momentarily." Madeline heads into her office, which is behind the reception area, but keeps the door open.

I know this ploy. She likes to arrive to a meeting after everyone else is already there. To make a grand entrance. So she'll listen out for the CozMoz team's arrival and wait a minute or two and then come to the boardroom.

The client arrives at ten past ten, full of profuse apologies for their tardiness. I show them into the boardroom, where Imani waits, looking utterly bored. But she brightens up when Madeline makes her entrance.

Imani is always on her best behaviour in front of Madeline. Not because she wants to impress her professionally, but because Imani is best mates with Amelia, Madeline's daughter, and Madeline is a kind of mother figure. And, I've observed over the past year, someone else for Imani to wrap around her finger to get her own way.

To my surprise, Imani does a great job of presenting her slides, clearly loving everyone's attention squarely on her and enjoying the sound of her own voice. Perhaps public speaking is her thing. It took me a lot of practise to build up my confidence, but Imani's a natural.

We take it in turns to speak while the client team chips in with questions now and then. Madeline sits back and silently observes, like a monarch presiding over their court in full swing.

I stand for emphasis and position myself next to the big screen, with all eyes on me. "This is one of the highlights of the year. The YouTube video by home influencer DecorDiva, who has four hundred and fifty thousand followers on Instagram. She used CozMoz Paints in shades Starry Night and Mercury Rising to decorate her kitchen. To date, the video has had forty thousand views."

I smile brightly and nod at Imani to click on the slide on my laptop, where the video is embedded. As she does this, I say, "Dun, dun, dunnn!"

The clients smile and look on expectantly. They've seen this before, of course, but it's always good to remind them of our best work.

The screen changes from the slide to an image that is not DecorDiva's kitchen. It takes me a moment to realise what I'm looking at, but the accompanying noise flicks the switch in my head.

Hardcore porn is playing on the big screen in the boardroom. One woman, numerous men. The grunts, groans and "Fuck me, big boy!" encouragement echo off the walls.

I freeze, horrified. It's as if my insides have turned to liquid and are trying to escape through my feet to get away from the embarrassment.

Imani laughs.

The lead client, a sweet-natured middle-aged man called Phil, says, "Crikey," but in a tone that suggests he'd rather have shouted a swear word.

Phil's younger assistant goes deathly pale and looks like she might vomit, and the older manager chuckles along with Imani.

Madeline slaps the table and yells, "Imani, turn it off!"

Imani snaps to attention, the jollity subsiding immediately, and presses pause on the video. For a moment, there's a still close-up image that none of us wants to see before she manages to get it off the screen.

Although I'm cringing so hard that I want to fold into myself again and again until there's nothing left of me, I recover my senses. "I'm so, so sorry. I've got no idea what just happened."

Madeline glares at me but then takes control of the situation by making light of it. "Well, that woke us all up. A technical glitch. Imani, find the right video and play it. Quickly." She smiles her warmest smile at the CozMoz team, who look stunned, like rabbits caught in headlights, but allow her to soothe them. Movement slowly comes back to their faces and bodies.

Phil clears his throat and attempts a joke, "I don't think that was one of our paints on the wall."

We all force laughter just to push the moment along. I sit back down, my hands shaking and my cheeks on fire. Imani finally plays the right video, and DecorDiva's voice describes how the satin-finish navy colour of Starry Night perfectly complements the metallic silver of Mercury Rising on her kitchen island.

But in my head, it can't quite drown out the sex grunts that still ricochet there. I scan the others. They watch with fixed smiles and fixed interest, but it's obvious that they can't forget what they've just seen or heard either.

The video ends, and Imani clicks to the next slide. I'm meant to be talking through it. It's the coverage figures for the year that Imani added in at the last minute. It's the last slide of the presentation, and I swallow, attempting to quash the mortified flames that are still licking up my neck and raging across my cheekbones, but Madeline steps in.

She talks through the figures as if she were meant to all along and, being Madeline, nails it. Phil and his two assistants are impressed. And happy that the results are more than the previous year, although they spent less this year on fees and activities. They talk around me, but I'm still stuck in the hardcore porn moment and can't seem to drag myself out of it.

How did that happen? I embedded that link in the presentation. It was correct. I know it was. I checked it twice.

I hear the word 'contract', and I jolt back into the present. Madeline is talking as if CozMoz Paints renewing with MBW for another year is a done deal. They've been with us for three years, and we do an incredible job for them, so it's almost a dead cert that they'll renew.

But Phil shakes his head.

"I'm sorry, Madeline. Lauren, Deb, and Imani have done a spectacular job, but I think we'll be considering our options for next year."

The younger assistant frowns at Phil, and the manager looks confused. It's clear they weren't expecting that announcement.

"I'm sorry to hear that, Phil. Can I ask why?" Madeline replies.

"We, er, we, um..." Phil squirms. He's only just

decided this, it's obvious. "Various reasons," he finally says.

Madeline graciously smiles at him and indicates for Imani to show CozMoz Paints out. We all shake hands, and when it's just Madeline and me left in the board-room, she gently closes the door and hisses, "What on earth was that, Lauren?"

I shake my head, thinking on my feet. "Maybe I acci-dentally copied the wrong link?" As soon as I say it though, I know it's not true. Yes, I'm tired, stressed and grieving, but I don't watch porn. How could I just find that link in the first place to copy?

Imani comes back into the room. "That was hilari-ous," she announces before bursting into uncontrollable laughter.

"Enough, Imani," Madeline chides. "This isn't funny. We just lost a lucrative client."

Imani bites her lip, to keep the laughter behind her teeth, but it's still there in her eyes.

Madeline continues, as if she's a headmistress admonishing naughty children, "I'm exceedingly disap-pointed. Mistakes happen. But don't ever let that happen again. We'll say no more about it."

She strides out of the boardroom. Imani smirks at me and follows her.

As I unplug my laptop from the big screen, the ques-tion *how did that happen?* Plays over and over in my head. I was the last person to look at that presentation when Deb shared it with me last week. I added that link because Deb had forgotten to, and I checked it, and it played DecorDiva.

I walk back to my desk and sit, unlocking the screen on my laptop with the plan to check my emails, but I can't focus.

I grab my phone and my handbag and head to the

toilets to freshen up. As I'm in a cubicle, I hear someone else come in. I finish up and head to the sinks; a moment later the other person joins me. It's Cleo.

"Hi," I say.

"Are you okay? You're as white as a ghost."

"Just had a nightmare meeting."

"Oh?"

I catch myself before I talk about the porn incident. Cleo is on her way out of MBW. This is her last week. The last thing I need is for this story to get out and bounce around the Manchester PR scene as hot gossip. Or even the news that CozMoz is unlikely to renew, that doesn't look good on the agency, or on me.

"Yeah, didn't quite go to plan," I reply, but I'm obviously rattled as I stumble over my own feet on the way to the hand dryer.

"Sorry to hear that. Must've been awful. You look really shaken."

I smile as she joins me awkwardly under the hand dryer, both attempting not to touch the other's wet hands. Why have four cubicles, four sinks and only one hand dryer? Who knows.

I decide to change the subject. "So, your leaving drinks on Friday after work. Deb's booked an area at Cuba Cuba. Should be fun. Madeline's putting some money behind the bar so we can work our way through the drinks menu."

I try a laugh, but it curdles in my chest and sounds all wrong. I'm still stuck in the boardroom, reliving the *dun dun dunnn* shocker.

"Yes, they do some great virgin cocktails there," she says.

Dammit. Once again I've forgotten that Cleo doesn't drink alcohol. Has never really drank, as far as I can tell. Although being sober doesn't stop her from enjoying herself on nights out – which is probably why I always forget. Most of us need a bit of booze lubrication to loosen up when out with colleagues, but not Cleo. She's often the life and soul of the party.

We both move to the mirror to check our appearance, and Cleo pulls out her lipstick. It's almost right down to the nub, so she tucks her long hair behind her ears and leans in close to apply it carefully. I notice the big nick out of her left earlobe and the ugly scar that stretches right across it. I try not to look, but it must've been some nasty injury that caused it. Cleo has never mentioned it, and I've never asked.

She immediately untucks her hair to hide her left ear.

"So how's your job hunting going?" I say to cover the fact that I was looking.

"Oh, just fine," she replies brightly.

But she's not asked me for any time off for interviews, and I haven't had any requests for references, so I'm not sure it's going all that well. But perhaps I'm not down as one of her references, and maybe she's been going to interviews before or after work or in her lunch break. And I know her fiancé is wealthy, so there could be no need for her to rush to find another job, or possibly there's no need for her to work at all.

She turns to me, and I notice her slightly run-down look from earlier has almost entirely transformed. She's practically bursting with life, her eyes glowing and skin radiating joy. She continues, "In fact, I have some big news. I've just landed the most *amazing* new job."

"Oh, wow! Good for you." I smile, genuinely happy for her, but when she doesn't offer any further details, my curiosity gets the better of me. "Whereabouts?"

"Oh, it's confidential at the moment. They want to do a big announcement, you know. I start on Monday. I honestly *cannot* wait. It's a *massive* step up from this place."

I baulk slightly at that remark, and Cleo must notice because she adds in a rush, "Not that I didn't have a great time here and learnt so much, but it was time to move on. I needed the push, and it was perfect timing because I wouldn't have gone for this opportunity if I hadn't been *encouraged* to hand my notice in."

Oh gawd, I groan internally, I don't really want to get into the nitty-gritty of Cleo's exit all over again without the HR woman in attendance.

But she waves her hand and grins. "Honestly, it's fine. Water under the bridge. I couldn't be happier right now. Yes, it stung initially, but all turned out brilliantly for me in the end."

"Glad to hear it," I say as we leave the toilets and head back to our desks: Cleo on cloud nine, skipping ahead, me dragging my feet.

As I sit, Imani turns back to her desk after gossiping with Mikey. She glances at me with laughter still dancing in her eyes, and Mikey grins, and I know she's just told him about the porn. I'll need to send an email to the team minus Cleo to tell them to be discreet and not to mention it outside these four walls.

I open my laptop to do just that, and on my screen is the last slide of the presentation. My pulse quickens.

I wasn't the last person to look at this presentation before the meeting.

Imani was sat in the boardroom for a good ten minutes on her own with my laptop and this presentation before we came in. Did she plant that link? Why would she do that?

But before I can ponder this more, Lorna, the receptionist, appears at my desk and tells me Madeline wants to see me in her office. Now.

8

All of my team side-eye me at this demand from the boss delivered via Lorna, apart from the intern Tara, who has her headphones on and is diligently working on a task. It's never good if Lorna is sent to fetch someone.

"Coming," I reply and stand.

During the few steps from my desk to the reception area, Lorna makes polite, sweet chit-chat. This is a sign that Madeline is in a *seriously bad mood*, as Lorna feels the need to compensate for the reprimand she knows a summoned team member is about to receive. Lorna looks at me sympathetically as she sits back down behind reception.

I knock on the MD's door and then push it open. Madeline beckons me in, but she's typing something on her keyboard. The way she's bashing the keys foretells trouble for me. She said that we wouldn't speak again about the porn incident – and Madeline means it when she says something won't be spoken of again – so I wonder what I'm doing here. I close the door behind me and wait.

She finishes typing, then turns her chair to face me. "Sit," she commands.

I sit on her sofa. She clasps her hands together and just looks at me.

The scrutiny makes me squirm, and I blurt, "I've honestly no idea how the porn thing happened. I think maybe it was—"

But she flicks her hand to make me stop.

"Lauren, you are a very valued member of MBW. You've grown that PR department since you arrived four years ago, and clients love you. You excel in new business and have an enviable network of contacts both in Manchester and London and across the country. I'm always very impressed with how you deal with issues and lead your team."

I swell at the praise. Compliments don't usually come out of Madeline's mouth apart from at annual performance reviews. And then they're often couched in between ways to improve.

She pauses and I know a 'but' is coming.

"But this is unacceptable. I understand we all need to vent. And we all get frustrated with colleagues. But really, I thought you'd be above this." She gestures at her laptop screen.

I have absolutely no idea what she's talking about. The confusion must show on my face because Madeline tuts.

She continues, "You sent the bitchy email about me *to me*, Lauren."

We've all done that – accidentally sent an email to the wrong person. My stomach lurches, but then I remember: I didn't write any email about Madeline to send it to her.

"What email?" I ask.

"Oh, for goodness' sake. You don't need to play dumb."

"I didn't write any email about you, and I didn't send any email about you to you."

She shakes her head in annoyance. "I'm looking at it right here." She points to her screen.

"What does it say?" I ask, desperate to jump over her desk and look at this email I'm meant to have sent her.

She glowers at me. "I'm not going to read the damn thing out to you. You wrote it!" She recovers her temper and takes a deep breath. "Lauren, I understand that we don't all get along with everyone. I'm not upset that you feel the need to rant about me and my behaviour – everyone has issues with their superiors – and I'm not going to ask to who you planned to send this to, whether someone in the agency or outside, but I'm exceedingly disappointed that you did it using your work email. Just as you made an error sending it to me, you could've sent it to a client or a journalist by mistake, and that is unacceptable. That could damage MBW's reputation."

My mouth falls open, and I gawp at her. Is Madeline making this imaginary email up? Why? Is it because we lost a client earlier today with the porn incident that she blames on me? Have I seriously fallen out of favour with her so dramatically that she's now trying to discredit me?

It wouldn't be the first time she's used these kinds of underhand tactics. Once she takes a dislike to someone, then they're out. She did something similar a year or so ago with a creative director who resigned suddenly after he got too big for his boots and called her 'Mads' – a nickname she loathes – and talked over her and criticised her ideas in an all-staff meeting.

Or is she trying to force me out so she doesn't have

to pay me the large pay rise I've been promised at the end of this year? She hates spending money on her staff, wanting the agency to look as profitable as possible to potential buyers. But I negotiated heavily at the end of last year and set high targets for the PR department that she agreed to, which I've now surpassed. And if we win the supermarket pitch from Friday – which I'm super confident we will – then I'll have doubled my new business targets.

Madeline grows impatient with my silence and gestures to the door to dismiss me. "Please think before you do something like this again. And we'll say no more about it."

But I don't move. I have to know more about this supposed email. "When was that email sent?"

She purses her lips at me, but when she realises I really want an answer and won't be going anywhere until I get one, she squints at her screen.

"About fifteen minutes ago. Soon after we came out of the CozMoz meeting."

"I went to the toilet straight after," I exclaim, as if I've solved the mystery. "I wasn't anywhere near my laptop to write it."

She shakes her head sadly at me as if I'm still trying to weasel my way out of it. "Did you take your phone to the toilet?"

"Yes."

"And you have your work emails on your phone, yes?"

"Er, yes…" She's got me there.

She shrugs and opens up her hands. "Well, there you go."

Yes, I could've written an email while sat on the loo having a wee. But I flipping well didn't.

"And it's *definitely* from me? From my email address?"

Madeline tilts her head and raises her eyebrows, as if to say: *do you think I'm stupid? Of course it's from your bloody email address.*

But I persist, "Can you check? Please?"

She looks at her screen, clicks twice, and says, "Yep. Definitely sent from you."

I can see by the look on my MD's face that she's bored of this conversation now, and if I push it any more, I'm likely to be frogmarched out of the building by the security guard on the ground floor.

So I stand and leave her office. Inexplicably – and automatically – I say, "Thank you," on the way out and reprimand myself because that somehow suggests I'm guilty.

I fly back to my desk, curse as I have to unlock my screen and my laptop takes the longest few seconds to load up. I open my emails, clicking straight into Sent Items and scroll through the top few emails.

There's no email there to Madeline. I order the emails by name, and I see the last email I sent to Madeline was on Friday – and it's now Tuesday.

I click into my Deleted Items folder, in case it's in there. It isn't. Could it have been permanently deleted out of there? Why though?

"You're kidding me," I exclaim and sense my team's ears perking up.

"Something up?" Finn asks.

"All fine."

He nods.

But everything is NOT fine. There is no email. What is Madeline going on about?

. . .

I DELIBERATELY WORK LATE. I've stewed all day over this non-existent bitchy email and realised I have to see it to believe it. Everyone on my team has already left for the night. It's not unusual for me to be the last person to leave.

One of the website designers sticks his head around to our area and confirms I'm about to be the last person in the office. I say goodnight and listen as the door shuts, and there's complete silence. I count to ten, put on my coat and grab my bag, then wander around the office, shouting, "Hello? Anyone still here?" and looking in all the meeting rooms, just to double-check.

When there's no reply and I'm confident I'm alone, I stand in front of Madeline's office. I spend a moment geeing myself up because snooping and being sneaky is absolutely not my usual modus operandi.

My legs want to turn and hurry away, but I force them through my boss' door. I have to know about this email. I'm not a liar. I have never sent spiteful, rude emails about other members of staff. I'm offended that Madeline even entertains the idea that I did. But her word is law in this organisation, and if she says I sent that email, then I did – and no one, not even HR, will believe otherwise.

I don't turn the light on in case someone on the street below should see, somehow know this is her office and that she's already left, and then go and tell her. I creep towards her desk and past her chair and marvel that this is the first time in four years that I've ever been on this side of it. My heart pounds, and I take a mental note of exactly where the mouse is before I shake it to see if Madeline's office laptop is still on.

It is – she hasn't powered it down. The lock screen pops up, and I type in Madeline's password that she so casually told me on Friday: Whittaker123.

I open her emails and look in her Inbox. As I see emails from clients, colleagues, HR and personal contacts, I feel as if I'm violating an unspoken rule – you don't look in other people's emails! – and guilt hits me.

But I have to find this email I was meant to have sent.

I try not to read any subject lines and skim through the senders of today's emails to find my name. Not there. She's probably filed the email somewhere. She has a lot of folders, and to look through them all would take hours. I find one called 'People' and guess it might be HR related so click in that. It has about fifty subfolders. I notice one called 'Rick', the name of the creative director who mysteriously resigned, but can't see my name. I click into the 'PR' folder and see emails from me, but mostly about recruitment and performance reviews.

Finding this email among thousands is proving harder than I thought. I decide to look in Sent Items in case she forwarded it to someone – maybe the outsourced HR woman – but no joy. Then I search for my name, and thousands of emails come up. I scroll through, but there's no email there that I haven't sent.

So I search for 'bitch' but only find a couple that I've sent moaning that a journalist was a 'bit of a bitch' at an event. What other words might I have used in the email? I try 'doing my head in' which is a favourite phrase of mine, but only one email pops up from three years ago where I was moaning about a nightmare client, who we ended up firing. I check in the Deleted folder, but nothing to be found.

Frustrated, I slap the desk. I spot the printer in the corner – Madeline has her own while the rest of the office, all two hundred-odd people, share just two others. There are a few sheets of paper on top. Perhaps she printed it out?

I sift through the sheets of paper. Not there.

"Argh!" I shout out loud. "Where is this sodding email?"

I go through Madeline's Inbox a second time. But the email is definitely not there. Has she deleted it entirely from her system? Did she make it up?

Something is seriously wrong here.

Leaving the mouse precisely where I found it, I exit Madeline's office, leaving the door ajar, just how she likes it. Movement catches my eye, and every hair on my arm stands on end – there's someone else in the office. I look up.

A few metres away is the graphic designer. He stares straight at me, and we eyeball each other. My heart thuds in my chest. I've just been caught coming out of Madeline's office, looking guilty as hell.

"Just popping a doc on the boss' desk," I say quickly and plaster on my thickest smile. It does nothing to help my cause: I still look – and now sound – guilty as hell.

"Yeah, sure, cool," he replies and shrugs. Then, as if he feels the need to explain his presence in the office, he adds, "Was having a drink over the road, and an idea for a client just like – ping – came to me, and I have to get it down before I forget it."

His voice slurs, and I expect he's had more than one drink. "Great idea," I say cheerily as I head towards him. His desk is right by the door to the car park. "Sometimes my best ideas come to me when I least expect them."

He hmms, but isn't paying me any attention. He intently focuses on sitting and on turning on his computer. He puts his satchel bag on his desk, and it clinks.

He winces and glances at me. It's obvious he's got a

few bottles of beer in there. And alcohol is only allowed in MBW on Fridays. I pretend not to notice.

"See youuu," I singsong as I pass him, and he half-heartedly waves at me.

He's drunk. And, by the sounds of it, about to get even more plastered. He hopefully won't even remember seeing me exiting Madeline's office, let alone tell her in the morning. I let out a very long breath. *Whew, close call.*

I hurry to my car. It's the only one left in the car park, and I walk round to the passenger side to see BITCH scratched in tall letters. With that, the porn, and the bitchy email, I realise I haven't made any progress on finding out who sent those texts and the lingerie last night.

I sigh. What a day. I can't wait to get home to talk to Akshay about it. Yes, he was a bit off with me this morning, but I'm certain that will have passed. We're a unit, a team, soon to be married. He'll help me work this out.

9

I drive home with my mind working on overdrive and the guilt of prying in Madeline's emails churning in my gut. It was necessary, I keep reminding myself, but that doesn't placate my conscience, which tut-tuts disapprovingly in my head. And all it did was throw up more questions.

I see Akshay's car parked up outside our house. I find a space up the road and pull my hood up to run through the pouring rain to the front door.

I let myself in. The house is quiet and dark, but Akshay's car keys are on the sideboard near the front door. Strange he hasn't turned any lights on – he usually always switches the front porch light on if he gets in before me.

"Babe, are you home? I've had the most bizarre day! OMG, I need to talk it through with you."

I wrangle with my damp coat, hang it on a hook and pull off my sodden shoes. Why isn't he answering me? I listen for the shower but can't hear anything. Maybe he's gone for a walk. But in this rain? Doubtful.

But I sense his presence. At least, I hope it's *his* presence.

"Akshay?" I try again, more tentatively this time.

There's a faint glow coming from the lounge, so I head there. The light is from the telly, which is on, but seems to be paused with a fuzzy image on the screen that I can't make out.

Akshay is sat bolt upright on the sofa, staring into space. He's still in his suit. Odd. He likes to preserve his workwear and is very particular about getting changed as soon as he gets in. The suit is crumpled and his shirt creased. His face is ashen, and his hair, normally so neatly gelled, is chaotic, sticking out at all angles as if he's run his fingers through it or grabbed and twisted at it.

I move nearer to him. "Are you okay?"

But he doesn't look at me. He doesn't even acknowledge my presence.

My heart leaps up my throat. He's not moving or blinking.

"Akshay!"

But his chest faintly rises and falls, and the horror that I was looking at a dead body subsides. I wave my hand in front of his face to break his trance.

"Babe?" I say softly and gently sit on the sofa next to him.

He finally turns his head to look at me. It takes a long time, as if he's been sat in that same spot for hours and all his muscles have locked into place. I can almost hear the creaking.

His haunted, red-rimmed eyes pierce my soul as he looks at me, as if I'm the harbinger of doom and he's resigned to his fate. I see trails of now-dry tears on his cheeks. He's been crying? Oh no. Has one of his family had an accident or… worse?

"What's happened? Talk to me." I reach for him.

But his harsh voice stops me short and cuts me in two. "How could you?"

He chokes on the words, and tears stream down his face.

Akshay upset is awful, and I would do absolutely anything to comfort him, but I'm puzzled by his words. "How could I do what?"

He gestures to his lap, and I see a small plastic tub on his knee, the kind that takeaway food comes in. It's full of what look like scraps of paper and handwritten notes. I stare at the tub and then at him, attempting to make sense of it.

"I don't understand," I say.

He looks at me with undisguised contempt for so long that I want to shrink into myself and away from his severe gaze. I don't though. I hold his eye contact. This is not how Akshay usually behaves, and it's clear something is very off.

Eventually, he says, "I didn't go into work today."

Oh, crap. There's a problem with his job? He's worked at that place for twelve years. Has he been made redundant? What does that bundle of notes have to do with it?

He continues, "I pretended to leave this morning, then headed back here after you left. I searched the house top to bottom. I had to see if the letters that guy mentioned on text yesterday existed. I couldn't find them. But then I thought to look outside. And I discovered this tub. You hid it pretty well out there, didn't you, Lauren. But I found it."

There's now no mistake. This is about the dirty texts from yesterday. I reel from the revelation that he deceived me about going to work, but that's not a priority right now. I point at the things in his lap. "I've never seen that stuff before in my life."

"I read the letters. They're all dated over the two months I've been away."

"What letters?"

Akshay picks one off his lap and reads it out loud. "'Sexy Lauren, missing you today. Us both being at work sucks. But so happy I can drop this off at yours so you can see it the moment you get through the door. I hope your work event went well. Can't wait to see you tomorrow night. I also can't wait for the time we'll be together. I know you're waiting for A to get home from New York to do it, but I wish it could happen now. I want to scream our relationship from the rooftops. All my love.'" He flaps the note in my face. "That was dated on October tenth. I checked back through our messages, and you had a work event that night. The following night, a Friday, you told me you were knackered and having an early night. But you weren't, were you? You were seeing *him*."

I shake my head, completely perplexed. Disoriented as if lost at sea and facing a huge incomprehensible storm. Confusion crashes against me in great chaotic waves, and I cling on as Akshay's accusation flips everything upside down.

"Listen to me, that's not mine. I have never seen it before. I have never read it before. I don't know who is doing this or how they know so much about us, but it's made up. It's not real. It's not what you think it is."

But Akshay is not swayed. "I found the USB."

"I've got no idea what you're talking about," I insist, but Akshay isn't really listening to me. He's still in a daze.

"The note said 'thought you might like to see our

home movie from last night at mine'. I plugged the USB into the telly and…"

He picks up the remote, which is resting on his other knee, and presses play.

For the second time that day I see porn on a big screen. I look away. "Turn it off!"

"Watch it," Akshay growls so emphatically that I look back.

This isn't the slickly filmed porn from earlier, this is obviously a video shot on a phone of a man and woman having sex in what looks like a normal bedroom. It's not clear what's happening and is a bit dark and blurry, but then the couple change position, and there's a straight-on glimpse of the woman's face before it's obscured again.

That face is mine.

My legs turn to jelly and give way. I drop down onto the rug between the sofa and coffee table and cup a hand over my mouth in shock. Akshay rewinds the video, presses play, and pauses it precisely on my face as if he's been doing this all day.

"That's you," he says very slowly, very deliberately, with zero doubt.

"That's not me," I say, but it comes out so weakly that it sounds like a lie.

For the second time today I'm denying something that others are convinced I've done. I couldn't find the email that Madeline accused me of sending, but this – this movie – is irrefutable. *I'm looking at my own face on the telly.* And Akshay is looking at my face attached to a body that is having sex with a man who is most definitely not him.

Even though it's not me, it is me.

"It must be fake. My face edited in somehow," I say,

but it sounds implausible even to my own ears, and I know it's the truth.

Akshay explodes off the sofa, his arms in the air, the tub and notes scattering. "You're having an affair! Just admit it. Stop lying to me. I can't bear it."

"I'm most definitely *not* having an affair!"

"Lauren – stop. Just stop." He points at the telly. "That is *you*. With another man."

"It's my face, yes, but that isn't me."

He yells and chucks the remote at the telly. The back cracks off, and one battery flies out and hits the coffee table with a clunk. The sound gives me a start.

"You're a liar!"

"I'm telling the truth – you have to believe me. It's fake. This is all fake."

"Shut up. Everything that comes out of your mouth is poison. I loved you so much. I gave you everything I could. I devoted myself to you, and you betrayed me."

He lunges towards me on the floor but stops himself short and instead grabs the edges of the coffee table and tips it over onto its side. Magazines, candles, a small vase of flowers, and drink coasters fly everywhere.

Akshay turns to me, and I scuttle backward out of the way. I've never seen him so enraged. He pants heavily, his face is screwed up tight in an ugly, dangerous expression, and a taut vein pulses in his neck.

He leans over me and shouts in my face, "You've shamed me, Lauren. I can never forgive this disloyalty." He must see the terror on my face, for he pulls away and composes himself.

His nostrils flare, and he scrunches his mouth. He gestures to me and then to him. "This. Us. It's done." In a calmer – but just as vicious – tone, he says, "We're over. The engagement is off."

Thunder booms in my ears, and lightning strikes across my vision. I slump against the sofa.

"Don't do this." I reach out for his hand. "You're making a mistake."

But he yanks his hand away, stomps out of the lounge without a second glance and up the stairs.

I can't move.

My world, my love, my heart shatters. No more engagement? He's leaving me? This can't be real. I must be trapped in some kind of nightmare.

I can't even begin to imagine my life without him – all my visions of my future include Akshay. All my dreams of our family, of our marriage and life together that I cherish, that I can't wait to make reality, vanish as if scrubbed away, permanently deleted from my mind. I feel hollowed out, blank, lost.

I hear him thumping about in our bedroom, and a few moments later he flies down the stairs, grabs up his car keys and heads out the front door, slamming it with an almighty bang.

In the still aftermath I sob.

How could he not believe me?

The grief of my mother's loss and now this. Akshay gone, the engagement off. The love of my life just walked out on me, and I haven't done anything wrong.

I attempt to get up off the floor to follow him outside even though I know he's long gone. But I can't manage it, as if there's an earthquake and the ground is shaking so much I can't find my balance.

So I stay on the floor, curl up in a ball, and hold my breath against the rumbling that brings my entire world down on top of my head and crushes me into pieces.

10

Eventually the shuddering subsides, and my limbs ache from staying in the same position for too long. Laboriously, as if my body were on pause and is just coming back to life, I sit up. And then stand, trying not to look at the coffee table on its side, trying not to remember Akshay's rage.

This is ridiculous. I haven't had an affair, I didn't receive any love letters, and I sure as hell didn't make a sex tape with another man.

Someone is doing this to me. And I'm going to find out who.

I turn on the lights in the room and wince as my eyes adjust. I scowl at the letters, scraps of paper, and the plastic tub scattered on the sofa and on the floor – not just everyday inanimate objects but the things responsible for bringing poison into my home. Although I don't want to touch them and contaminate myself any further, I know I need to look at them to solve this mystery. Taking a deep breath, I remind myself that they're not going to bite, and scoop them up and take them to the dining table.

I sit and survey the bundle. First, I look at the plastic tub. It's just a bog-standard container that any takeaway or café might use. It has no brand name and, I concede, could actually belong to me. Akshay and I are partial to a takeaway every now and then, and yes, I wash out and keep the containers to reuse for work packed lunches or to store leftovers. I have no idea how many of these containers I own. We have an entire drawer over-flowing with plastic containers, and I only ever rummage in there to find a container and lid that fits. I've never taken an inventory. So maybe this is my tub. But more than likely, it isn't.

Next, I look at the letters and scraps of paper. I spread them out. There are seven notes. Some are A4 pieces of paper folded up, and some are smaller, written on the back of what look like envelopes or ripped out of a lined notebook. I turn each over, but the A4 is blank, and the other pieces have no distinguishing marks or logos. One note is in a plain white, generic envelope.

I study what is written on the letters. Each is dated in the top left corner. Which seems very pedantic. But Akshay was right; the dates all correspond with when he was away in New York. Each has been handwritten in an untidy, large scrawl. I don't recognise it.

I organise them by date and read each through in the order they were apparently written. Much of the same love babble as the one Akshay read out, but peppered with mentions of work or personal information.

One talks about my mother's passing and how they wish they could've been there for me but how they were pleased my auntie Joyce was with me. The date is correct. Another talks about us going to one of my favourite restaurants when Akshay is out of the picture. And the note in the envelope indicates that I left one of my grandma's pearl earrings – which I always wear – at their house, and the reason for the envelope was to give it back to me by posting it through my letterbox.

Someone knows *a lot* about my life.

I reread all the notes, but they don't give anything away about the sender. Occasionally they say, 'thanks for your note', as if I've replied, but mostly they talk about undying love, me dumping Akshay and about all the incredible sex we've supposedly had.

I stand and go to the telly, reaching behind to pull out the USB. It's a common one that you might find in any shop, with no company name or logo. I grab my work laptop, which I always bring home with me, put it on the dining table and power it up. I sit again, plug in the USB and note there's only one file on it: the sex tape movie. It's an MP4 video file labelled with characters and numbers in the same format as many smartphones use.

Although I'd rather be watching anything else, I grit my teeth and press play.

The video is dark and unclear, but I study it carefully. It looks like a normal bedroom, a bit messy and cluttered, rather than a hotel room or movie set. I don't recognise it. The curtains are closed, and there's a low light coming from behind the camera, as if a table lamp is on. The bed looks like an Ikea jobbie with a bland wooden headboard. The bottom sheet is white, and the navy-blue duvet is crumpled on the floor, as if kicked off in the throes of passion. There's absolutely nothing remarkable about this bedroom. There's no gadgets or trinkets or pictures on the wall. There aren't any books on the nightstand.

I pause it at the moment Akshay had – where there's a glimpse of my face. I lean forward to scrutinise the still image on my screen. Yes, it's definitely my face. And it looks like my hair – but I have pretty normal hair similar to many other women. I rewind the movie to check the body. It does look similar to my own. But, as with my hair, I have an average body shape and height, with average boobs. But it's clearly *not* my body. This woman has a flatter stomach, skinnier arms and larger calf muscles.

If Akshay had looked, *really* looked, past my face he'd have seen it wasn't me. But the video quality is poor, and the lighting is murky. The man is not anyone I recognise. White, average build, a bit of a belly, short hair that could be dark blond or brown, and beard stubble.

I didn't notice before, but there's sound. It's very faint. I turn it up to full volume and hear the usual sex groans, but neither man nor woman say anything. I can hear traffic noise and the beeping of a truck reversing in the background but nothing that might locate where it was shot.

It looks exactly how it's meant to: an everyday, normal couple having sex in their bedroom at night and filming it on their smartphone.

How is it possible to edit my face into this?

I open a browser on my laptop and google 'edit face onto video'. I'm shocked at what comes up. One result says 'want to change the face of someone in a video? It's a piece of cake with this software'. I read a few entries and learn that face replacement to make a video look authentic is a thing. It's called deepfake.

I'm both terrified and fascinated.

Someone went to the trouble to produce a deepfake video of me having sex with another man. And to plant it on a USB along with some fake letters in my garden. I glance out the window into the garden. It's dark out there, but I immediately see the fallen fence panel and the row of garages behind. The gap in the fence offers easy access into my garden. I should've asked Dad to fix it as soon as it happened, but Akshay was away, and I was so busy with work and spending all the time that I could at the hospital. And then Mum passed away. I just didn't think about it, but it left me open and exposed.

I get up and check the sliding glass door is locked. It is. Then I close the curtains across the door and pull down the blind on the window. I go back to the dining table and sit once again. The thought that someone is watching me from out there flickers in my mind, but I cast it aside. There is no one out there, of course there isn't. I need to focus on the task at hand.

Whoever it is also knows my phone number to be able to send those dirty texts. They also know my address, to have posted the lingerie and sex toy, both of which are now in the bin.

Maybe they'll give me some answers? I fish the package out of the black bag, thankful that I started a new bag and it's not covered in food waste. I put the box on the side. The bra is in the correct size. Alarming. How does whoever this is know *that*? My bra size isn't exactly something that I broadcast. And the matching knickers and babydoll are in the correct dress size.

I don't bother looking at the sex toy, not sure what that will tell me, but I do scrutinise the packaging. The bag has my name and address on it and the delivery slip too. It looks exactly as if I've ordered it for myself or someone's purchased it for me. There is no bank card detail or other information on the delivery slip. I dump everything back in the bin.

It's someone who knows a lot about me, both my personal and work life. And who wants to destroy my relationship with Akshay.

But just like this morning, I don't have any suspects.

I decide to do an inventory of everyone in my life:

work, romantic partners, family, friends, acquaintances and even neighbours. I think back as far as I can remember, to school, college, university. I tick off everyone I can remember and ponder whether or not they might have a grudge against me that I'm not aware of. I come up short.

The biggest emotional turmoil in my life was splitting with my first fiancé a decade ago. It was tough at the time, but years later I bumped into him, and he was happily married with a baby on the way, and he'd actually said 'thank you' to me for leaving him.

I've had friends come and go, as everyone does, but none that have ended sourly. I've had one-night stands and flings but nothing that traumatic or unusual. I did have a minor falling-out with a neighbour who had a habit of playing loud music at 2 a.m. on Wednesday mornings. And I've had work colleagues over the years who I've not gelled with, but never any major drama.

Although the palaver with Cleo recently was pretty awkward. She'd been less than honest about an incident with a client and got found out. HR got involved, and it was decided it would be best for Cleo to hand her notice in. It was uncomfortable, but she accepted it and, by the sounds of it, has landed on her feet with this awesome new job. I just can't imagine her doing this. She has a great life – she's about to get married and is moving up in her career. So what would be the point?

I start thinking about Akshay's family and friends, but there's absolutely no one who I think would want to split us up. I got on with his parents from the first time we met. I'd even go so far as to say his mother adores me – outwardly anyway. Perhaps it's a front? But I really don't think she's anything other than genuine in her affection.

A name pops into my head that I hadn't considered: Jenna.

Jenna shouted how she wanted to ruin me when Toby kicked her out of the house for making a scene at the funeral reception. I discounted it at the time as drunken, empty nonsense, but what if it wasn't?

No. It's not Jenna.

She isn't bright enough to engineer the texts, the delivery, the letters, and to produce that video. Although there's deepfake software on the internet, it would need someone with some skill to actually create a video that looked so real. Or it needs to be someone who'd know where to find someone with those skills. Jenna knows how to contour her nose; she is not tech savvy or streetwise. And Jenna had nothing against Akshay, so why would she involve him if she wanted to ruin me?

Although I try to convince myself, I just don't believe it's my brother's ex. But who else? I can't believe it's anyone in my family. My best friend lives in Brighton and adores Akshay; she wouldn't want to split us up. I run through everyone again, but there's no one. And what motivation would they have?

But it has to be *someone*, because one thing is for certain – it wasn't me.

11

I wait for the kettle to boil in the kitchen at work and take some deep breaths to steady my racing thoughts.

I wasn't the earliest person here this morning. I couldn't sleep last night in a bed so empty of Akshay. I tossed and turned, going over and over who could have wanted to split us up and why. It felt as if I'd only just nodded off when my alarm blared. I pressed snooze one too many times and ended up leaving the house late, then getting stuck in morning traffic. I dropped my bag on my desk and headed straight for the kitchen to make an extra-strong coffee.

The kitchen door opens, and I look up. Madeline steps in, and we both robotically smile at each other.

"Morning," she says.

"Morning," I reply.

Remorse for sneaking in her office and going through her emails swims in my veins. But it was necessary, I remind myself. And what am I going to do? Tell her and apologise? Not a chance.

The atmosphere between us is strained enough after

yesterday's boardroom porn and bitchy email. That drama feels so insignificant to me now that Akshay is gone. I hadn't even thought of it until I saw Madeline's slight hesitation about coming into the room a moment ago. If she could've, she would've turned and avoided me. But that's not Madeline.

She edges around me and grabs a mug from the cupboard, places it next to my mug, pops in a tea bag, and stands with me, listening to the kettle rumble.

I know I should make small talk, make the move to smooth over the cracks from yesterday, but I just don't have the energy, and after a bad night's sleep – I sleep like a log usually – words escape me.

The kettle clicks off, and Madeline breaks the silence. "Is there enough water in there for me?"

"Yes," I reply, but my hoarse voice breaks, still full of emotion. I haven't spoken out loud since Akshay dumped me last night and walked out. I swallow, but my throat is still raw from so much crying. The distress bubbles and boils over like the water in the kettle and must show on my face.

Madeline, alert as ever, picks up on this. "Are you okay?"

My MD is the absolute last person I want to speak to, but I couldn't get hold of Kemi or Toby last night to talk to, and my mother – the first person I would've called in a situation like this – is no longer on the other end of the phone. Mum would've known what to do, would've soothed and listened, would've been there for me. She'll never be there again to console me. Fresh grief stamps in circles around my heart, and I press a palm into the painful spot on my chest.

"Lauren?" Madeline probes gently.

She's the first person who's shown me any kindness, and I crack. "It's Akshay," I say before I can help myself.

"Oh?" Madeline looks concerned.

She's met Akshay before, knows all about him. She even graced our engagement party with her presence for all of thirty minutes.

"We've... split up." I heave back a sob at saying it out loud. It sounds so brutal, so final.

"Oh, I'm so sorry to hear that. Always painful when relationships end. Do you need some time?"

Time off, she means. But I want to be at work. I can't bear the idea of sitting alone at home, traipsing around the endless whodunnit maze in my head. The idea of work, and focusing on something else, is more appealing. My brain likes to come up with solutions to problems when I'm doing or thinking about something entirely different and not paying attention. I was hoping an idea, or even the teeniest hint of an idea, as to who did this would pop into my head while I was in the shower this morning. It didn't.

"No, I'd rather be here."

Madeline nods, gives me a sympathetic smile and then pours the hot water into my mug and then hers. She splashes some milk in her mug, gives it a quick stir, removes the tea bag, bins it, and exits the kitchen in her brisk and efficient manner.

In contrast, I feel as if I'm wading in a thick soup and am physically unable to move that quickly. Slowly I add milk to my coffee and put the carton back in the fridge. I know what she'll be thinking: will heartbreak affect Lauren's performance at work? Because for all the sympathy and saying the right things, the bottom line is if this will have an impact on Madeline's business. She doesn't really give a monkey's about her employees as individuals. Never has done, never will.

After sipping my super-strength coffee, I shake myself off and pull it together.

Much to my surprise, I actually do feel slightly better for speaking to Madeline – or maybe it's the caffeine kicking in? – and head back to my desk. I need to compartmentalise everything and take control. I hate the feeling of powerlessness that I felt last night when Akshay didn't believe me, like a tortoise on its back, legs flailing, unable to right itself. But I put that to one side. I'm at work now. And there's tasks that need crossing off my to-do list, clients to manage, and team members to lead.

After an hour or so of focused work, I check my emails. As I'm replying to Deb about the collection for Cleo's leaving gift, an email arrives from the contact at the supermarket we pitched to on Friday.

I click it open immediately and see it's been sent to me with Madeline cc-ed in. That'll piss her off no end, but I read on. It's a reply to the last email I sent confirming the time and date of the pitch.

I read:

Lauren,
Great to meet you and the team on Friday. As I mentioned at the meeting, MBW was the last agency to pitch to us. We've discussed it internally, and without a doubt you guys smashed it. So, we'd like to award you the business for next year.
There'll be a handover period with the incumbent, and we'd expect MBW to start in January.
Let's organise a call to talk everything through and sort out the contract.
Looking forward to working with you and the team.
Best,
Stephanie

I jump out of my seat, punch the air and shout

"YES!" at the top of my lungs. Finally, something is going right for me. Madeline will have to honour my pay rise now. I've smashed my targets for this year. I knew we'd done an awesome job even with the undesigned presentation. It will be the biggest contract won by MBW, and I led the pitch team. I swell with pride that all my blood, sweat and tears has paid off.

The PR department is depleted of people apart from Imani, who has her Beats headphones on and glances at me, sees me standing and pulls off one ear.

I do a little jig and sing, "We won the supermarket business!"

Imani watches me with a raised eyebrow, radiating disgust, and manages a half-hearted, "Yay," before sliding the headphone back into place and turning back to her screen.

I run towards reception. "Lorna, is Madeline in?"

"She's just popped out for a croissant."

I nod and then skip over to the creative team area and find the creative director to announce the win. He high-fives me, and I head over to the web team to relay the message and then to the content department, who whoop and cheer. After that little lap of honour, I head back to the PR department past reception.

I notice Madeline's door is open, but Lorna shakes her head at me, to say: She's back, but now is *not* a good time to disturb her.

Disappointed, I walk back to my desk and force myself to sit down. I'm giddy with excitement. It's a bright spot after all the crap of the past few days. I can't wait to tell Akshay... oh. The memory of him stomping out of the house slices through my elation, and my mood sinks.

To rekindle my high, I reread the email from supermarket Stephanie, as we've been referring to her in the

office. I get that same buzz as the first read, but I notice
that it says I've replied to the email. I click onto conversation view and see that not only have I replied all,
copying in Madeline and two of Stephanie's colleagues
who were copied on the original email, but Madeline
has also replied all immediately afterwards.

Odd. I click into my reply to supermarket Stephanie.
It reads:

> *Stefaney,*
> *Fuck off. We don't want your bollocks contract. We*
> *don't want to work with you or your shitty team. Your*
> *supermarket is an embarrassment and we wouldn't*
> *want it on our books. MBW is SO above your brand.*
> *You also had the most wet-fish handshake I've ever*
> *encountered. Get some meds or something for those*
> *sweaty palms already.*
> *Regards,*
> *Lauren*

I reel back from my laptop, feeling very hot, then
very cold, then very hot again as shock pitter-patters
around my body.

What is this email? Why does it say I sent it?

I was across the other side of the office. I would
NEVER reply and say that. I would never misspell a
client's name for starters. I don't even talk like that.

Scrolling up, I read Madeline's reply. It's excruciat-
ingly grovelly. She apologises profusely for my email
and insists it's a mistake and then goes on to talk about
organising the call and the times and dates she can do.

OMG.

I look in my Sent Items and – unlike the bitchy email
that Madeline claimed I sent – this email is right there.
Sent just minutes ago. Who sent it? It's definitely not

Madeline; she wants the lucrative contract more than anything.

Someone is trying to sabotage me at work – why?

Before I can fully process what has happened, a voice screeches my name.

12

"What the hell do you think you're playing at?" Madeline shouts at me.

The full force of her yell smacks me in the face and incapacitates me. All I can do is open and shut my mouth like a fish out of water as all the life drains from me.

Imani turns to stare, slowly removing her head-phones as if any sudden movement might make the Madeline bomb go off again. It seems the entire office goes silent, listening in.

Cleo, Mikey, and Tara come out of the nearby meeting room, chatting and laughing, but immediately sense the charged atmosphere, go instantly quiet and stand still, not daring to get any closer to the snarling beast that the MD has turned into.

Madeline continues her tirade, "Have you actually lost the plot? I cannot *believe* you would send that email, Lauren! Was it meant for someone else? I mean, *come on!* My office. Now."

She marches away, red-faced, and we all watch her back.

I turn to my team. Tara, the intern, is wide-eyed and frightened. Imani smirks. Mikey studies his feet, but Cleo takes a step towards me.

"Are you okay, Lauren?" she asks.

I nod and shakily gather up my notebook and pen to take to Madeline's office as if we're about to have a normal catch-up. "Yes, thanks, all good," I lie, but my voice quivers and gives me away. Trying to retain some level of respect from my team, I say, in as unruffled a tone as I can muster, "Imani, please can you share with me that media list by the end of the day?"

"Mmn," she replies noncommittedly.

I walk towards Madeline's office in a way that I hope looks as if I'm in control – shoulders back, chin up, not too fast, not too slow. The last thing I need is for my team to lose faith in my leadership after a public bollocking from the MD.

I enter Madeline's office and close the door. She's sat on the sofa already with her arms crossed. She indicates for me to sit on the matching armchair.

"I didn't send that email," I say as soon as my bum hits the fabric.

But Madeline holds up a hand. "Lauren, I'm extremely worried about you. You've had a lot on your plate recently, what with the grief of losing your mother, the stress of the supermarket pitch on top of your usual workload – which I know is exceedingly heavy at the moment with Cleo leaving and no replacement confirmed just yet. And from what you told me this morning, it sounds as if you're experiencing some relationship troubles too. I think it has all just got too much for you."

"I didn't send that email," I repeat, firmer, but Madeline either doesn't hear me or chooses to ignore me. I suspect it's the latter.

"Up until this point, you have been a reliable, hard-working, steady member of the team. I value your contribution to MBW highly, but I honestly think you need a break. There's no shame in needing to take some time for personal self-care. You look exhausted, and I'm concerned you're having some kind of mental health crisis. I want you to take the rest of the week off. Go home, relax, sleep, reflect. Read a book, have a bath, binge-watch some Netflix. Just do whatever you need to do to switch off for a few days."

"Madeline, I don't need to go home. I need to find out who sent that email."

She stands. "Go home. Right now. I'll speak to the team and check in with you on Friday afternoon to see how you're feeling."

She ushers me up and out the door, and I realise there's no point arguing with her. She's made up her mind that I'm on the brink of some kind of monumental breakdown, and that's that.

I head to my desk and gather up my things, my fingers trembling. "Guys, I'm heading home for the rest of the week," I announce to the team. Although it pains me, I say, "I won't be working." My second and third in charge are both still out of the office. "I'll let Finn and Deb know."

Cleo, Mikey, and Tara all nod supportively. But Imani grins and doesn't even do me the courtesy of trying to hide her glee. I catch her eye and hold the contact with her. She brazenly stares back, with a suggestion of a challenge behind her smug expression. An expression that says: *I won. Dare you to say otherwise.*

I turn and march out of the office, feeling all eyes on me as I walk past the other teams. Everyone heard Madeline's raised voice; everyone knows I've fallen from grace. All I need is someone ringing a bell behind me, shouting 'shame, shame', as suffered by Cersei in *Game of Thrones*.

In the car, I sit but don't leave immediately. Who sent that email to Stephanie? I have to find out.

I find my phone and call the IT guy, Rob.

He answers on the third ring. "Hi."

"Hi, Rob, it's Lauren."

"Lauren, the PR group account director?"

"Yes, that's me."

"Hi, Lauren, do you have an urgent request? Otherwise I'm going to have to ask you to email me so I can log it on the queue and deal with it after all the tickets in front."

"It's urgent. Very urgent."

"Okay, sure. Go ahead," he says.

"An email was just sent from my email address, but I didn't send it. It was a rude email to a new client, and I have to find out how it happened because it's very damaging to the business." When he doesn't reply immediately, I add, "And Madeline is *extremely* upset about it."

"Oh. I see. That is strange. Well, I can look at the IP address to see where it was sent from. What email was it? Do you have a time or subject line or keyword so I can find it?"

"Yes." I tell him to search for the misspelled name: Stefaney.

"Here we go. Found it. Give me a moment."

I can hear a few mouse clicks and Rob's breathing on the phone. It takes him what feels like forever, and I look in the rear-view mirror. Madeline was right – I do look exhausted. I fidget and check my nails and chew the side of my mouth.

Finally, Rob speaks. "That email was sent from the

office's IP address. Which means it was highly likely it was sent from your laptop."

"I absolutely did not send it."

"Right. Someone could've logged on to your webmail while in the office from another laptop, which is doubtful, as they would need to have your login details."

"Is there any chance that I've been hacked? And someone outside the office sent that email? Or is the virus still on my laptop?"

"No," Rob answers. "I removed the virus, and we have the highest security measures in place to prevent hacking. I ran a scan when I had your machine and ensured all the security software was up to date."

I wait for him to elaborate, but he doesn't.

After a pause he continues, "Is that all, Lauren?"

"Yes. Thanks, Rob, you've been really helpful."

"No problem. Have a nice day." He hangs up.

I start the engine and head home. That email to supermarket Stephanie was sent when I left my desk to tell the teams across the other side of the office that we'd won the business. The only person near my laptop was Imani, the rest of the PR team being away from their desks or out of the office. She could've jumped on my laptop while no one was looking. In my excitement, I left it unlocked. Wide open. It would've only taken her a couple of minutes.

Did she do it to spoil my obvious joy at winning? She knew how important that pitch was to me – she'd seen me working on it, heard me talking about it. The entire agency knew how important it was to the business. Perhaps Imani didn't like that I was about to be Madeline's golden child, usurping her from the position and stealing her crown? Or maybe she just doesn't like me and is trying to force me out by ruining my credibility and casting doubt on my professionalism and ability. Maybe this is tit for tat and she's getting back at me for pulling her up on her tardiness on Monday and refusing to let her leave for her nail appointment on Friday.

And wait. She had access to my laptop yesterday – I left her with it in the boardroom for ten minutes.

Could she have also sent the bitchy email to Madeline yesterday? Maybe she scheduled it to send right after the meeting? As well as swapping the link in the CozMoz Paints presentation so it showed porn?

Imani is entitled and believes I'm always on her case, even though I'm just doing my job as her boss to get her to do her job.

I sigh as I stop at a traffic light, and a car pulls up in the lane next to me. I glance across. The driver looks over at my car, and his eyes flick downwards. He catches my eye and nods down at the passenger side door. I nod, thinking he's trying to flirt or something. But then I remember.

I have BITCH emblazoned on that door.

An epiphany hits me square between the eyes as the lights turn green, and the car behind beeps when I don't move. I put it into gear and pull away.

Could Imani have scratched that into my car? That morning she was the second person in the office after me, so she would've been alone in the car park with my Mini. Cleo arrived soon after and said there were only our three cars in the car park. The entire floor is allocated to MBW, so there wouldn't have been anyone else there.

The more I think about it, the more I'm convinced that my account executive is attempting to undermine me at work.

Imani, you little cow, I won't let you get away with it.

13

I fly through the front door and straight into the lounge, determined to work out the best way to confront Imani about this.

But I stop dead in my tracks. Something is very wrong.

My cosy, safe place feels all rigid with jagged edges that poke me. As if the house is telling me: 'Beware, Lauren, BEWARE'.

A prickle dances across my shoulder blades, and I can sense another person or persons have been in the house.

The coffee table is still upended from yesterday, but it's not that. The sofa cushions have been pulled off the sofa, and the big flat-screen telly is no longer on the wall. All of Akshay's Apple gadgets, surround sound speakers and numerous video game consoles are gone from the cabinet under the telly. Books have been pulled off the shelf and are scattered on the floor. Akshay's rare vintage wine from the wine rack is gone, and the bottle of twenty-year-old single malt scotch whiskey proudly on display on top is not in its usual place.

I glance at the kitchen and notice a gaping hole on the counter where the expensive coffee machine should be. And next to it, Alexa is gone. The cupboard doors are wide open.

A break-in. Someone has trashed the house and stolen our things.

My heart pounds. Is the intruder still in the house? I reach for one of Akshay's eye-wateringly pricey professional chef knives out of the block, but they've been taken. Without making a sound, I carefully pull open a drawer and take out another less fancy knife. I stay very still and listen hard. But the house is quiet. Knife in hand, I creep upstairs and into our bedroom. Akshay's expensive Apple HomePod speaker is no longer on his bedside cabinet.

"Shit," I say out loud.

We've been burgled.

This is the last thing I need right now. I curse myself again for not getting that fence panel fixed, for making my home a target for burglars. My precious home violated. Everything feels dirty, even the air. I have the urge to throw open all the windows and to clean, clean, clean. To scrub the intruder's breath off my surfaces, to wipe away the dirty fingerprints that have touched my belongings.

I turn to head back downstairs to find my phone and call the police, but I notice my Mulberry handbag. It's still hanging on the hook by the chest of drawers. This strikes me as strange. One thing the bastards missed. Then it dawns on me. My equally expensive Coach handbag, a gift from Akshay, which was also hanging from the same hook, is gone. Why would a thief take one but not the other? Did they think the Mulberry's a fake – it most certainly isn't – or do stolen Mulberry handbags not fetch as much money?

I open my jewellery box. The most precious, expensive items I own, I'm wearing, including my grandma's pearl earrings, but the Tissot watch that Akshay got me for my birthday, which I wear on special occasions, is gone. But my Fitbit smartwatch, which I self-gifted last January when on a short-lived and overzealous health kick, is still there.

Spinning around, I fling open the wardrobe doors. Akshay's side is empty. All his clothes are gone. I open his drawers – all empty. I dash to the spare bedroom, looking above the wardrobe. His suitcase is gone.

The truth of the situation settles over me like a heavy, suffocating veil. He's been in the house and ripped out everything that belonged to him or that he paid for. Including expensive gifts that he gave me.

I sink onto the bed in the spare bedroom and hold my head in my hands. It's definitely over. Akshay has well and truly left me and taken his things to prove that point. I had a glimmer of hope that I could rectify the situation, that he was just staying away for a few days, because all his things were still here; his home with me was still here. But this is so final. My relationship is over. The man I loved more than anything is gone. No wedding, no marriage, no family. We wanted to start trying for babies as soon as we were married. I'm thirty-eight, he's thirty-nine; we weren't going to wait any longer. He was the man I was meant to be with for the rest of my life.

My mouth dries out, so parched it hurts. I slouch downstairs, wiping away tears, and head into the kitchen to get a glass of water. And there I see it. A handwritten note on the side, propped against the toaster.

I open it and read:

*Lauren, I want my money from this house, so we'll
need to sell it. I'll organise an estate agent to come and
value it next week. I've taken what's mine. We'll need
to sell the stuff we bought together and go halves. I
want this over with as soon as possible. My solicitor
will be in touch via email to get the house sale underway. The less we have to deal with each other, the
better. Akshay.*

Not my house, my beautiful house. Where will I
live? I'll have to buy somewhere else on my own. Somewhere smaller and not in such a nice area, and somewhere without Akshay in it.

Or I could move into Mum's small one-bedroom
apartment… but that thought is distressing. How could
I sleep in her bedroom? How could I inhabit the rooms
that were once so full of her? I'll expect to see her
around every corner, at the sink, in her favourite
armchair and then remember she's not there, will never
be there. My brain says: it's a roof over your head. My
heart says: you'll be living with her ghost. I'm
distraught at the prospect.

I take in the room, the open-plan area, all the furni-
ture that fits just right. We've been here for six months
and made it our own, our nest, our starter home to raise
our young family. We've made so many good memories
in this place already, and I was so excited to make many
more. This is my safe space, my happy place. Somewhere I love to come home to every single day. Damn.

I put the cushions back on the sofa and sit looking at
the big blank space where Akshay's telly once was,
taking stock of the past few days. The desperate grief of
my mother's funeral, the frustrating issues at work that
led to me being sent home by Madeline, my fiancé
leaving me and now this – ejected from my lovely home.

Maybe if I speak to Akshay, I can make him see sense.

Before I can talk myself out of it, I find my mobile and call him.

"Yes?" he answers abruptly.

"Oh, Akshay…" I mumble, the sound of his voice so familiar, but so, so distant.

"You've seen my note? My solicitor will be in touch."

"I didn't have an affair. This is all…"

But I trail off as I hear a woman's voice in the background shout, "Akshay, lunch is here." My words turn sour, as the voice has a very distinctive American accent.

"What do you want, Lauren?" Akshay asks impatiently.

"Where are you?"

"It doesn't matter. I'm hanging up now."

And he does.

My secure, stable life is falling through my fingers like water. But why now? It was all going so right for me. I've worked hard to build a great life. Cancer took Mum, not anything anyone did.

But losing Akshay? The work drama? My car getting keyed?

I must have some serious bad luck for all of those things to happen at the same time and so close to Mum's funeral. We all have our fair share of misfortune – but all at once? There's a proverb that says bad things come in threes. But am I really that unlucky?

These incidents aren't innocent or by chance. They are premeditated and calculated to inflict major damage. There's no mistake, I'm clearly the target.

I've been looking at this all wrong. The timing of these events isn't a coincidence. They're not random or isolated. The drama in my personal and work life is connected. It has to be.

I switch into doing mode. I can't sit and mope all day, that's just not in my nature. I need to work this out, set Akshay and Madeline straight, keep my home, head back to work.

Imani is suspect number one for the trouble at work. But the dirty texts, lingerie, letters and deepfake video? I just don't know.

Thinking about work, I realise I need to do a handover of sorts to cover my absence. I know how frustrating it is to pick up other people's work with no clear understanding of where things are up to. I drill it into my team before they're away for any length of time. I have to set an example; I can't let my standards slip. When this is all sorted, I don't want to return to angry clients, a chaotic team and missed deadlines.

I open my work emails on my phone and tap out a couple of quick messages to Finn and to Deb with a rundown of what was on my to-do list for this week that can either wait until I return or will need to be picked up by them or one of the team.

Satisfied I'm not leaving any loose ends, I scroll quickly through my new emails and see there's no reply from supermarket Stephanie. I wonder if Madeline has called her to apologise again. There are numerous emails I can leave for one of the team to pick up. But I see an email from Imani.

Just seeing her name grinds my gears, but I open it. It's the media list I asked her to share with me earlier. I'm surprised she's actually completed a task without me chasing her for it at least five times. She's attached it to the email, the message reads:

Media list attached. Have fun at home. Don't watch too much porn. Maybe now's the time to start making your own?!

I fling the phone down before I reply with something I'll regret later. What the hell does she mean about making my own porn? Is that a reference to the porn played in the boardroom, or is she referring to the lingerie and sex toy? Or that deepfake video of the couple having sex and my face edited in?

Hold up. How does she even *know* about that?

My hunch that everything is related becomes a knowing, a certainty in my gut. I try it on for size: Imani is responsible for the work drama and all the troubles in my personal life too. She's getting back at me for coming down hard at her at work. She's played a cruel and senseless joke on me with the affair stuff, which Akshay has massively overreacted to and taken at face value. It fits. It all fits.

Imani certainly knows my phone number, email, and home address. She came to this very house for my engagement party along with a few others from the office. And there she met Akshay. She brazenly flirted with him at that party, as well as with most of the other men there.

She has access to my work diary, as my calendar is public so people can check when I'm free before sending me meeting requests. And we have full team meetings every Monday morning, where we go through every client, discuss upcoming work, check the status of ongoing work, and everyone shares what they have on that week. So she could've written those letters that mention specific work events.

And we all talk about our personal lives at work, within reason. I know all sorts of little facts about my team – I know Finn's girlfriend is ten years older than him, that Mikey is learning to play the piano – so Imani knew, as the whole team knew, that Akshay was away for two months, when he left and when he was back because I talked about it. And she was well aware of the day Mum passed away because I told my team that morning I was going to be at the hospital all day.

But could Imani have managed the deepfake video editing by herself? She's certainly smart enough when she applies herself and always surprises me with her knowledge of tech – and not just smartphones. But maybe she had help? She certainly has the money to pay someone to do it for her. And she always makes out that she knows a lot of people. Perhaps some techy kid in Eastern Europe looking to earn a quick buck made it for her. It's not hard to find people like that on the internet – you can outsource pretty much everything these days and find the appropriate freelancers.

How do I go about stopping her? Or proving she did it?

I'll cut straight to the chase and confront her. No messing about. The direct route is nearly always the best route. But I need to handle this right. Imani is Madeline's darling. One false move and Imani will have me fired; she has Madeline's ear.

Precisely because I want to rage at her and shake her until the truth comes out, I decide face to face is probably not the best idea. I'll call her. Then there's no record in writing if I'm wildly wrong. And ask her if she knows anything about that email to the supermarket client, ask her if she saw anyone near my laptop. Be subtle. Let her trip herself up. Listen to her voice, pinpoint the lies.

I find a notepad and a pen, poised to jot notes as if on a business call, breathe in and out to the count of four to ready myself, and pick up my phone to call her. But it rings in my hand.

14

"Hey, Kemi," I say.

"Hey! I'm so pleased you answered," Kemi says.

Her voice is a bit echoey, and I know she's in the bath. She has Wednesday afternoons off teaching, and her three kids are either still at school, at after-school clubs, or with her wife, Gillian. This is Kemi's me-time, and she always has a long bath, telling me there's nothing more luxurious than a daytime bath. "I read your message. Jeez. A lot of shit has happened to you. I just can't believe you have an enemy that has it in for you *that bad*."

"Well, I think I've worked out who did it."

"Really? Who?"

"A junior member of my team."

"Seriously? Wow. Which one? Actually, hold up. Before you get into that, I have to... well... talk to you about something."

Her tone worries me. Kemi sounds almost reluctant to tell me something, which never happens. We've been friends since we were eleven and have shared absolutely everything with each other since then – no matter how gross or personal or awkward. I heard all about Gillian's abnormal discharge at one point.

"Come on, out with it," I say.

"I just checked Facebook, and you've posted a ranty update and then shared a really, and I mean *really*, offensive post."

"What? I haven't been on Facebook since I woke up this morning." I always check my social media channels and emails the moment I wake up, and then again in the evening. I'm not the kind of person who dips in and out multiple times a day. I'm usually too busy at work to check. "Are you sure I posted it?"

"Yes. Very sure. And, mate, it's a good job that I know and love you. Because, well…" She trails off.

"Hang on, let me get it up on my laptop and have a look, and then I can stay on the phone with you."

I grab my laptop, power it on and go to the desktop version of Facebook. I put in my login details using PW-Protekt, my password manager, and click OK, but an error message comes up saying I've entered the wrong details.

I tut.

"What is it?" Kemi asks.

"Facebook isn't recognising my flipping password."

"Annoying."

"Let me try again." The same thing happens. "Urgh."

"I'll hang up, screenshot it and message you."

"Okay."

We hang up, and a moment later I receive Kemi's message with two screenshots of my Facebook posts. It's definitely my Facebook profile. I see the familiar picture of me that Akshay took, where I'm standing against a backdrop of endless lavender fields in Provence, France, just before he proposed to me. It is – was? – his favourite photo of me and is – was? – his background image on his phone.

I read the rant first:

This is it, wankers. I've had enough. I'm tired of lying, tired of saying and thinking things that I'm told to, that are meant to be polite and politically correct and "acceptable" when I don't believe it. I don't believe ANY OF IT. From herein, I'm speaking my truth. If you can't handle that, then fuck off. I don't need your goody-two-shoes shit in my life anymore. Because my feed is about to be full of the truth as I see it. I'm about to tell it how it is. So, here goes, you arseholes.

I scan the second post, shared minutes after the rant, and swallow back the bile that immediately rises. It's a disgusting racist meme with a comment – apparently from me – saying: 'YES to this!'

Another message pops up from Kemi:

Another one's just been posted.

She messages another screenshot. This post is a reshare of a sexist, anti-feminist rant that enrages me.

Kemi:

There's more…

More screenshots come through. The fourth post talks about denying the World War Two Holocaust, peddling a horrifying conspiracy theory that the Jews made it all up. Then a fifth, which is shockingly homophobic and links to a video that I don't even want to click on, and a sixth about how climate change doesn't exist and that everyone who believes the 'fake science' should be 'shot for stupidity'. All of it spewing hatred and discrimination.

I can't believe that this kind of evil even exists on the internet, let alone that it's been shared on my Facebook page. It's distressing and terrifying, and the complete polar opposite to my beliefs.

They're followed by Kemi's message:

Definitely think your account has been hacked!

Another few screenshots come through with the message:

And looks like your profile is public because you're getting all kinds of freaky comments...

I look at the screenshots of some of the comments under the first racist post, and Kemi is right. There are fifty-two reactions, ranging from likes to loves to angry and sad faces, and twenty-two comments, many from people I've never heard of before, definitely not my friends. But then there are replies from people who *are* my friends saying that they don't agree with me or that I need to rethink my attitude or that they're de-friending.

My cheeks burn – how could anyone think I'm saying these things? I would never post this poison because I don't think this poison.

I tap a message back to Kemi:

Fucking hell! I'm going to log on now and delete everything.

She replies with a thumbs-up emoji.

I put my phone aside and try to log in to Facebook for a third time. Again, the password that PW-Protekt adds in automatically is incorrect. I search for my Face-book page, which, although I've always had the strictest privacy settings from day one, is now public, and see the offensive content plastered across it.

This is insane.

My social media is like an extension of me, and it's frightening that I'm not in control of what is coming out of my mouth. Someone is polluting my online world, appropriating my voice, aligning me to beliefs that are most definitely NOT my own. They are deliberately alienating me from my friends and acquaintances, oblit-erating my network.

I click on PW-Protekt and enter my master pass-word. All my many passwords are saved in this piece of software – for social media, emails, Spotify, Netflix, all the various work platforms that we have to use. Nearly ninety passwords are saved. And for security, PW-Protekt generates random passwords to use, and each is different. I've used it for about a year, and it's been bril-liant. I just have to remember the one master password to log in.

There's a split second after I click OK, and then an error message pops up: Password incorrect.

The bottom falls out of my stomach, and I feel as if the ground beneath my feet is now a yawning chasm and I'm tumbling, tumbling down into nothingness.

How can my master password not work? It's always worked. It's the only password I have to remember.

Shit.

I click on 'Forgotten password?' and put in my personal Gmail email, which is linked to the PW-Protekt account. I open Gmail and go to log in to my account. But I can't. The password that PW-Protekt has automati-cally added is incorrect.

I start to sweat: a trickle down my spine, armpits

dampening, palms going clammy. This cannot be happening.

Grabbing my phone, I open the email application. But it bars me, asking for my password to proceed.

"I don't know my password," I yell.

I click on 'Forgotten Password?' on Facebook too, and it says it's sent a code to my email – my Gmail email that I can't access.

"Oh shit, oh shit, oh shit."

I tap out a message to Kemi:

Can't log in. Pls can you post a comment saying that you think I've been hacked. Am working on getting it sorted!

Sure. There's been some more posts.

My Facebook profile is now a hotbed of right-wing extremist bullshit, and I can't do anything to change it. I see Kemi's comment on one post, but it's right at the end of a long stream of comments.

My body shakes. It hurts to inhale, my vision falters, and terror crawls through my belly. I feel completely out of control. It's the same feeling I had when I had an accident while on a skiing holiday with Kemi when we were twenty-two. That skidding, slipping, falling, sliding. Down, down, down. Picking up speed with no way to slow up. Then, I thought I was going to die. I ended up with lots of bruising and a broken wrist. That out-of-control sensation before a tree broke my fall comes back to me now. The same rush of nausea. The same flood of panic.

Am I having some kind of panic attack? Calm down, Lauren. *Calm. The. Fuck. Down.*

And think.

I trawl through the Facebook help page to see if

there's anything about what to do if you can't log in with the email or phone number associated with the account and go through the straightforward account recovery steps. But I'm still blocked. I search what to do if I think my account has been hacked and spot immediately that I can report a compromised account. I follow the instructions to do just that. Easy.

But it tells me it's sent an email to the email address associated with the account. And I can't log in to that sodding email. I slap the sofa's armrest in frustration.

Lauren, I hear Mum's steadying voice, *now's the time to use your practical, logical, solutions-orientated brain to fix this.*

I can use my other social media channels to let everyone know. Yes. That's it. I try to log in to Twitter, but once again, the autofill password is incorrect. I search for my profile on Twitter, which is public, and see – to my horror – the offensive content has been posted there too, as well as retweets of awful, awful things.

The same has happened on my LinkedIn and Instagram accounts. I see my follower numbers have dropped and read comments from my friends, acquaintances and contacts in my personal and professional networks saying that they don't support what I'm saying so don't want any association with me anymore.

Scarily, I also read messages of support. There are some seriously messed-up people out there, and currently they're all congregating online on my social media channels.

I have to get back into PW-Protekt. There must be a way. I look at the help page, follow the various steps but don't get anywhere. Links are sent to the email I can't log into or texts to a blanked-out phone number, which ends in three digits that *aren't mine.* Another burner phone? It's clear my password manager software has been hacked – but how? It can only be accessed with the master password on the website, via the app on my work laptop or the app on my phone.

It had been so easy to use up until now, the app starting and opening automatically when I logged on to my laptop. It had made me feel almost smug that I was taking such good care of my online security – as if my personal information and passwords were now infallible. I recommended PW-Protekt to anyone who'd listen. How did I first hear about it? It had been a recommendation from...

Imani.

I saw her using it at work and asked her about it. She said that she used it not for security, but that it was the ultimate lazy-girl hack – it automatically filled in passwords on every site and saved them so you didn't even have to expend energy or brain power in remembering them all. Imani uses it. Imani knows how it works.

A boulder drops squarely into the bottom of my throat, and I choke to get my breath out. Imani had access to my laptop before the CozMoz Paints meeting when the porn was played. She could've deactivated my account or changed my passwords. Or found out my master password or given herself 'emergency access' and then logged in on the website earlier today.

I've not been targeted randomly by some faceless hacker. *It's her.* She's the one posting appalling content on my social media accounts. I picture her rubbing her hands together with glee: *evil cackle* Oh, what fun to wipe out Lauren's entire online life! Mwahaha!

I need to stop this malicious bitch before my reputation is well and truly left in tatters.

My phone pings. It's a message in my WhatsApp uni friends' group, which is always pretty active. Apart from Kemi, the seven in this group are my closest mates.

It's from Farida, one of the first friends I made during freshers' week.

> Lauren, we've discussed, and we don't agree with what you're posting online. I'm the admin for this group, and we've all agreed to remove you.

I immediately type a message, but it won't let me send it, and I get the text: 'Farida removed you' and 'You can't send messages to this group because you're no longer a participant'. I find the direct chat between Farida and me and type out a message to say I've been hacked. But it doesn't deliver and only shows one tick. My heart sinks. She's already blocked me.

My landline phone trills, and I jump. It rarely rings and is usually junk calls or my aunt, who prefers to call people on their landlines for some inexplicable reason that makes sense only to her.

I pick up the phone. "Auntie Joyce?" I ask, desperate to talk to her all of a sudden.

"Yes. Hello, dear."

A rush of warmth floods through me. My aunt's soothing, steady voice calms me. She sounds so much like Mum.

She continues, "I don't have long. We're about to board a flight to Portugal, and my phone battery is almost at zero. Kelly's told me that you seem to have put some funny stuff on Facebook. I don't have it, as you know, but she wanted me to talk to you. Kelly says it's not too nice what you've posted and is quite angry about it, saying you've brought shame on the family and whatnot. Now, I know you're a wonderful person and grief affects us all in different ways, my dear, and can make some people go off the rails a little. So I think you should see a grief counsellor. That'll help you get your head sorted. Your mum made it her mission in life to spread happiness and kindness, and I know it's not like you to be unpleasant or impolite. Your mum would be ever so disappointed if she knew that."

Brought shame on my family? Disappointed Mum? That is the last thing I'd ever want to do. Of course my cousin Kelly has seen it and said something. All of my extended family has now probably heard about it one way or another.

"Oh, Auntie Joyce, so much has happened—"

But I get the dead tone and suspect her battery has gone flat. I replace the receiver and scroll in my mobile phone contacts for my uncle's number, but before I can dial it, my mobile rings in my hand.

15

"Toby! OMG, have you *seen* my social media—"

But my brother cuts me off abruptly.

"You told Mum and Dad," Toby yells.

"What?" I reply, confused by his fury.

"Don't pretend not to know, Lauren. You're the only person I told, and I told you not to tell them. And you did, didn't you? Couldn't keep your mouth shut for a few days. Had to blab."

"I haven't said anything to them, I swear."

"You sent an email to Dad! He told me."

"I'd never do anything to hurt you, Toby. Someone has accessed my email account and must've sent that email—"

"Did you do all this to keep hold of your favourite-child status? Did you think your shine was fading? Believe me, it wasn't. Dad already favours you over me. And you clearly wanted to bring me down even further in his estimation. But I honestly didn't think you'd have it in you to be so cruel."

"That's not true, Toby!"

"Bullshit." He hangs up.

The silence booms in my ear. I slowly lower my phone. I didn't tell anyone about Toby, not even Akshay. It was my brother's news to tell. Toby messaged me on WhatsApp when I was at work yesterday, just before the CozMoz Paints meeting…

Aargh.

My WhatsApp web app was open on my laptop. Imani must've read Toby's messages. They would've been right at the top. And now she's sent this email to Dad just to upset me further. My disgust and revulsion at the offensive content and panic at not being able to get onto my social media channels turns to anger at someone screwing with my family.

I call Toby. It rings once and then goes to voicemail – I guess he's cancelled my call. I don't leave a voicemail, as I know he'll never listen to it. Instead, I send him a text message reiterating that I've been hacked and that I didn't tell Dad. I know he's more likely to read that.

I'll go to his apartment. And if he's not there, I'll wait for him at his bar. I need to explain everything to him, to make him understand this wasn't me.

I gather up my handbag, but my laptop, which is sat on the coffee table, flashes. I look at the screen. It's white with red blobs fading in and out. It looks like… blood splatters.

I click on the mouse touchpad, but aggressive earsplitting heavy metal music blares out. I jerk so violently that I almost leave my own skin. I cover my ears with my hands in an attempt to block out the shouty male vocals.

The blood splatters shrink to nothing, and just as abruptly, the music stops. My desktop reappears with my folders and shortcuts. Was that some kind of tech meltdown? I lean towards my laptop, and the screen glitches. Imperceptibly at first. But then it gets wilder until it's like a blizzard.

A message pops up in red letters across my screen:

I KNOW WHAT YOU DID, LAUREN.

My pulse quickens. I haven't done anything. I know I haven't done anything. She's just trying to scare me by messing with my laptop.

Angry, I shout at the screen. "Stop playing games, Imani! You've seriously taken your little joke too far by involving my family. That's it!" I jab the power button and watch as the screen fades to black. I slam down the laptop lid.

My flash of fury dissolves as I realise I'm sat in darkness, and a shiver ripples down my spine. I look towards my sliding glass door and see my reflection and the gloom beyond. In the silence and darkness, I feel watched, as if there are eyes everywhere, observing my every move. I spring up and switch the outside light on.

It illuminates the patio and most of the garden. I stare just past the edges of the light. I get the distinct feeling that I've locked onto eye contact, that someone is staring right back at me, but I can't see them.

Is Imani out there? Has she been watching me this entire time? I have to know. I grab the little just-in-case torch that Akshay keeps in a bowl by the back door and switch it on. I open the sliding glass door and step out into the night. I shine the torch to and fro along the back of my garden and stride purposely towards the fallen fence panel.

I scan the beam in every dark corner. But there's no one in my garden. I look past my garden boundary at the row of garages behind. I shine the torch, but it doesn't reach that far and just creates deeper shadows.

A gust of wind rattles me, and my whole body does one big shiver from top to toe. I realise my socks are getting damp, and every leaf rustle, every creak of a branch, every bang of the next-door neighbour's loose shed door in the wind sends fear coursing through my veins. It's creepy out here. I feel exposed. My bravado fades faster than a summer tan, and I need to get back inside. I whirl around and see the door into my house wide open. Oh shit, did someone creep in when my back was turned?

I'm paralysed with indecision. Stay put or face whoever might be in the house? No, I would've heard someone stepping on my patio, wouldn't I?

There's a crash from the garages, and I look over my shoulder to see a metal dustbin spilling its guts onto the concrete, the top rolling to a clattering stop.

That's it. I run back into the house, slam closed the door, make sure it's locked and the windows are shut, and close the curtains and blind. I go to the front door and put the deadbolt across.

It was a fox, I tell myself, *only a fox looking for a meal. And there's no one in the house. Don't be ridiculous. Get a grip, girl.*

I'm so, so cold all of a sudden that I need a hot drink. In my kitchen, I turn the kettle on. As I take a mug from the cupboard, my hands shake so much that I drop it, and it shatters on the tiled floor. The sight of the smashed pieces of my favourite mug overwhelms me. I grab hold of the counter before my legs buckle. I take long, deep breaths and try to process everything that's just happened.

My emotions, thoughts and feelings all swirl, and it takes me a while to pinpoint exactly how I'm feeling: under attack.

First, infuriating issues at work that make me look

incompetent, then my relationship ripped apart, my stable and comfortable home life pulled out from under my feet, my professional and personal reputation set on fire online, and now my family targeted and deliberately hurt. It's like all the spinning plates of my life that I've worked so hard to keep in perfect harmony are crashing down around me, and I can only watch, desperate to save them, but my hands are tied. The vulnerability of my happy life has been laid bare, ripe for the picking by someone cruel enough to pluck it apart bit by bit.

A spider runs out from under one of the cabinets and pauses next to a chunk of mug. I recoil, as I hate spiders, and Akshay's name forms on my lips. But he's not here. I'm on my own. I find a glass and a piece of paper without taking my eyes off the creature, then trap it and fling it out the window without completely freaking out. This small act gives me the boost of confidence I need.

As I find the dustpan and brush and sweep up the pieces of my mug, I work out a game plan. I have to take charge of this situation. Imani might have the upper hand now, but the tables can turn.

First things first, I find my phone and call Dad. I need to explain about Toby.

He answers his mobile with an *mmm hmm*, indicating that he's angry – too angry to even say hello to me.

"Dad, I didn't send that email to you about Toby. I think someone at work has got it in for me, and they must've read my texts. I would never have gone against Toby's wishes by telling you."

But he's not listening. "I wondered when you might call. That's all part of your plan, isn't it?"

"Plan?"

"What were you thinking? Posting all that homophobic crap about Toby on my Facebook page."

Dad has more friends than me on Facebook. He and

Diane are social creatures, out all the time and with a huge group of acquaintances.

"Dad, that wasn't me. My social media accounts have been hacked, just like my email."

"Not only did you tell on your brother, blabbing about his sexuality before he could tell us, you've also told all our friends and family about it too."

"Dad—"

But he's got a bee in his bonnet, and there's no getting through to him when he's on one.

"And that's not what disappoints me the most. Your brother does not deserve to be treated with disrespect because of his sexuality. He is free to love whomever he pleases. And why would you think I'd agree with all this homophobic nonsense that you've covered my Facebook page with? Hmm? Because I'm in my sixties, you think I'd disapprove. Well, I'll have you know that Bob and Andy at our bowls club are gay, and they are both decent, friendly, perfectly nice chaps. They've been over to ours for dinner many a time. Did you think you'd win my favour by letting the cat out of the bag about Toby before he got the chance to tell us? Hmm?"

I raise my voice to try to get through to him. "Listen to me! I'm not doing these things. Someone else sent you that email. Someone else spammed your Facebook page. It was NOT me."

"You've lost the plot like your mother. Hurting people just to get attention."

"What are you going on about?"

"Judy had a number of issues before you came along, let me tell you. I'm beginning to wonder if you're that way inclined too."

I'm stunned at this revelation about my mother's mental health and can't form a reply.

Dad continues, "You're my daughter, and I love you.

But this behaviour isn't acceptable. Hurting your brother and then trying to hurt me by shaming him isn't acceptable. Understood?"

But before I can reply, Dad says, "Speak to you in a few days." And – like his son before him – hangs up on me.

Solid, dependable, practical Dad is incensed at something I haven't done. He's always been there for me, no matter what. Mum's gone, and now I can't turn to my father or brother. And what was he talking about with my mother's mental issues? That's never been mentioned before. Mum was always so happy, fun-loving, and bright.

I look at Dad's Facebook by googling it on my phone and see some of the homophobic comments on his profile. As I'm looking, one post is no longer available, then the next. Dad, obviously working his way through and deleting them all.

How could anyone be so cruel? To deliberately destroy a happy relationship between parent and child, between siblings. I feel severed from my family, cast adrift. Like an untethered astronaut desperately floating away from the mothership with no hope of reconnection.

But I'm a survivor. And there's some fight left in me yet.

16

I f Imani thinks I'm going to take this sitting down, she's got another thing coming. Hurting my brother and now my father. And doing so in a way that they don't believe me when I tell them it's not me – by using my own email and social media accounts.

Scrolling through my contacts app, I find Imani's number, take a deep breath and press dial. It rings. And rings. And then goes through to voicemail. I hesitate but don't leave a message. I need to talk to her and get her to stop this campaign against me and rectify the damage she's wreaked so far. I'll give it a few minutes and then try again.

I stand up and put the coffee table upright again. I don't know why I haven't done it sooner. This simple act makes me feel a modicum of control and bolsters my spirit, as if fixing my life will be just as easy.

As I'm putting everything back in its place on the coffee table, my phone rings. Imani calling me back. I sit on the sofa, back straight, poised for action. I pick up my phone and check the screen. Disappointment soars.

It's not Imani. It's a local landline number that I don't recognise and which isn't saved in my contacts.

I answer. A friendly voice explains she's from the supermarket and that I was meant to have a food delivery that evening, but there's something that she needs to check. The normality of the call and the friendliness of the voice is like a balm. Dealing with mundane everyday matters is manageable after all the drama of the past few hours. It reminds me that normal, regular life does still exist and that I'll get back to it soon.

"I'm afraid the card on account has been declined. Perhaps it's out of date?" she asks helpfully.

"No, it shouldn't be," I reply.

I fish my wallet out of my handbag and find my debit card, the one I use for most things. I read out the details, and the supermarket employee confirms that's the card they have on file, and that's the card that isn't working.

"But it doesn't go out of date for another two years," I say.

"Sorry," she says. "It's been declined. Do you have another we could use to take the payment?"

That's odd. Must be some glitch in the system. "Yeah, sure." I find my credit card and read out the details.

"Thanks, will just take a moment."

I'd completely forgotten about the food delivery. At the thought of food, my stomach gurgles. I haven't eaten anything for lunch, and it's now nearly dinner time.

"Hmm, sorry about this, but that card has been declined too," she says apologetically.

The dread rises. Once is bad luck, twice is... something else. How can both cards not be working? "Can you try again?"

"I have done, dearie, twice, and both times it's not worked. Don't suppose you have another card to try?"

I pull out my second credit card, which I only use for big purchases like holidays and in emergencies. I read out the card information.

"Thanks," she says brightly, but then I hear her 'hmmm', and she says, "Sorry, dearie, my system's not liking that one either."

All three not working... Has Imani messed with my bank cards somehow?

"Shit," I blurt, and the supermarket employee thinks I'm swearing at her.

Her tone changes to defensive as she replies, "I can't do anything about the system not accepting your cards."

"I'm sorry, it's not you or the system. There's an issue on my end."

"I see."

"I need to hang up now and go and sort it out."

"Certainly, but we won't be able to deliver your food unless it's paid for three hours in advance. I'll get an email sent out now for you to reorganise the delivery time."

"Thank you. Bye."

I end the call and stare into space. My finances now too? She must've cancelled my cards through my online banking. The password of which was saved in PW-Protekt, along with all the other security information required to gain access.

I attempt to log into my online banking account, keeping everything crossed – and hoping beyond hope – that the PW-Protekt autofill password and details will work.

They don't.

I can't access my money. I CAN'T ACCESS MY MONEY. The horror of this takes a while to sink in.

When it does, I feel well and truly hobbled.

I've had the same bank account since I opened it at fourteen. It was my first one. My savings account is with the same bank. And one of my credit cards. I trusted all the pieces of plastic, all the numbers on the screen. That's how we live, isn't it? That's how we do anything. And now the cards – my direct line to my cash – are useless.

What else has she done? Cancelled all my Direct Debits? My mortgage payments? My entire life will come to a grinding halt.

And what if she's stolen my money? Moved it to other accounts? Taken it all and left me with nothing. I've always worked hard to earn money to live comfortably, to eat well, to survive. I've always saved for nice things, to splurge every now and then. And I'd been saving more recently for the wedding and honeymoon. I had a tidy sum put away – the most I've ever had in savings.

I have to hope and pray she's not done that. Just restricted access to shit me up. Imani has no need for money – she's swimming in it.

This is a disaster. It's as if I've been thrown overboard amongst the sharks and they're slowly picking off every last bit of me before pulling me under.

How much worse can it get? What's next?

I dial Imani's number again.

"Hey," Imani answers, bored. "It's after work hours," she adds as if I'd better have a very good reason for calling her at 7 p.m. on a Wednesday.

I'm furious but force myself to switch to my calm and collected, in-control boss tone, thinking it the best way to get her to do anything, to reverse the harm she's caused by pressing the explode button on my life. I can still pick up the pieces and put things back together again as long as I handle this right: steady but firm. "Imani, this isn't cool. You need to stop."

She groans. "I knew you'd lose your shit. I was just trying to be funny."

"Funny? Are you *kidding* me?"

"Jeez, chill out. It was jokes."

"A joke? It has gone way too far to be a *joke*. You've made your point. You don't like me coming down on you heavy at work. And you're getting back at me. But this is not how it's done. If you have an issue with me, we talk about it like adults. We go to HR if necessary, but attacking me like this is not the answer."

"What the fuck? HR? I thought you had a sense of humour."

"I know you sent those emails at work, that you're responsible for the porn in that presentation. I know you sent those dirty texts and the lingerie—"

"Whoa. Stop. I've got no clue what you're talking about and seriously do NOT want to hear about your personal life. Dirty texts? I mean, eww."

"I've found you out. You had access to my laptop before the CozMoz meeting."

"You do know you're talking to Imani, from work, don't you?"

"Yes. You're not so clever. Did you think I wouldn't work it out?"

"Work what out?"

Frustrated at Imani's complete show of ignorance, I lose patience and shout, "That you've been targeting me and trying to ruin my life!"

Imani sighs impatiently. "Duh. I have zero interest in your life. I'm far too busy living *my own*. Screwing with you would take time and energy and headspace. And, you know, I have none of that for you. Ever."

This is unexpected. I thought she'd capitulate as

soon as I called her out. Or perhaps gloat and rub my nose in it for a while and then relent. But she's not concerned. She sounds utterly blasé.

Imani continues, "I thought you were calling me to tell me off for joking about watching and making porn in that media list email. But you're going on and on and on about shit I've got no idea about. And, to be honest, it's giving me a right headache."

I hear voices and laughter in the background, then a tannoy announcement. Imani adds, "My movie starts in five minutes. I can't be dealing with you calling me just to be... like... *weird*. Madeline said you weren't feeling well, but call a therapist or someone, you know, I'm *busy*."

I decide to change tack. "Did you see anyone near my laptop around the time I told you we'd won the supermarket business?"

"Huh?"

"Do you remember? I did a little dance?"

"Not especially," she replies.

"Not especially as in people near my laptop or that you remember?"

She huffs long and loud.

I continue, "Imani, this is important."

"I don't recall your 'little dance', and I don't remember anyone near your laptop."

"You're sure?"

"I don't spend all day looking at it. I'm not your laptop bodyguard now, am I?" she snaps.

"No, of course not."

There must be something that will trip her up. "Did you access my PW-Protekt?"

"You use that?"

"Yes. Did you access it?"

"No, why would I?" Someone in the background

shouts her name. "Look, is there something you actually need from me, for work? Like a client emergency or something?"

All the wind is knocked out of my sails, and my bluster fails. She's genuinely unfazed. All her responses are textbook Imani. If she's not going to admit to this, then I'll need to find some hard evidence.

"That's all for now, thanks. Enjoy your movie," I reply and hang up.

17

tumped. That's the word. I confronted the
perpetrator, and it didn't work. So what next?

I take stock of my situation. A part of me just
wants to retreat. To curl up in a ball and hope this'll all
blow over. Be realistic, Lauren. That's not going to
happen. There must be some evidence that points to
Imani. There has to be something that I can do... or
somewhere I can start... or someone who will help...

My money. I can't just let it disappear. I'll start there.

I scrabble in the 'important paperwork' box in the
front room for the letter from the bank with my telephone banking details. I so rarely call that I didn't
bother to add the information to my password manager.

I dial the number on the back of my bank card, listen
to various menus and press the right numbers. I'm told
I'm in a queue, and an earworm pop song cuts in. When
it finishes, it starts again. The same fecking song. I put
my phone on speaker and drum my fingers on the sofa's
armrest. A notification pops up on my screen – battery
running low.

Gah. I pick up the phone just in case someone

answers while I'm on the move, take the stairs two at a time and grab my charger from the bedroom. I bring it back downstairs and plug it in a kitchen socket. I stand there looking at the phone and listening to the same song again and again. I pace, do some shoulder stretches, which make me yelp – the tension of the past few days settling in my tight muscles there, and then put my forearms on the kitchen counter and cradle my head in them.

Thirty-five minutes later, after the music lulls me into a half-conscious state, a human says, "Hello?"

It startles me, and I fumble for my phone and almost drop it.

"Hello! Hello! Yes, I'm here."

I tell him my telephone banking number, which – thank the heavens – still works.

"I just need to ask you some questions to make sure you are who you say you are."

"Of course."

"What was the last transaction you made on your debit card?"

"Umm, paying for some shopping at Tesco Express in Chorlton on Thursday night? I think it was around thirty pounds?"

"No, that's not correct. Let's try another question. What is the approximate balance on your account?"

"Around two thousand." I know this for certain because I always keep about that amount in my current account after my salary is paid in every month. Anything over that goes into my savings account.

"Hmm, that's not quite right. What's the first line of your address?"

"Number twenty-four Three Acres Road."

"Have you moved recently? Is there a possibility that your account details need updating?"

"I moved here six months ago and changed my address then. I get post from you guys, so you've definitely got this address."

"Ah."

This is NOT going well. I desperately reel off information that isn't so easy to change. "My full name is Lauren Virginia Cohen. I've had the account for twenty-four years. I opened it in the Salford branch in February, just after my birthday. I have a credit card with you guys and a savings account. I took out a loan when I graduated and paid it off four years ago – I know this because it was just before I started at my current job—"

He cuts me off. "Thank you, Lauren. Can I just confirm your date of birth?"

I tell him, and when he replies with "That's what we have on our system," I almost weep with joy.

"However," he continues, "I'm not able to confirm your identity."

"That's because I think I've been a victim of fraud. I think someone has accessed my account without my approval and changed my personal details and password. I can't log on to my online banking, and none of my cards work," I say, trying to remain calm.

The call centre employee puts me through to the fraud department, and I'm on hold for another ten minutes. With every minute that passes, I can feel my blood pressure rising.

Finally, the call is picked up, and I'm asked the same questions to confirm my identity and have the exact same conversation. The fraud department employee asks me some more questions specifically about the fraud claim and determines that I'm probably telling the truth.

"Is there any money left in my account?" I ask.

"Because I can't verify your identity, I'm not able to

tell you that information," the fraud department employee replies.

"Are all my cards cancelled?"

I get the same reply.

"Is there *anything* you can tell me? I'm freaking out a bit here," I say.

"We'll investigate these claims as a matter of urgency and come back to you."

"What can I do to prove that this account belongs to me?"

"You will need to go into a branch with your passport and driving licence and potentially some other forms of ID to prove your identity."

"How long will it take for you to come back to me?" I ask, already plotting the route to my nearest branch to be first in line when it opens in the morning.

"It's going to take between twenty-four to forty-eight hours," he replies.

I can't access my money. It's probably all gone. And the bank is telling me to wait for up to two days. *"Seriously?"* I say in a tone brimming with exasperation.

"Please be assured we'll look into it as quickly as possible. Is there anything else I can help you with today?"

Maybe he can help me to rebuild the ruins of my life? To pin down the entitled twenty-something who's doing this to me? I say no, thank him, and end the call.

A broken heart I can just about cope with. It'll take time but it'll heal. But suddenly not having any money? That blows my mind. And all those years of saving for a rainy day? Well, it's absolutely pouring down, and I have nothing to fall back on. All of it, gone. Yes, Mum left me some money. But that isn't enough to live off for any length of time.

All that financial security, just… vanished. Poof. Up in smoke.

I google cybercrime UK. There's a dedicated centre to report financial fraud and cybercrime to the police. It has a hotline. I go to call it, but it's only open until 8 p.m., and it's now 8.17 p.m. FFS.

There's no way I'm waiting until tomorrow. So I navigate to the online reporting tool. I have to sign up first and automatically put in my personal email address, curse when I remember that is the account that's been compromised and change it to my work email, which I can still access at the moment. I complete the online report, write the report number on my notepad, and read the fine print: someone from the relevant police department will get back to me in… 'up to forty-eight hours'.

"You're taking the piss," I shout out loud. Why does it all take so long? My life has imploded, and everyone who might be able to help will 'get back to me'. I don't have forty-eight hours. It's all going tits up *right this very minute*.

Right. I need evidence. I know there are no cameras inside the office, so I know I can't find CCTV of Imani jumping onto my laptop and sending that email to supermarket Stephanie. Perhaps there are cameras in the car park that picked up Imani keying my car? But I remember the graphic designer's motorbike got stolen when he decided to leave it there over one weekend after a few heavy nights. He'd told me that there was CCTV only at the entrance/exit and not on each of the floors. Work's a dead end, then.

But what about the personal things? Perhaps I could compare a sample of her handwriting with the letters Akshay found in the tub outside? I rack my brain. There must be a time when I saw her handwriting. A memory pops up. I have seen it, and it's surprisingly neat and tidy, considering her completely impractical fingernails. It's nothing like the looping scrawl on the notes. But she could've got someone else to write those notes.

Or maybe I could somehow check her bank statement to see if she purchased the underwear and sex toy – but how would I even go about doing that? Or maybe I could ask Rob if he can check her laptop and see if she has some kind of deepfake software on it? But I discount that, because the IT guy would want to know why I needed to snoop on another colleague's laptop and likely inform Madeline.

What about the burner phone she used to send the dirty texts? Long binned by now. And even if it wasn't, where would she keep it? At home, I expect, and I can't exactly rock up and say, "Hi, Imani, can I just search through your belongings?"

There's nothing quick and simple I can think of that wouldn't involve some kind of highly irregular or illegal activity. And that's just not me. A twang of guilt about looking at Madeline's emails yesterday reverberates again. But if that's what I have to do... An uncomfortable knot forms in my chest.

I feel so isolated and impotent. Like someone has sucked out all the goodness of my life and left me with an empty husk. My brain aches from the mental torture, and I rub circles on my temples. Is this what Imani wants? To grind me down so completely that I self-destruct?

But an idea pops into my head. I check the time on my watch. There is *something* I can do.

18

I hunch down in my car in the car park at work, my eyes trained on the route down to the exit. I'm on the floor beneath the MBW floor. I drove up, saw Imani's car still parked there – hers was the only car – and then strategically parked so I could see when she left but so she wouldn't notice me.

She's still at the cinema. The movie must be ending soon, they all last around an hour and a half to two hours, and there's always a good twenty to thirty minutes of adverts at the start. And she went in around 7 p.m., after I'd called her. It's now gone nine.

I know exactly which cinema she goes to. It's just across the road from the office. She's told me before that she goes with three friends who also work in the city centre. It's a regular conversation within the PR team about what movie she might watch, and what she thinks of it the next day. She always goes on the same night because it's two-for-one Wednesdays. Not that I imagine Imani is bothered about saving money, but perhaps her friends are.

The lights on my floor go out, and I wait in the

gloom. They're automatic, and if I don't move the car, they won't come on again. Perfect.

But agitation crawls under my skin, and I can barely sit still. I'm sweating. Following people like some kind of private investigator on the tail of a cheating spouse isn't something I ever thought I'd do. I wrapped up warm in my big coat and scarf, as it's a cold night, but now I've got way too many layers on. But I don't dare take my seatbelt off to wrangle off my coat in case that's the moment Imani's car whizzes past.

The glass is beginning to steam up with my body heat, so I wind down the passenger-side window, which isn't facing the route that Imani will take. I doubt she'd notice a car with its window down, but you never know.

There are two other cars still parked on this floor, and I hope the owners don't come out any time soon. They're sure to spot me and wonder what I'm up to, hiding in my car, my head just high enough to see out the window. I switch my phone to silent, not wanting it to ring and somehow give me away.

I'm not entirely sure what I'm hoping to achieve. But I have to find some kind of evidence to prove that Imani is the one doing this to me. And if that means tailing her for a while, then so be it. I can't think of anything else to do right now.

A light snaps on from the floor above. Here we go. My finger hovers above the ignition button. A few moments later, headlights spin around, and Imani's in-your-face metallic pink Range Rover flies past on its way down to the exit. I catch a glimpse of the driver – it's definitely her.

I count to three and then follow, without turning on my headlights. As I turn into the exit barrier, I see the back of the Range Rover turning right. The car park empties onto a one-way street, so I know which way she'll go. I turn on my headlights and follow at a discreet distance.

The Manchester city roads are busy with traffic, but her car is hard to miss and hard to lose. It sticks out like a sore thumb among the drab cars around it. She drives south out of the city centre towards Wilmslow, where I know she lives. But I've never been to her house and don't know her address. I've never had to pick her up for a meeting or had any reason to go there.

As we get closer to where she must live, turning off the main road into a smaller, upmarket, new-build estate, I hang back. I've no idea whether she's noticed a car following her or not – and my Mini at that – and I've no idea what I'm doing. I watch from afar as she turns into the driveway of a small detached house. I drive past at a normal speed and glimpse her getting out of her car and heading towards her front door.

I turn at the end of the road and then head back, parking on the other side of the road not quite opposite. I see the light in a downstairs window come on. It's the kitchen. She doesn't bother pulling the blind. I watch as she puts some bread in the toaster, looks in the fridge and pulls out a tub of butter, opens drawers, puts a plate and knife on the counter.

My mouth goes dry, and I get an achy feeling in my side like a stitch. This is so intrusive. It doesn't feel right. She's oblivious to my presence. How would I feel if I found out someone was watching me in my home like this? It's awful to imagine. She looks so vulnerable. And I feel so... sleazy. Nausea squirms, and I almost turn away and drive off. But I'm rooted to the spot. I have to find out who's doing this to me. And if this is the only way, then I need to persevere. I decide to approach this with a clinical, unemotional mindset. It's a job I need to get done.

I swallow back the bile and continue my observation. The toast pops. She inspects it, finds it wanting and puts it back in the toaster to brown a little more. She wanders out of the kitchen, and I can no longer see her.

Movement in my mirror catches my eye, and I see a dogwalker coming towards me with a tail-wagging golden retriever. I scramble for my phone in my bag and hold it to my ear, pretending to have an intense conversation and saying loudly, "That's not right... I told you... No..." as the man walks past.

He glances at me, but the look is disinterested. I'm just someone who's pulled over randomly to take a phone call. Not someone who's spying on the woman in the house over the road.

When he's gone far enough, I drop my phone and turn back to Imani's house. She dashes into the kitchen and shoves open the window with a grimace, then wafts a tea towel. The toast must've burnt.

Her head jerks, and she picks up her phone. She drops the tea towel and wafts her hand in front of her face as she leaves the room again, talking on her phone. For a long while, nothing happens. No other lights come on at the front of the house.

She must be in a room at the back. Perhaps she's getting ready for bed. What's my plan now? Stay here all night? Or head home?

I look at my location on my GPS app and drop a pin so I can find this place again should I need to.

As I'm looking at my phone, the light in the kitchen clicks off. She's heading to bed, she must be. I might as well go home.

But the front door opens.

Shit. I slouch right down in my seat. Has she seen

me? Does she know I've followed her all the way from work? She's peeped out of a dark window and seen me in my Mini outside her house like a crazy woman.

What the hell am I going to say? Should I speed off or confront this? My sweats from the car park return with a vengeance, and I can feel my brow breaking out with perspiration. It balls up and streams down the sides of my face. My armpits are sodden, and the creases in my stomach fill with an uncomfortable dampness.

She's got changed into a different outfit: oversized hoodie, joggers, and trainers. She steps off her front porch and closes the door, heading down her driveway. If I'm going to go, it has to be *now*.

But she opens the back door of her car, tosses in a large overnight bag, then gets in the driver's side and starts the engine, the headlights popping on.

She's going out? At almost 10.30 p.m. on a Wednesday? I'd be getting ready for bed right about now, if not tucked up already. I can't keep my eyes open any later on weeknights. But she's fourteen years younger than me and clearly doesn't need the sleep.

She reverses off her driveway and accelerates away, thankfully in the opposite direction to where I'm parked and not passing me. I watch her taillights and then look back to her house.

I haven't been rumbled. Thank god for that. I breathe a sigh of relief so huge it fogs the windowpane briefly. As it dissipates, I notice something.

Her kitchen window is still wide open. She's gone out and forgotten to close it.

I'm torn. Follow or... break in? I gulp at the thought.

And decide to follow her.

She drives for about fifteen minutes to a smart townhouse closer to the centre of Wilmslow. She pulls up outside, and I pull over up the road, on a slight hill. She grabs her overnight bag off the back seat, then heads to the front door. She doesn't once look in my direction. Cars zip past. It's a much busier road to the one her house is on.

I watch as the door is opened by a man, and Imani jumps into his arms. They kiss and hug on the front doorstep for quite some time. Her boyfriend? Is this the man she was with when I called on Monday morning? She's never mentioned a boyfriend at work, but that doesn't mean anything. This could just be a booty call, not anything serious. Eventually they pull apart, he takes her bag, and she heads inside. He closes the door behind her.

A light pings on from an upstairs room, and I see the man come to draw the curtains. As his arms are spread, a hand on each curtain, Imani puts her arms around his waist and nuzzles his neck, putting one hand up his jumper, the other edging under the waistband of his jeans. He yanks the curtains shut.

She's obviously going to be there a while. And, judging by the bag, more than likely she'll be there overnight.

I have a choice to make.

19

A s I drive back to Imani's house, my conscience attempts to convince me this is a VERY BAD IDEA.

But I'm on it. This is an opportunity I can't afford to miss. When else will I get a chance to look in Imani's house? To find proof that she's behind this attack on me?

It has to be now.

I park up the road, not directly outside her house. Just in case someone sees me, or happens to spot my car, or something goes horribly wrong. I unstick my fingers from the steering wheel, which are holding on for dear life, and take three deep breaths. I place my phone in my coat pocket and stuff my handbag under the passenger seat. I unwind my chunky scarf and leave it in the passenger footwell, knowing full well it's only going to get in my way…

… when I break into my account executive's house.

Eek. The thought of what I'm about to do stalls me once again. But I can't delay. It's now or never.

I check my mirrors and look around. The road is

quiet. No more dogwalkers. I jump out of the car, shut the door and lock it, dropping the keys in the other coat pocket. I run to Imani's house, keeping to the shadows of fences, bushes, and the occasional tree along the pavement.

I turn up her driveway, edge past her front door, and stand by the open window. It's higher up than I thought it would be, the front garden sloping down to the house. The bottom of the window is about level with my chest. I put my hands on the inside of the window frame, rally my courage, and then haul myself up. It reminds me of attempting to get out of a swimming pool along the sides when the steps are busy. Except I don't have the water to kick in for a boost.

I let out a grunt with the effort and immediately go silent. Did anyone hear that? Oh god, this is not me at all. Hurry up, hurry up, hurry up. I manage to get my body up and balance on my waist.

Beneath the window is the kitchen sink. I readjust my arms and lift one knee up and wedge it on the window frame, then the other, and then I'm through. I spill into the sink and knock over the washing-up liquid and soap, and a mug on the draining board clatters over but, thank heavens, doesn't shatter. I can set those right on the way out.

I untangle my limbs – which I know will bruise up a treat with all the knocks – and jump to the floor, immediately spinning around to see if there are any bystanders in the street disapprovingly watching this performance and already on the phone to the police. But there's no one. Everything is still and silent outside. And everything is still and silent inside.

Now I'm here, where do I start? What am I even looking for?

A dog barks nearby. I drop down under the countertop, out of sight. My breath comes in short pants. Has another dogwalker spotted me? Or has a neighbour clocked the open window and come to investigate?

I huddle against the cupboard door so anyone coming closer to peer through the window won't see me. But the barking quietens until it sounds far away.

A car drives past, and it reminds me that Imani could be coming home at any minute. She might decide not to stay over. I need to get a move on.

Her laptop. Let's start there.

I spring up and scan the kitchen, the hallway and the lounge. There's another room downstairs, which is full of gym equipment. Not there. I take the stairs two at a time and go into the first door. The bathroom. I scan what looks like a spare room slash overflow closet with clothes, handbags, and shoes tossed everywhere and then the master bedroom, which is the complete opposite and is surprisingly tidy. I open the final door, and it's an office. A laptop sits on the desk, lid closed. It's an Apple and brand new, so not her work one.

Bingo. I fling it open, hoping beyond hope it might be unlocked and on. It isn't. A black screen stares indignantly back at me. I press the power button. There's a chance Imani doesn't use a password. As it whirs to life, I look around the room. It's pretty bare, with a beanbag in one corner and a floor-to-ceiling shelving unit filled with books and folders. There's a pile of papers and letters on the desk.

The screen comes to life with a prompt to enter a password. Dammit. There's no chance I can guess her password. I switch it off again and close the lid.

There must be something... perhaps the burner phone she used to text me those dirty messages? Long shot, but worth a look.

I rummage through the desk drawers, careful not to

move anything too far out of place. Then I flick through the paperwork pile and the folders on the shelves. It's all official documents from a mortgage company and letters from her solicitor about the house purchase. Just the usual correspondence. She has a folder full of old university coursework, books, and leaflets.

I head into the master bedroom and straight to the bedside cabinet. There's what looks like a journal buried under other odds and sods. I hesitate. Breaking in is one thing, but reading a private journal? That's something else entirely. I'm crossing a line here, and there's no going back. But she might've written something in there about me, about what she's doing to me. I have to know.

I pull it out and mouth *sorry* to the sky. I can feel my mother's disapproving eyes on me from up there. She was very strict on boundaries and privacy when I was growing up. Prying was very much frowned upon. Sorry, Mum, but this is necessary.

Gritting my teeth, I flick through the handwritten pages to the last entry, dated three weeks ago. I skim read, and it's some trivial crap about an argument Imani had with her father. I find the entry before, dated two years earlier. Clearly not an avid diarist, then. And that doesn't help me. I've only known Imani for a year.

Still, I open at random and skim read the contents just in case I see my name. I do this twice more, coming across Imani's graphic description of her seduction and conquest of a married man – a friend of her father's, no less. I gag at the image it conjures. Clearly not going to find anything to do with me in these pages.

I slip the journal back and continue the search. In Imani's chest of drawers is one drawer dedicated to lingerie. I grimace, pout my lips, and push aside the disgust at what I'm about to do. The idea of the reverse – of Imani going through my underwear drawer –

makes me shudder. But she could be hiding something in there. I tentatively lift and move items with my fingertip and hold my head away as if whatever I might find is going to slither and hiss.

A flash of red catches my eye, and I pull out a slinky babydoll. It looks exactly the same as the one that arrived for me with the sex toy. I check the label. *Trudy's.* It's the same lingerie brand.

Imani has exactly the same lingerie as was sent to me – is that proof of anything? Or simply a coincidence? Did she buy this at the same time as she purchased one for me?

I stare at it for a while until a bang from outside startles me, and I drop the underwear back in the drawer and push it shut. I stand very still. I hear distant chatter. Male and female voices. And car doors slam.

Is that Imani come home? What would I say if she found me in her house? What would she think? That I've completely gone off the rails. I called her, rambling, and now I'm in her house. She'd call me a stalker, a freak. And say there was something very wrong with me. The last thing I need is for everyone to think I've now got an unhealthy fixation on my account executive. Would she call the police?

I should've brought my scarf with me to wrap around my head as a disguise. I could hide and then charge out of her house when her back's turned. As I'm looking around for a scarf or something of Imani's that I could use to cover my head, I realise something: the front door remains closed. I'm still the only one in the house.

It must've been her neighbours. I need to hurry up and get the fuck out of here. I check my watch; I've been thirty minutes already. I get a rocket up my bum and lift up her mattress, scan under her bed, flick through the clothes in her wardrobe, look in a few shoeboxes, and riffle through the make-up, wigs, and hair products on her vanity table.

I peek in the spare room, decide against fighting my way through the mounds of clothes-shoes-handbags, and hurry downstairs. In the lounge I look through drawers. But there's nothing. I head into the kitchen and do a quick scan in the top drawers and cupboards. Aargh. There has to be something else.

A cool breeze ruffles my hair, and I stare at the open window. I need to get out of here. I've already been here too long. I see my car up the road, and it seems to say to me: *C'mon, Lauren! I shouldn't be here. We shouldn't be here. This isn't our neighbourhood. That's not your house.*

But the lingerie isn't enough. I can't leave with nothing. Just one more sweep. I must've missed some vital clue. I'll be fast.

And I should take a photo of the babydoll. I curse myself for not thinking of that earlier.

I turn to leave the kitchen and pull my phone out of my coat pocket. It's still on silent, and a notification pops up on the screen. I've had sixteen missed calls. *Sixteen!* As I frown at my phone, it lights up with another call. An unknown local number. Someone really wants to speak to me.

"Hello?" I answer quietly, stiffly.

"Hello, Lauren?" a female voice asks.

"Er, yes."

"Sorry to wake you. It's Mrs Simpson, Judy's neighbour."

"Oh, hi, Mrs Simpson…" I reply, baffled, realising my whispering must sound as if I've just been woken from sleep, and am not creeping around someone else's home while they're out. "Everything okay?"

"Well, no, love, it's not. I've been trying to get hold of you for a while."

A bubble of alarm rises in my chest and pops. All I can think about is why my mum's neighbour, who came to the funeral on Monday, is calling me. Suddenly I don't care where I am. No longer whispering, I say in a rush, "Has something happened?"

"I'm sorry to say this, but there's been a fire."

"A fire?"

"Yes, at your mum's flat. I think you should come here…"

"I'm coming right now," I say and hang up.

20

As I pull into the quiet Salford cul-de-sac, I'm faced with an almost apocalyptic scene of four fire engines and two police cars, flashing lights, and people everywhere. Neighbours stand in the street and stare while firefighters come and go and the police prevent people getting too close.

I stop the car in the middle of the road and jump out, leaving the door open and the engine running. I run towards the two-storey detached building that once housed my mother's ground-floor flat and another flat owned by a young couple on the first floor.

Wispy smoke and what looks like steam trickles out from the melted window frames, the glass jagged and shattered or missing completely. The red-brick walls and just-about-intact roof are blackened with soot.

"Ma'am," a police officer says and catches me before I can go any further.

Although I see no flames, the heat and smoke stench coming off the building is palpable. Firefighters haul a water jet out of a downstairs bay window, the last few drops of water dripping out of the tip. Mum's bedroom window, I know.

Mrs Simpson comes running over. "Lauren!"

I nod, not able to form any words.

Together, Mrs Simpson and the police officer lead me a few steps away from the burnt-out building and try to stand me so I face away, but I turn back.

Mrs Simpson talks, but it doesn't register. The police officer heads over to one of the firefighters and points back at me.

I can't tear my eyes away from the torched wreck in front of me. My mum lived in that ground-floor apartment for nearly fifteen years. It has a small garden out the back. When she moved in, she had a dog called Alfie. The sweetest Staffordshire bull terrier from a nearby dog shelter. When Alfie died, we buried him in that garden.

Fifteen years' worth of memories are in that place. *Were* in that place.

All her photos, trinkets, clothes, jewellery, books, stuff. Her presence still lingered there, her *smell*. Everything I had left of her that wasn't my own memories was within those four walls. I thought I had all the time in the world to sort through it. To cherish the things that weren't worth anything money-wise, but were worth everything to Mum, and so, to me.

But no. It's gone. All gone.

A gigantic crack emanates from inside the building as a beam or some piece of wood succumbs. For a moment I think it's my devastated heart wrenching apart, damaged beyond repair.

How could this have happened?

Mrs Simpson is still talking, clearly on a high from all the drama, and I tune in. "Thank goodness the couple who live in the flat upstairs are on holiday. We're feeding their cat, you see. Flossy likes to do the rounds, and she was in with us for some fuss and ham when I noticed the smell." She nods towards her house, next to my mum's building, and I see Mr Simpson in the front window, holding a cat. He waves at me.

Mrs Simpson continues, "I called the fire service immediately, and they arrived in under ten minutes. I told them that the building was empty, and they contained the fire pretty quickly, and it didn't spread to any other houses, thank the lord. You should've seen the flames – thick, black, and yellow. And the smell, what a pong. Apparently, that's the plastic going up. And not long after the fire engines arrived, the front window blew out. A huge bang! So dramatic. They asked me to call you, and then we couldn't find the darn address book where I'd written your number. By the time we found it – in the cupboard under the stairs of all places! Both of us are getting so forgetful these days – they'd pretty much put the fire out. Very efficient."

"Is there anything left?" I mutter.

She shakes her head sadly. "The firefighters have said it's gutted in there. Not much survived on the ground floor. I'm sorry."

She catches me as I stumble, and holds me upright with an impossibly firm grip for a nearly eighty-year-old. I slump against her. I have this urge to cry, but nothing comes. As if the fire has sucked out all the moisture from my eyes too. My eyelids scratch as I blink.

All I can think of is my mum's precious photos. Boxes and boxes of them. She'd sorted through them all when she was nearing the end. I picture them in her lounge, exactly where she left them, and imagine fire eating at the edges and licking up the sides and then consuming them in one big whoomph of flame.

I choke out a dry sob, which turns into a wail that goes on for a long time.

Mrs Simpson pats my hand in sympathy. When my wail abruptly ends, as if I'm completely spent and have absolutely nothing left in me, she says, "This is Fire Officer Amy Wilson. She's in charge here."

I look up to see a firefighter and a police officer.

The firefighter nods at me. "Ms Cohen, this must be a shock. But I need to ask you some questions. Mrs Simpson confirmed that there was no one in the building when we arrived, and there hadn't been anyone in the ground-floor flat for weeks and the upstairs flat for nine days, so there was little chance something had been left on like a cooker, hob or washing machine. Is that correct?"

"Yes. Everything was switched off."

"We thought as much. The fire is out, and we're just turning everything over and dampening down. We've had a fire investigator in there. He's almost certain that the fire was started deliberately, but will need to do some additional analysis in the daylight."

"Huh?"

"It was likely set on purpose about two hours ago, not long before Mrs Simpson called us. There's a broken pane in a back window, which someone possibly used to get in the house. It looks as if the batteries were taken out of the fire alarm, as no one heard the alarm going off. There were dining chairs and what looks like an armchair pushed into the corners of the bedroom, lounge and kitchen with piles of stuff on top of each. An accelerant was used, probably petrol, to set these chairs on fire. Because the positioning against the walls created chimneys, as such, the fire took hold quickly and spread. These three separate seat fires indicate this was a deliberate act rather than the fire starting in one place and travelling."

My mum's favourite armchair... up in flames.

"For that reason, we're pretty sure it was arson," Fire Officer Wilson continues. "We've briefed the police, who will be involved from herein." She indicates the police officer, who nods. "If you'll excuse me, I need to get back to my team."

I say thanks as Fire Officer Wilson walks off.

The police officer turns to me. "Lauren, I'm PC Timothy Sarpong."

"Hi," I reply weakly.

"It was possibly kids," PC Sarpong says. "But who can say why they'd target this place specifically? Perhaps they noticed that it had been empty for a while. Mrs Simpson said Mrs Cohen had been in hospital for weeks before she passed away."

"Kids," I repeat.

He nods. "Nothing appears to have been stolen. All the high-value goods, like the flat-screen television, were still in there. So it doesn't look like a robbery gone wrong, or a thief covering their tracks."

He pauses, and I force my scratchy eyeballs to blink at him. The smell of smoke filters through my nostrils and gets in my mouth. I swallow and it seeps down my throat. I cough. It's as if the lingering smoke in the air is permeating through my skin and getting into my body through every pore. It's like the ash of my mum's burnt possessions wants to cling on to me. I begin to tremble. PC Sarpong notices. He steps away, finds a foil emergency thermal blanket from somewhere and puts it around my shoulders.

He continues, "I'm sorry, but I need to ask you this. Did your mother have anyone who might have wanted to damage her property like this? I know your mother recently died, so could this person or persons be targeting you or someone else close to Judy?"

I stare at him as this sinks in. "You think the arsonist might have been targeting me?"

"Potentially. Do you know anyone who might've done this?"

Yes, I almost scream, the same person who's fucked up everything else for me: IMANI! IMANI! IMANI! But I don't. The timeline is off. What did the fire officer say? That the fire had been started about two hours ago?

Imani wasn't anywhere near this place two hours ago. I know because I was following her.

But I can't exactly say that, can I?

All the stuff happening to me is linked, and this was very deliberately done to hurt me, like all the rest. It's obvious. But how can I tell PC Sarpong that I think it was Imani when I know she has a watertight alibi? She was at the cinema with her mates, then popped home and then went to the house of her boyfriend, or whoever he is.

Could she have paid someone else to do it? If I try to explain all that, will he think I'm mad?

Because I take so long to answer, PC Sarpong says, "You have a think about it. Now, I think it's best if you head home. The fire department will conduct a thorough investigation of the place, and we'll take some statements from the neighbours in the morning. Someone might remember seeing something."

I shake my head. How can I leave? It would be like turning my back on a friend in need.

But PC Sarpong is adamant. "There's nothing you can do here. You can't go inside, as the structural integrity of the building needs to be assessed. It's past midnight. We'll be round at some point in the next day or two once we get the fire service's report."

"Okay…" I reply.

"Come on, Lauren," Mrs Simpson says, leading me to my car, trailed by PC Sarpong. Someone's turned the engine off, but the door is still wide open. She helps me in and steps back.

When I don't make any move, PC Sarpong frowns. "Will you be okay to drive? I can give you a lift home, and you could leave your car here? Or do you have someone who can come and get you?"

"I'll be fine," I say and force a smile at him. "I just need a moment."

"Sure," he replies and steps back so I can close my door.

I sit and gawp at the firefighters traipsing in and out of my mum's now-open front door. PC Sarpong watches me for a moment and then walks back to talk to the other police officers. I hold a hand up to Mrs Simpson, and she acknowledges it and then hurries back to her house. A few moments later I see her next to Mr Simpson at the window.

But I don't move for hours. It takes all my effort just to breathe, just to blink. Neighbours drift back into their homes. One police car leaves. The firefighters pack up their equipment and engines and drive away. The second police car goes. Eventually it's just me left on the street.

When the horrific reality of my mum's torched home and belongings finally registers and I know this isn't a nightmare I'm about to wake up from, I drive back home.

21

I get home around 4 a.m. and go straight up to bed, not bothering to undress, not bothering to get under the covers. I just sprawl face first on top, the smoke still in my nostrils, the loss aching in my chest. They were just things, I tell myself soothingly over and over. I still have all my memories of Mum.

But it doesn't help, and I can't sleep.

I reach out a hand to where Akshay should be, and the emptiness cuts open that wound again. No more fiancé. The love of my life gone. I don't blame him for doubting me – that video looked so real, so definitive. How can you argue with video 'proof' like that? If the shoe were on the other foot, I would've believed it too. Such a clever, awful thing to do.

I attempt to empty my mind and lull it to sleep, but there's a doubt niggling that won't go away. It's migrated up from my gut, a feeling, a knowing, that I just can't ignore. This doubt pinballs around every corner, bouncing off the sides until it settles and reveals itself.

And this is it: is Imani really responsible? Have I got it all wrong?

Imani is the laziest person I've ever come across. Would she really go to the effort to engineer all of this? She's hostile and entitled, but is she really that cruel and petty? And yes, she has a certain amount of protection from Madeline, but I just can't believe she would push it this far.

I groan. Madeline. Imani is sure to tell her about my accusatory phone call. I'm already slipping down my boss' good books, one step away from plummeting over the cliff.

My eyes ping open, and I stare at the ceiling, playing back the phone conversation. Imani was so disinterested. It could've all been an act, of course, but I know she spoke her truth. She always speaks her truth. She's selfish and only cares about herself and her own pleasure. I'm such an insignificant part of her life, why would she invest any energy bothering to ruin me when she has herself to focus on?

Yes, she doesn't really want the job. She's only there because her ex-footballer-now-property-mogul daddy told her she needed to work and earn some money and couldn't just live off him. Although she once boasted that her annual allowance from Daddy was more than her salary. And also that her plan was to work outside his business for a while, to gain 'experience', before she went into his business. She'd begged her bestie, Amelia, to persuade her mum, Madeline, to get her a job. And that's exactly what had happened, because Madeline and Imani's daddy run in the same affluent circles in Cheshire, and Madeline wants to keep him on side.

And would Imani really go to all the trouble of finding someone willing to commit arson? That's a dangerous, illegal act with some serious consequences and not something to casually ask a mate. And as far as I know, there aren't freelancers lining up to take on that kind of job either. I know *she* didn't torch my mum's apartment because she was nowhere near it. She has a rock-solid alibi.

It's been such a traumatic whirlwind these past few days that I latched onto the only person I could think of who would do this – Imani – but perhaps I'm missing something or someone. The more I reflect, the more I think I've made a mistake. I had tunnel vision and need to cast my net wider, broaden my investigation. Maybe it's not even someone I know. Perhaps it's a nutter who has targeted a random stranger for a sick thrill.

I decide to apologise to Imani for the phone call, to nip this in the bud before she blabs to Madeline, if she hasn't already. I flip onto my back, grab my phone off the nightstand and open my work emails. I haven't looked at them since I was sent home mid-morning by Madeline and have hundreds. I ignore them for now and, holding the phone above my head, type a short, polite but professional email to Imani that doesn't give too much away:

Imani, my apologies for the phone call earlier. I made a mistake. I hope you had a good time at the cinema. I'm resting up. See you next week.

I deliberate for a moment but then press send. Hopefully she hasn't already mentioned anything to Madeline and reads this email when she first gets into work tomorrow and decides to keep schtum.

Mindlessly scrolling through the other unread emails, a name pops out at me in the subject line: Jenna Robinson. That's Toby's ex-girlfriend's name. Surely it can't be the same Jenna Robinson?

I open the email. It's from a North-West PR industry body that runs a website and newsletter and puts on events and networking opportunities for PR professionals. I've been to a few, and they are always excellent. This is an event they are putting on with a Jenna Robinson as the guest speaker. I scroll down the email and see Jenna's heavily made-up face smiling at me.

WTF. The phone slips through my fingers and bops me on the forehead. Wide awake, I scrabble in the sheets to find it.

I read the event's blurb. Jenna is speaking about being a beauty influencer; the importance of being able to create and edit video content; how she taught herself and how you can too. And how she now regularly gets hundreds of thousands of views on her YouTube beauty videos.

Hundreds of thousands of views? Huh.

I click on the link that takes me to Jenna's YouTube channel and sit upright in bed. I shuffle back to sit against the headboard and switch on the bedside lamp. Jenna has hundreds of videos, all with huge numbers of views. I click on one at random, and it's super slick, with Jenna demonstrating how she achieves such thick, bushy, perfectly shaped eyebrows. It really has been edited to perfection. I find myself mesmerised, and I couldn't care less about my eyebrows.

I follow Jenna on Instagram, as a favour to Toby when she'd first set up her channel and needed numbers, but don't pay much attention, always scrolling quickly past when I see her posts. I click onto her Instagram profile and see she now has almost eight hundred thousand followers. Her latest post is a video. The caption tells me it's an ad from an up-and-coming make-up brand, and I wonder how much she got paid for that one sponsored post. It has to be hundreds of pounds, maybe even in the thousands.

I massively underestimated her. I didn't think she was this bright. She'd always tried to get Toby to be her Instagram boyfriend, following her around and taking photos of her, but he point-blank refused – and moaned to me about it. So she must've learnt to do it herself and gone into videos.

A memory plays in my head of Jenna drunkenly shouting, "I'm going to ruin you!"

Maybe she really meant it. Maybe I discounted her too quickly.

Perhaps she does have the skills to edit my face onto that clip of another couple having sex. And the intelligence to plan and execute this attack on me. I didn't initially suspect her, I immediately wrote her off as a ditzy, harmless idiot, but I was wrong. She's business savvy and switched on. I was so fixated on Imani that I didn't see it.

Jenna was in my house at the funeral reception. In my garden. She could've planted the letters and USB then. So many people were milling about and coming in and out of the house that she could've easily gone unnoticed.

But what about all the work emails, social media hacking, and bank account issues? I realise my laptop was in the front room during the funeral reception. It was on, and it was open – I never lock it when I'm at home; it just goes to a bubbles screensaver rather than a lock screen if I don't use it for a while. I'd checked my work emails first thing before the funeral, the CozMoz Paints presentation was open, as it was the last thing I was working on after the pitch on Friday, so she could've planted the porn link then, and my PW-Protekt app would've been open. I mentally trawl through our past conversations. Did I recommend it to her? Highly probable. I recommended it to everyone. So maybe she found out how to use it?

Just as she could have planted the letters and USB in the garden, she could've easily snuck into that room unnoticed. She said she'd been in the house for a while before she made herself known to us, claiming she'd been talking to my cousins who'd recognised her from YouTube.

And my car. She could've keyed it when Toby booted her out of my house, but I only saw it the following day.

She also knows exactly where Mum lived, as she'd been round to her apartment for Sunday roast with Toby on a few occasions when Akshay and I were there too.

Jenna knows everything about me. She knows my address and phone number to have been able to send those dirty texts and post the lingerie and sex toy.

All the pieces of the puzzle slot into place, and I berate myself for not seeing it earlier.

But why? What motivation does she have? I think back, and it's obvious. Jenna shouted, "You ruined our relationship, Lauren!" She wanted to split up Akshay and me as punishment for me splitting up her and Toby. She blames me for encouraging Toby to dump her and has a gigantic grudge. Perhaps she knows I told him to dump her when he called me on Friday.

She said she'd ruin me – and she has. She's chewed up my life and spat it out; found every way to publicly humiliate me and privately torture me and gone after everything I hold dear.

Jenna's threats at the funeral weren't empty. She meant every word.

I've been such a fool to discount her on the false belief that she's stupid. I look at the time: 4.45 a.m.

Sod it.

I find Jenna's mobile number and dial it. It rings and rings. Do I really think she'll pick up at this time? I always turn my phone to silent at night, but I know a lot of people who don't in case of emergencies.

But she doesn't answer, and it goes to voicemail. I leave a message:

"Jenna, it's Lauren. I know what you've done, and you need to put things right immediately! Call me back ASAP."

I also send a text message saying the same thing.

Twiddling my thumbs impatiently, I know it's unlikely she'll reply until she's awake in a few hours. More damn waiting for someone to get back to me.

I switch off the lamp and wriggle down in my bed. But every time I close my eyelids, they slide open again, as if the close function is faulty and will never work again. I refuse to wait for her to reply – what happens if she never does?

My need to be in control of a situation kicks in.

What do I know about Jenna? I've never been to her apartment and don't know her address – and the one person who does, Toby, isn't speaking to me right now.

Think.

OMG. That's it. Dredged up from the depths: on Thursdays, Fridays, and Saturdays she works at a beauty counter in the beauty hall of a department store in town.

And today is Thursday.

I check the time: 5.05 a.m. In a few hours she'll be there. And in a few hours, I'll be there too.

22

At 9.02 a.m., after zero sleep and zero response from Jenna, I call the department store and am directed through to the beauty hall.

I know exactly what I'm going to say, recalling a time when Jenna went on and on about how her biggest dislike is seeing strangers wearing the wrong colour of foundation. "I just want to take them under my wing, wash it off and find them the right shade," she'd said. "They'd be soooo much happier, I just know it."

A woman answers. I put on the friendliest, happiest, lightest voice I can muster.

"Hi there, I know this is a long shot, but last Thursday I came in, and there was an *amazing* sales assistant who matched me a foundation *perfectly*, and I wanted to come in again today to find some more items, and I was really keen to speak to her again. She was soooo good, such excellent customer service. She had such an eye for what suited my skin tone."

The woman gushes, "I'm so happy you enjoyed our customer service. All our staff are excellent. Do you happen to remember her name?"

"Oh gosh." I pause to pretend I'm thinking. "It was something like Jenny or Jennifer?"

"Jenna? On the All Yours Make-up counter?"

"Yes, that's it."

"Yes, Jenna is very talented. Really knows her stuff and loves make-up. She has a YouTube channel, you know. Maybe ask her about it when you see her. Anyway, let me check the rota... Okay, here we are. Jenna's due in at ten."

"Wonderful. Until when?"

"Seven this evening."

"Perfect. I'll be in later today. Thanks so much for your help."

"No problem."

I jump in the shower and get changed, too jittery to eat any breakfast but forcing down a cup of coffee. Although I haven't slept a wink, I'm not tired. I'm running on adrenaline, finally having worked out who is doing this to me.

At 9.30 a.m., I put on my coat, and as I'm wrapping my scarf around my neck, my phone rings.

Jenna?

I dive into my handbag and yank out my phone. No. Madeline.

My heart sinks. Imani has spoken to her.

I'm torn briefly between my need to get to the department store and confront Jenna, and my need to preserve my relationship with my boss and reinstate my position at work. I sigh and answer.

"Hi, Lauren, how are you feeling?" Madeline asks briskly.

"I'm really good, thank you," I reply in the same chirpy voice I used earlier.

"You're at home?"

"Yes," I reply cautiously. Where is this going?

"Good. I need to come to your house to discuss a few things."

"Right now?"

"Yes. Does 10.30 a.m. suit?"

Bloody hell. No, it does NOT suit.

Madeline senses my hesitation and continues, "It's urgent and can't wait."

My insides knot with apprehension. Imani has mentioned my phone call, and Madeline, playing mother wolf, thinks it's urgent. Sorting my life out is urgent. Getting Jenna to admit to everything and putting everything – and everyone – straight is URGENT.

But Jenna is at work until 7 p.m. I know exactly where she'll be all day. This is a minor delay, that's all. I can go after meeting with Madeline.

I swallow back my annoyance at the delay and reply through gritted teeth, "Sure. That's fine. See you then."

For an hour I hover by the front door, pacing back and forth and checking out the window. I know this is a gigantic waste of time, and if I went and did something else – like attempting to sort out the aftermath of Mum's burnt-out flat – the minutes would pass quicker, but I can't drag myself away or concentrate on anything else. This meeting needs to be over fast, and then I can get to Jenna.

I see Madeline's car pull up and spring towards the front door, opening it before she can ring the doorbell.

But Madeline's not alone.

Behind her is Ursula Craddock, the agency's outsourced HR consultant. I know her well from many meetings a while back regarding Cleo's departure.

Ursula here is a bad sign. I calm my panic. I'm jumping to conclusions. Maybe it's to do with someone else on the team. Maybe Imani hasn't made a complaint about me.

"Hi, Madeline. Hi, Ursula," I say brightly. "Come in."

They return my greeting, and I show them through to the back of the house. I indicate the dining table, but Ursula suggests we sit in the lounge. I offer them a drink, but both decline.

We sit, and I bring out my work notebook and a pen, as if I'll need to take notes. But I'm twitchy and jumpy and can't sit still. I chew the inside of my cheeks and corners of my lips.

Madeline takes in my appearance, and a strained expression settles across her brow. She's never seen me without make-up or with dirty hair scraped back in a messy bun. With two nights of no sleep and no undereye concealer, I imagine I look a right state. But my appearance really wasn't a priority this morning. And still isn't, to be honest. I haven't even looked in a mirror.

Madeline begins, "At MBW we pride ourselves on being equal and diverse, and championing job opportunities for all with a fair and open approach. We make every effort to eliminate discrimination and create a workplace that champions great working relationships between all."

I think of Madeline's penchant for hiring pretty, young things with a certain look for the junior roles and know that isn't strictly true.

She continues, "We strive to be inclusive and to improve ourselves and our policies continually. We don't tolerate any discrimination of any kind, and quite frankly, we do not condone the content you have been posting on your social media channels, especially as they relate to your work and employer – us. You posted a number of offensive posts on both Twitter and LinkedIn yesterday. They've snowballed out of control overnight, and unfortunately MBW has been brought into the narrative. Clients, fellow staff and media have contacted me expressing their concerns."

I gape at her blankly. Snowballed out of control? Shit. Dealing with the awful content took a back seat after everything else that happened afterwards. I haven't looked at any of my social media channels since.

Ursula shifts forward on the sofa. "Lauren, you are entitled to your opinion, everyone is. But it does not align with the values of MBW."

"No, you've got this all wrong—"

Madeline cuts me off. "I have to distance myself and my business from you. Immediately."

But Ursula steps in more diplomatically. "Unfortunately it is unacceptable for the agency to be linked to you in the manner in which it has been. And therefore we need to take the relevant action, as your content, although on your personal channels, is still linked to your employer – it even names Madeline – and is very serious."

I shake my head in disbelief.

Ursula continues, "We would like to offer you the benefit of the doubt, however, and will be instigating a full investigation. But in the meantime, you will be suspended pending investigation for a serious incident of misconduct."

"My social media accounts have been hacked. It wasn't me who posted that content. I'm not like that. I don't believe any of those things. You know me. You know that's not who I am."

Madeline shakes her head sadly. "I thought I did know you, Lauren, but recently you've not been yourself. What with those emails and playing that ex-rated video in a client meeting."

"That wasn't me either. It was *her*."

"Her?"

"My brother's ex," I say, exasperated. My lack of sleep is manifesting itself in emotional, impatient outbursts that I'm aware make me sound half-deranged, but I can't stop myself. "She's targeting me because she blames me for splitting her and my brother up. I was on my way to confront her, but then you showed up."

Ursula observes me neutrally, but Madeline's incredulity is etched for all to see across her face.

"I refuse to believe that far-fetched story. I'm very worried about you and think you might be having some kind of breakdown and are self-sabotaging. Perhaps in your head you think someone else is targeting you, but actually it's all your own doing. You're doing this to yourself, Lauren. I honestly think you need to see your doctor and get referred to a therapist."

"The mental health of our employees is very important to MBW," Ursula chimes in.

My voice rises a few notches. "There is nothing wrong with my mental health. I'm not imagining this or doing it to myself. Someone has got it in for me!"

Madeline's eyebrows shoot up, and she looks almost smug, as if I've just confirmed her thoughts.

I continue, "And that person burned down my mother's flat last night!"

"There was a fire?" Madeline asks.

"Yes."

"I'm sorry to hear that, but I imagine it's completely unrelated," she says.

"It is *not* unrelated," I bellow.

"Let's just calm down," Ursula soothes.

I deflate. "I'm doing all I can to get this issue sorted, trust me."

Ursula smiles, but it doesn't reach her eyes. "I'm sure you are. But in the meantime, we'd like to ask that you don't come into the office, use your emails or contact any MBW staff, and we'll get the investigation underway as soon as possible. You can keep your laptop and phone for now, as you'll possibly be required to do some handovers with the team in due course."

Ursula glances at Madeline as if to say, *we're done here*, and Madeline stands.

"Do you have a bathroom I can use?" Ursula says, and she pats her pregnant belly. "When I need to go, I need to go." She fake-laughs to break the heightened tension.

"Sure." I stand too and lead them to the hallway, pointing out the small downstairs loo to Ursula. She jumps in with a look of relief on her face.

Madeline and I are left in the hallway. Static hisses between us. She shifts closer to me, and the movement is like a spark. I twitch.

"Just so you know," Madeline whispers, "you are as good as sacked, and your career is finished. But we have to go through the official procedures. You'll never work in PR in Manchester again. I'll make sure of that. Mental health breakdown or not, no one damages my standing or my business' reputation. No one."

I stare at her open-mouthed, but the toilet flushes, and Madeline moves to the front door and opens it while I'm frozen in place by the venom in my MD's pronouncement.

A moment later, Ursula comes out of the toilet with a smile. "Ah, that's better. Thank you, Lauren. You take care of yourself."

Ursula sees Madeline by the door and follows her

out. I watch them cross the road and get into Madeline's sporty Mercedes, Ursula struggling to manoeuvre her unbalanced pregnant frame into the low seats, but getting zero assistance from Madeline. I almost dash out to help, but she manages it, and the instant she closes the car door, Madeline speeds away.

I shut the door and stand motionless in the hallway for what feels like forever.

Jenna has well and truly fucked up my job – and my career. Madeline will make good on her promise, that's for sure. Years and years of hard work down the drain. Years of building up my professional reputation and network scratched out in an instant. I was just meant to be off work for a few days, and now I'm unemployed and unemployable.

Rock bottom.

It rankles that Madeline cut me loose without a second thought after all that I've done for her and her business. But, just like with Akshay, the evidence is damning. And that's all Madeline can see right now.

I have to get to Jenna *immediately.* To get her to confess and to give me access to my accounts again, to admit to Akshay that it was her who produced that deepfake video and that I didn't have an affair. To apologise to Toby and Dad and to write an email to Madeline to put her straight. And Jenna can bloody well face the music with the police for starting that fire.

When I finally move, everything goes fuzzy, and I grab the stair banister to stay upright. Holding onto the walls, I make my way into the kitchen for a glass of water and – although I'm not hungry – I force down a granola bar.

I need to be on form for what I'm about to do.

23

The light-headedness passes. I grab my bag, put on my coat and scarf, and find my car keys. I step out into the dreary day and close my front door, ensuring I double lock it. I walk the couple of steps onto the pavement and look up and down the road for my car, having completely forgotten where I parked it but knowing it won't be far.

As I pause, a small group of people appear from nowhere and crowd around me, making me feel ever so slightly uncomfortable and blocking off every opportunity to escape apart from retreating back into my house.

"Excuse me," a man says.

I look at him. He's tall with tattoos on his neck and up the back of his head. He also has tattoos on his hands.

I glance around the others in the group before replying. Two more men and a woman. They all smile at me, but alarm bells blare as a sense of menace emanates from them. Perhaps they're just lost? Or trying to sell me something for the house like new windows.

I smile tightly back, wanting to get this encounter over with as soon as possible so I can drive into the city centre and get to the department store. "Can I help you?"

"Are you Lauren Cohen?" asks another man. He's smaller than the first, overweight and wrapped up against the cold in a red-and-white scarf that reads England and has the national flag on each end before the tassels.

"Forgive us," the third man says and takes a step closer to me.

He has a skinhead and small squinty eyes that look a little too hard at me. I edge instinctively back towards my little front garden and closer to my front door. I still have my keys in my hand and clutch them tightly.

The skinhead continues, "It's an honour to meet you is all, petal, and Adam 'ere has forgotten his manners."

Confused, and a little threatened by their presence, I stay quiet, hoping this entire situation will become clear if they keep talking. I glance at the woman, who's middle-aged and unremarkable, and she continues to smile at me, with what seems to be a look of awe.

Scarf guy says, "We're from Our Pure Nation Now, or OPNN. Have you heard of us?"

I shake my head in the negative.

"Not surprising. We've done some digging and see you're not affiliated to any group in particular. Which is why we're here," tattoo guy says.

Group? Affiliated?

Then skinhead pipes up. "There we go getting all ahead of ourselves again." He laughs. "My name's Terry. This is John, Adam, and Vanessa." He points each out, but I immediately forget the names – I don't have any desire to remember these people. I know immediately they are not my kind of people.

Skinhead continues, "OPNN is one hundred per cent on board with what you've been posting on Twitter. You're so bold to just put it all out there, and we admire that. That one tweet that's gone viral globally really struck a chord with us."

Gone viral globally? Oh, crap. It has to be the same one Madeline mentioned.

Excitedly, tattoo guy adds, "We'd like to recruit you to OPNN, to be the poster girl for our next campaign. With your reach now, and your values aligning with ours, we know it'll be the perfect fit. Our Manchester branch has a healthy number of members."

"What do you say?" scarf guy asks.

I weigh my options. If I deny posting that content to my Twitter, what will these right-wing extremists – for that's precisely what they are, I realise – do? They're ever so slightly aggressive now, and they're meant to be on my side. Instead I say, "How did you find out my address?"

"Ah, well, we have a number of IT whiz-kids in our group. It's easy to find out things like that if you know where to look, petal," skinhead replies.

A brief thought flickers across my mind: should I ask these people to help me to get back into my accounts? But I dismiss it as quickly as it appeared. I don't want anything to do with them. Just being this close to them turns my stomach.

I anger. The nerve of them accosting me in front of my own house. "I think you need to leave. I am not, and never will be, interested in your group."

Tattoo guy crosses his massive arms and frowns.

"Have you had any lefty freaks bother you yet?" scarf guy asks.

"What?"

"It's just as easy for them to find out your information as it is for us," skinhead says.

"That's why you need us," scarf guy adds.

I glimpse movement to my right and turn to see the woman with her phone up, either taking photos or a video of me. I put my arm up to cover my face as a shield.

"Stop that," I say to her, but she doesn't.

"You can't put all that out there and not expect kick-back," tattoo guy says, and takes a step towards me.

He's too close, invading my personal space, and my flight or fight mechanism kicks in. I take flight, straight back to my front door. I fumble with my keys, open the front door, curse that I've double locked it and finally get inside.

Before I close the door, I glance behind and see the four of them stood on the pavement, watching me, not coming onto my property but blocking my exit from it. It creeps me out, and I slam the door.

My heart hammers as I hear the letter box flap, and a business card drops on the mat. Then from outside the door, one of the men says, "That's our number. We're 'ere for you, Lauren Cohen. You can't take on the world on your own, petal."

I run up the stairs and lock myself into the bathroom as if that might offer me some extra protection. I obsessively wash my hands, attempting to scrub away all the grimy hatefulness that just standing near those people has drenched me with. I stop when the skin is red and stinging.

I sit on the bathmat, find my phone and look at my public Twitter account. It's dreadful, truly. There are hundreds of tweets from my account spewing hateful rhetoric, spreading awful conspiracy theories and inciting 'my people' to commit acts of far-right terrorism. All of them using popular, unrelated hashtags to get more eyeballs on them.

I only had around two hundred followers, but a lot of those were journalists and media contacts I knew from work. I see one influential online editor from a huge news agency has blasted me on a comment, and follow the thread to see it picked up by many of his contacts all weighing in.

Immediately I spot the tweet that has gone viral. It has three hundred thousand retweets and fifty-two thousand likes. It tagged a well-known, controversial right-wing commentator, and he retweeted it to his 1.1 million followers.

And there are *tens of thousands* of angry replies. I gulp as I click on one of the hashtags and see that #laurencohen is trending on Twitter. It's hard to even take in the enormity of that. It's overwhelming. The internet has taken it upon itself to publicly shame me, like a virtual public whipping. And – even though I didn't even post any of that crap – I do feel ashamed. My name is tainted, and it will take a miracle to disentangle it from this… scandal.

The content Jenna has posted has taken on a life of its own. As if she's simply lit a fire – just like she did at Mum's flat – and now it's raging out of all control.

I attempt to switch into crisis-management mode. What would I advise a client to do if something like this happened to one of their brands? But that part of my brain is wholly disconnected. There's not even a flicker of inspiration. I just feel completely… Blunt? Dull? Dampened? Muted? All of the above?

I google my name and change the settings to see the latest results. There are pages and pages of search results, my name showing up all over the place – not only in UK media but globally. I spot an article on a huge digital site with the headline: IS THIS THE MOST HATED WOMAN IN THE WORLD RIGHT NOW?

I click into the article and see my Facebook profile image of me in Provence. I read the first paragraph:

> *Who is Lauren Cohen? The 38-year-old from Manchester, UK, has catapulted into public awareness with a series of mind-bogglingly offensive, discriminatory and aggressive posts across her social media channels. And – unsurprisingly – has sparked a huge backlash across the world, including an announcement from Twitter that her account will be permanently suspended for violating its hateful conduct policy. With the other social media channels likely to boot her off too, one thing's for sure – this piece of dog turd has been CANCELLED.*

I stop myself from reading on and click out. I can't possibly feel any worse than I already do.

There's a post from OPNN on its social media channels with the photo of me that the woman took outside just moments ago and the text: 'Look who we've been talking to today. She's coming to our next Manchester meetup. Be there.'

Horrified, I click back to the search results only to see a post in what appears to be a far-left activists forum of my picture from the MBW website, along with my address and mobile phone number and a message that says:

TAKE HER OUT

Is that a death threat? Is my life in danger now?

Jenna has succeeded in getting the whole world to hate me, in turning not only my loved ones against me but complete strangers too. And now I have a target on my back.

My stomach somersaults, and I crawl to the toilet, put up the seat and vomit the granola bar.

24

There's nothing left in my stomach, but I continue to dry heave. Finally, that eases. I rinse out my mouth with water and brush my teeth.

I'm ruined. The entire world hates me. I call Kemi, the only friend I still have, but her phone's off. She always switches it off when she's teaching. I slump back to the bathroom floor. Never have I felt so desperate and so, so alone.

I hug my knees and try to make myself very small, willing the ground to open and swallow me up.

But there's a little voice in my head. It's my bruised and bloody optimism, clinging on for dear life, piping up. *This is still redeemable. You can make this right*, it squeaks.

But what can I do?

Only one thought pounds between my ears: I have to get to Jenna. I need to log on to all my social media accounts and delete all that shit. This is getting dangerous now. Jenna has made her point.

I have to stick to the plan.

Frightened to make any noise in case one of the

right-wing group has their ear to my door, I heave myself up and creep downstairs. I tiptoe into the front room and, taking care to stand far back from the window, open the still-closed curtain a crack.

Bollocks. They are still there, milling about on the pavement. The woman is on her phone, clearly the one to have posted my photo, scarf guy is talking on his mobile, but the other two men watch my house.

I know I should go out there, force my way past them and get in my car. How dare they trap me in my house. I'm a prisoner hemmed in by people. Perhaps I can clamber over the downed fence panel in the garden and sneak around the back and approach the car from a different direction? They might not notice me until it's too late and I've driven off?

Yes, that's what I'll do. It'll work, it has to work. Come on, courage, show yourself one more time. But movement outside distracts me from this pep talk. Scarf guy finishes his call and gives a signal to the others.

He gives one last look at the house, and then the four of them cross the road and walk off towards the main Chorlton high street.

Relief soars. I let the curtain go, count to ten, force my feet to move one step at a time and head back into the hallway. I reach out to open the front door, but the doorbell rings. Every muscle tenses. I don't move. There's no way I'm opening the door.

I listen hard, but don't hear anything. I edge closer to look out the peephole. I don't see anyone on the doorstep. But that doesn't mean they're not waiting for me to the side.

Creeping into the front room, I check from behind the curtain again. But don't see anyone. The street looks quiet. A cyclist goes past and doesn't even glance at my house, making me think there's no one crouching on my front doorstep or acting bizarrely that might catch their attention.

I wait a few moments longer. Whoever rang the bell must know no one's coming to the door by now. If they were still there, they'd ring again, right? I wait a little longer, then head back into the hallway and slowly, carefully, quietly, pull down the front door latch and open it a fraction. It's unusually sticky, as if something has warped the doorframe. I tug softly, but then yank.

There's no one stood on my step. The release of anxiety whooshes in my ears. I fight off the inexplicable urge to do a little dance.

But the outside of my pale-wooden door and the matching doorframe is blackened. As if someone has splashed paint on it.

But it's not paint. I inspect the wood closer, and it almost looks… charred? I slam the door and stagger back inside my hallway. Whatever it is, it's not good. No, not good at all.

My phone pings with a message. I fish it out of my coat pocket and see it's from a mobile number that is not in my contacts list.

It reads:

Next time it'll be acid on your face, Nazi scum.

Sheer terror boils over, and my vision swirls.

I COME to in a crumpled heap on the carpet. I must've fainted. I have no idea how long I've been out, but I massage my temples to bring my brain back to life.

As soon as my memories snap into place, I sit on the bottom stair and call the non-emergency police number on 101. Although someone throwing acid on my front door is frightening and makes me fearful for my safety, I'm not in any immediate peril. I'm safe in my house.

At least, I think I am.

I get through to a man who introduces himself, checks it's not an emergency, takes all my details and then asks me to explain what's happened.

His steady, competent professionalism reassures me and instead of a hysterical outburst, which so nearly comes out of my mouth, my heart rate lowers and my tone settles to match his.

"Someone threw acid at my front door and sent me a text telling me that next time it would be my face," I say matter-of-factly.

"Do you know who this someone might be?" he asks.

I'm about to say Jenna, but I know it can't be her – she's meant to be at work. "I think it was someone from a far-left group. My address was posted online on what looked like an activist's forum."

"Why was your address posted in this forum?"

"Because someone else has gained unauthorised access to my social media accounts and posted vicious, hateful, right-wing content, and it's got out of control, and everyone thinks I posted it, and now I'm being targeted."

"Okay, so this hateful content that's been posted on your channels, just to confirm, you didn't post it?"

"Absolutely not. I reported that I've been hacked to the police's cybercrime hotline. I have a reference number if you want it."

He says yes, and I haul myself up from the stairs, holding onto the banister as my head spins when I get up too quick, and plod into the lounge, my feet feeling like they're stuck in tar. I find the notepad I wrote it on and read it out for him. I head back as I do to sit on the stairs, my lounge feeling disconcertingly alien.

"Other than your social media accounts being taken over, is there anything else?"

"Yes!" I babble at him about the work emails that I didn't send, the porn playing in the presentation, the attack on my relationship with the dirty texts, the lingerie and sex toy parcel, the faked home movie on a USB, and the letters. The fact that my bank account has been screwed with too and that my brother and father have also been targeted. The fire at my mum's apartment that looks like it was deliberately started.

He listens patiently to this and then says, "I'll make a note of all that. Do you think this is all related?"

"Without a shadow of a doubt, yes."

"So a far-left group has done all these things to you?"

"No, I think it's my brother's ex-girlfriend."

"But she didn't throw the acid?"

"Um, no, I don't think so – I think she's at work now."

"Do you have any evidence that she's done these other things?"

"No... She shouted that she wanted to ruin my life, and then all this stuff started happening."

"Okay." He pauses a moment, and I imagine him assessing his notes. "I think the vandalism is because of what has been posted online. Are you able to stay with a friend or family member tonight? I'll be able to send round an officer, but it's unlikely to be today."

"When will it be?"

As soon as I ask, I have a premonition of what he's going to say.

"Between twenty-four and forty-eight hours."

I silently scream at the top of my lungs down the

phone. "Fine," I say curtly, clenching my jaw against the rage. I can't shout at a police officer, can I? That's not going to help.

He gives me another reference number, and we end the call.

Why is no one taking this seriously? Why does everyone think I've got all the time in the world to just sit by and watch my life be blasted into smithereens for the next twenty-four to forty-eight flipping hours.

That. Is. It. I have to get to Jenna. If I can just reach her, I can make all this go away, set everyone straight and get my life back on track.

I stand and grab my things and look at the front door. What if there's someone lurking out there ready to throw acid on my face? What if the OPNN are back and aggressively try to accost me this time? What if I get beaten up? Or kidnapped? Or worse?

What if, what if, what if.

My chest constricts, and an iciness pricks at my cheeks. I shiver. I could just stay inside my house, hide for a while, wait one to two days for the police to get back to me, for the bank to get back to me. But what could happen in that time? What else have I got left for Jenna to destroy?

My spirit. That's what.

And I refuse to be broken.

Reaching deep down, I pull upon my reserves of strength and fearlessness. There's some left. It might only be the dregs, but it's enough to get me moving.

I look out the front room window, but can't see anyone in particular milling around. I spot my car up the road and plan the most direct route I'll take to get to it. Through the massive puddle by the drain that I usually skirt around. But not today. I'm taking the fastest path.

Back in the hallway, I wrap my scarf around my head, pull my hood up, sling my handbag across my body and hold my car key in my hand. Taking a deep breath, I open the front door, slam it shut behind me and sprint towards my car, figuring speed and the element of surprise will deter any would-be assailants.

I splash through the puddle, the cold water immediately seeping through my boots, and jump in my car. I speed away without looking back.

25

I race into the city centre, not caring that I'm speeding, entering roundabouts with barely a glance and racing through traffic lights that have just turned red.

In my entire driving life, I've never had any kind of traffic violation, not even a parking ticket. But for once, drivers will have to wait or swerve or brake for me. This is urgent. I don't care.

A few times I glance in my rear-view mirror to see if anyone is following me, but there's so much traffic that I really can't be certain. As I pull to a stop at a traffic light, I look again behind me. I see a silver hatchback overtake the car behind me and cut in. It's going so fast I think it might shunt me, but it skids to a halt, earning it a few angry horn blares from the car it cut up.

There are four people in the car, and I see the driver and passenger clearly: tattoo guy and scarf guy. Scarf guy waves at me and gives me a thumbs up, while tattoo guy sticks his thick arm out the window and gives the middle finger to the car behind, which promptly stops beeping.

Oh, fuck, OPNN have caught up with me and are following me. This is bad. What are they hoping to achieve? To intimidate me so that I go with them or agree to attend their next meeting? Follow me wherever I go now and not let up until I've signed up with their group? Will they prevent me from getting to Jenna?

I look forward at the busy crossroads. The light is still red, and I watch as cars whizz past from right to left, left to right. I put the car into first gear and release the handbrake, attempting not to move my arms too much so tattoo guy won't get any hint of what I'm about to do. I see a gap in the traffic and then just DRIVE.

I screech forward, faster than I've ever pulled away from a stop before, and the engine revs powerfully. The Mini nips through the space, and I get honked at by oncoming vehicles. I swerve out of the way of one car and lose control of the steering, heading on a direct collision path with the traffic light pole. My insides tumble and lurch as everything slows right down. The pole is coming right at me, and I'm about to smash into it.

I'm going to crash. Oh god, I'm going to crash! I freeze in terror.

But my reflexes kick in, and I yank the steering wheel, mount the kerb with a huge crunch as it scrapes all the underside of my car, and knock the wheel arch on the pole. I right myself, turn away, and I'm clear – back on the road, racing away from the crossroads and leaving OPNN far behind. I don't look back.

Adrenaline pumping, I cut in and out of traffic and speed at twice the limit to put as much distance as I can between me and the silver hatchback. I turn off the main road and take a different back route into the city centre to throw them off the scent. It works, and I don't see their car behind me again.

Out loud, I thank the universe that I didn't just cause a huge collision and kill myself or anyone else.

Without thinking, I switch into autopilot and start heading towards the car park at work. I catch myself and change lanes at the last minute, receiving a honk from the car behind that brakes to miss me, and head to a city centre car park that I know is close to the department store where Jenna works.

As it's in the heart of the main shopping district, it's expensive. None of my bank cards are working. Shit. How much loose change have I got in the bottom of my handbag to pay for parking? A couple of quid maybe. Not nearly enough.

Keeping my eyes on the road, I rummage in the holder between the seats, shifting aside anti-bac hand gel, some breath mints, and a packet of tissues until my fingertips graze a couple of coins right at the bottom. Still not enough... The glove compartment. There should be a twenty-pound note floating about. The ever-practical Akshay put one in there when I first got this car in case of emergencies.

"Thank you, babe," I say out loud as I turn into the car park. I lean across as I'm waiting my turn to go through the barriers and open the glove compartment, pulling out the folded banknote.

I pull into the first space I see, not caring about the inconsiderate angle and half-covering another space. My wet foot squelches in my boot as I run to the department store. Shoppers stare as I dash past. I accidentally knock one man's arm and shout, "Sorry," without even looking back.

I fling myself through the department store's glass doors and pause to catch my breath. I wildly remove some layers, as I'm overheating. My coat snags in my cross-body bag, and I grumble loudly as I untangle my arms. The security guard watches me.

The beauty hall is in front of me, but the place heaves with shoppers. I scan the floor to find the right counter, but am momentarily disorientated, as the front displays are different to the last time I was here. I spot the All Yours Make-up brand logo and charge towards it, not even thinking what I might say.

There she is!

Jenna stands behind the counter, arranging some products on the shelf, her back to me. Her colleague is dealing with a shopper at the till.

Fuck subtlety, fuck handling this right. She's going down. I weave in and out of the crowd and practically slide to a stop inches from the counter.

"Jenna," I bellow, and I see her shoulders tense.

Time stands still as all my surroundings drop away, and all that's left is the space between me and her. There's movement in my peripheral vision, and I feel the disapproving stares of shoppers pricking me. But I don't care. My eyes are puncturing a hole through this snake's back.

Jenna slowly turns around to face me.

I point at her. "I know what you did! How could you? You need to put this right!"

Jenna's eyes go wide, and all the colour drains from her face. Not even that thick layer of blush can disguise the fact that she's shocked to see me. She glances at her colleague, who is staring open-mouthed at me, having forgotten about serving the customer, who also watches the scene with undisguised fascination.

I sense a presence next to me: the security guard is hovering.

"Jenna!" I repeat, louder this time, and I slap the counter. The make-up rattles and tinkles on the shelves.

"Madam," the security guard warns softly.

Jenna shakes her head slightly at me and then whispers to her colleague, "I just need a minute."

Her colleague nods vigorously as if to say: *get that crazy woman out of here, she's scaring the punters.*

Jenna edges out from behind the counter and grabs my arm, directing me towards the doors. She says to the security guard, "I've got this, Harry."

He nods and stands aside, but follows behind us as Jenna ushers me out of the department store. But I jerk my arm away and plant my feet, refusing to be silenced or pushed around. "Jenna, we need to talk, right now."

"We do," Jenna says gently. "But outside." She looks around at the staff and shoppers still watching us, at the security guard on high alert and readying to spring into action. "Please," she begs, appearing close to tears.

I grab her arm, and we head out the glass doors. She points to a side alley out of the way of the flow of pedestrians. I lead her there.

We face each other. Now I'm looking straight at her – the woman who has ruined my life – my fury rises from the tips of my toes and up my body ready to boil over and spew from my mouth in a burning torrent. It scares me; I've never felt so much rage.

"I'm so, so sorry," Jenna says before any words pass my teeth.

"How could you?" I shout.

"Oh god," she groans. "I thought I'd got away with it, but then you called me at nearly 5 a.m., and I just knew you'd worked out it was me."

"Damn right I worked it out."

"I'm so sorry, honestly. As soon as I did it, I felt awful about it. So impulsive and stupid. I totally overreacted to Toby's leaving me. He was my first long-term boyfriend."

"Do you know how much distress you've caused me? How much damage you've done? You need to put things right, immediately!"

"Of course. How much will it cost to respray it?"

Her reply flummoxes me. "What?"

"I'm guessing that's what will need to happen?"

I scowl at her. It's as if she's coming out with random words to deliberately trip me up and hoodwink me.

Jenna looks at me quizzically. "Have you been to a garage yet? Got a quote?"

"Are you talking about my car?"

She holds up her hands in a kind of surrender. "Yes, I admit it. I keyed it after I left the funeral reception."

"I couldn't give a shit about my car right now! You need to give me access to my social media and bank accounts, and you need to tell Akshay, Toby, and Dad what you did, and also my boss, Madeline. And you need to tell the police you started that fire."

Jenna frowns. "Huh?"

"For fuck's sake. I've had enough of this bullshit. You wanted to ruin my life. Well done, you did." I clap for emphasis. "Now, you'll put it right."

Jenna hugs herself, voice small and frightened. "I've honestly got no idea what you're talking about. Are we not talking about me keying 'bitch' into the side of your car? What do I need to tell Toby?"

This feigned ignorance infuriates me. "You told Keith that his son is gay! You blabbed before Toby could say anything, and then flooded Keith's Facebook page with homophobic comments."

For the second time the colour drains from Jenna's cheeks. Her hand shakily finds her face, and she cups it in front of her mouth.

"Toby's gay?" she whispers. With her other hand she

reaches out to the wall behind her to steady herself as her legs quiver. "Gay," she repeats.

My fury ebbs. It's obvious this is the first time she's heard this news. I scrutinise her. She must be acting. I underestimated her before; this has to be a performance.

But no actor can make the colour drain from their faces, can they? Affect such a look of shock that it even shows in the eyes? Make their entire body quake non-stop?

"You didn't know?" I demand.

She shakes her head, clutches her waist, and doubles over as if in pain. "Toby's gay," she says again, but this time it's a statement, and weeps noisily. I observe her every tremble. It goes on so long that I start to feel ever-so-slightly uncomfortable. Eventually she straightens, still whimpering. "I guess that makes sense," she snivels.

A thought comes to me: the fire. "What were you doing last night?"

She groans. "Ohhhh, how did you know? It must be written all over my face. I feel so bad about it. It was a one-off thing. It'll never happen again."

"You were in Salford?"

"What? No, it was at mine. He's my flatmate Cammy's older brother. He's a painter decorator and came over to help fix the hole in my bedroom wall. One thing led to another… and he ended up staying over."

"You had a one-night stand?"

"I'm not proud of it. It was just some rebound fool-ishness."

"Prove you were at home last night."

Jenna looks confused at this demand and goes to protest, but sees by my clenched jaw and hard glare that I'm deadly serious.

She pulls out her mobile from her uniform pocket,

taps in her pin code and then shows me a text from a 'Dean'. I take the phone from her and check the time and date it was sent: today at 8.33 a.m.

It reads:

Thanks for last night, sexy, and for letting me stay over. Made it to work on time. We had fun ;-) Let's do it again sometime xxx

I hand back her phone and study her face. Her make-up is ruined: mascara running, foundation smeared, lipstick smudged. There's no way this woman who cares so much for her outward appearance is putting this on. She's clearly devastated by the news that Toby's gay. And has an alibi for last night, so couldn't have started the fire. A cold numbness permeates under my skin. It alarms me more than the fury. A stillness. An emptiness I can't fathom.

"So you keyed my car?" I ask in a flat monotone.

"Yeah."

"And that's it?"

"Uh-huh."

I stare at her for a long time until she wipes her tears away.

She continues, "I'll give you the money to fix it. Whatever it costs."

It begins to rain. A splatter at first, then big fat drops. I pull up my hood, but Jenna shivers in her store uniform, her perfectly tousled hair sticking to her face.

She rubs her hands together against the cold. "How long has he been gay for? When did he know?"

"If Toby wants to tell you about it, he will," I snap.

She nods, then gazes at me. "So, what's all this that's been happening to you?"

A few moments ago, I believed this woman was my

arch nemesis, and now she's showing me concern. I consider her expression. She genuinely looks like she wants to help me and is ready to listen. But I just can't tell and, as the hustle and bustle of the busy shopping district suddenly begins to close in on me, I have an overwhelming urge to be anywhere other than here.

I walk away.

26

C ompletely deflated, I arrive on my road without even remembering the journey, my body taking over with familiar movements while my brain shut down.

OPNN's tattoo guy and scarf guy are on the pavement outside my house. But so are a number of other bystanders; I estimate about twenty. A few with professional cameras. Urgh. Media photographers. I probably know most of them from organising numerous photo-calls over the years for clients. They're congregating outside my house in the hopes of getting a photo of the *most hated woman in the world right now*. At least with this many people milling about, no one will attempt to throw acid at me or harm me in any way. I hope. Be grateful for small mercies, as they say.

Thankfully I see the crowd before they spot me and park a little way up the road. I wrap my scarf around my head so that only my eyes are peeping through, and pull my hood up over my head. This will deter the photographers – because if they can't identify my face in a shot, I could be anyone, and no newspaper will use it. I get out of the car and hurry towards my front door.

There's a flurry of activity as cameras are raised, and everyone huddles forward in an attempt to get closer to me. People shout my name and throw out questions. Tattoo guy steps in my path, but I sidestep him and mumble, "No comment."

As I let myself into my house, I notice the blackened, charred patch on my doorframe and front door, where the acid is eating away the wood. It shocks me for the second time that someone would do that.

I double lock the door and head straight to the lounge, peeling off my coat and scarf and dropping them on the floor as I walk. I collapse on the sofa and cry and cry and cry.

When my eyes finally dry, I shuffle through to the front room to peek out the window. It's dark now, early evening, and raining heavily. I can't see anyone. All the rubberneckers are gone. There's nothing to see here. Exhausted, I drag my legs back through to the lounge, but I can't bring myself to sit. Instead, I stand, swaying slightly, and hug myself.

The same questions circle:

Who is doing this to me?

Why?

What have I done to them?

I desperately want to talk to Mum, and the thought of her no longer on the end of a telephone, no longer a short drive away, makes me weep again.

I think about calling Kemi, but I don't want to talk to anyone right now apart from my mum.

Oh, Mum.

I've tried to live my life kindly, openly, non-judgmentally. I've always tried to tell the truth and be honest with others, to live by a code of personal values that I thought had integrity.

So what has gone so wrong?

Who have I upset along the way so spectacularly that they would want to rip me apart?

I have a yearning to hear Mum's voice and remember I have a video of her saved on my laptop, along with numerous photos that I collated for the funeral. At least I still have some digital copies left, with the physical printouts, old film, and memory cards from her camera all destroyed in the fire.

I grab my work laptop and put it on the dining room table. I sit on a dining chair and log on, navigating immediately to the right folder. I click through the photos, and grief strikes at me again and again as I see Mum's smile. Chubby baby photos on my grandma's knees; a photo of her as a child in the sixties, propped on the bonnet of a retro Mini Mark 1 by my great-uncle Bob; and a grinning photo of her and Dad on their wedding day.

I finally get to the video of Mum on her sixtieth birthday, from a couple of years ago. A video that I took on my phone of her blowing out the candles on her birthday cake. Auntie Joyce is waiting in the wings for her turn, my mum being the eldest by seven minutes. It's a perfect video of Mum smiling, laughing, whooping and talking.

A notification pops up and distracts me. I angrily move the cursor over the X to close it, but something jumps out at me.

A word: spy.

I move the cursor away and read the notification carefully. It's a reminder that my SPYR KEYLOGGR software needs updating with the latest updates.

It takes a moment or two for my grief-stricken brain

to click into gear. Slowly, slowly the mush clears, and the clarity sharpens.

What is SPYR KEYLOGGR software?

The notification fades away as they often do when you take no action, and I immediately open Google. I search for SPYR KEYLOGGR software and find what I'm looking for on the first page.

It's a keystroke logger. A type of monitoring software that records every key that is pressed on a keyboard. An 'insidious form of spyware', according to one article.

"What is *this* doing on my laptop?" I ask out loud. Someone must've put it there. That same someone who has been targeting me? It has to be.

Along the taskbar on my desktop, next to the Start button is a box that says 'Type here to search'. I click it, and a screen pops up asking where I'd like to search. Software isn't listed, so I select 'Folder', as the software must be saved somewhere on my laptop. I type in SPYR and press return.

The results tell me that the software is saved in a folder called LC Program Drivers, which is saved within four other folders. It's so buried that I would never ever have found it unless I'd seen that pop-up.

I open the folder. There is a file called SPYR-RUN, which must be the keystroke software. There are also perhaps twenty other files, all with weird names. One catches my eye.

I search in Google for 'Cam-Record'. Finally, on the third page of results, I find it. It's a piece of webcam-hacking software that allows someone to remotely take over your webcam, to watch you and hear you and take photos or video footage.

Shit.

Who has put this stuff on my laptop? I close the

browser and look at the folder again. There's a column that says 'Last Modified' with a date and time. All the files have exactly the same date in November. Almost four weeks ago.

What happened on that day?

I pull out my diary from my handbag. I always have a paper one which I jot down personal appointments and birthdays. A pang of sorrow hits as I realise Mum gave this one to me last Christmas. She could always be relied upon to gift me a diary and a pair of wholesome Marks & Spencer pyjamas. But I can't think about that now – I have to remain strong. I look up the date: 4 November. It's a Monday. And I have absolutely nothing noted.

A workday. Did I click on an email that downloaded all this stuff? Is this the virus that I had on my laptop that only reared its ugly head on Friday a few hours before my pitch meeting?

I open my work emails, which also has my work calendar. I'm a stickler for adding everything to my public calendar to stop colleagues from sending me meeting requests for times I'm unavailable. I click back to the first week of November and see I've got a few things listed for the fourth. I open the day to see the list in full.

And there it is – staring me in the face.

From 9 a.m. until 10 a.m. I was without my laptop. The calendar note says 'Laptop and Phone to IT'.

I'd given my work devices to Rob to sync due to an upgrade to our systems. Everyone at MBW had to do it, not just me. He'd given us all hour-long slots over the course of a couple of weeks, for some reason starting with the PR team on that Monday.

But had that been a ploy just to get my laptop? Or had someone grabbed my laptop while it was meant to be in his care when he wasn't working on it? No. That was impossible. He'd sat right next to me when he'd done it, at Finn's desk because Finn was out at a meeting. Rob had asked me to put in my password before he started.

And asked me to put in my pin code on my mobile phone too.

My mobile phone sits next to the laptop on the table. I pick it up. Did he do something to that too? Is it even possible to hack a mobile phone?

I turn to Google for the answers. Yes, it's possible to install spyware on mobile phones that lets the hackers remotely watch your phone activities. A person can do this by getting direct access to a device and installing an app. It's also possible to take over a mobile phone's camera.

Whoa.

I open my phone and search through the Settings app to see if I can find something there that I don't recognise. Nothing seems amiss, so I go through every folder on my home screen. It takes me a while, but then I spot it. An app called SpyDEM.

I immediately turn to my laptop and search for it. It's actually a parental control app that allows parents to 'spy' on their children's phones. It includes a GPS tracker, the ability to read all messages as well as look at what phone calls have been made and received. It tracks the internet browser history and can see all the photos and videos in the photo app. If you upgrade, you can even listen to phone calls happening in real time.

Did Rob do this? The geeky IT guy? It takes a while to sink in.

Rob. The IT guy. WTF.

He's been watching me through my laptop and phone, tracking everything I type and look at, reading all my messages and emails. Following my every movement through the GPS tracker on my phone – which I take everywhere. Seeing all my passwords, viewing all my photos.

My whole life has been monitored. Literally everything. For the last month.

Mentally I tick off everything that has happened over the past few days and whether Rob could be responsible:

My laptop dying hours before my big pitch and losing my presentation from the cloud – tick.

The emails sent from my work account to Madeline and supermarket Stephanie – tick.

The porn added to the CozMoz Paints presentation – tick.

The dirty text messages, the delivery of the lingerie and sex toy. He knew my address, as I'd sent it to him on Friday so he could deliver my laptop back on the Sunday, and he had my number from work – tick.

The letters and USB planted in my garden. This one gives me pause. When did he come to my house? He came to deliver back my laptop, but never went outside. But he would've seen my fence panel was down and the easy access from the row of garages behind. And the USB with the home movie of me and another man – he most definitely has the tech skills to find deepfake software and edit that. And he could've easily found a photo or video of me off my phone to use.

Taking over my social media accounts and flooding them with racist, sexist, homophobic, and other outrageous offensive content, as well as freezing my bank accounts – tick. This would've been simple for him to do, as he would've been able to find out my master password for PW-Protekt by just watching me type it in with the keyword logger.

The email to Dad about Toby and spamming Dad's Facebook profile with homophobic comments would've been a piece of cake too. He just needed to log into my personal Gmail account and Facebook profile, accessing Dad's page through mine and... voila.

I know he didn't key my car. Jenna admitted to that. But what about the acid thrown at my front door and the threatening text after? I blamed it on far-left activists upset at the content on my social media. But could that have been Rob too? I remember seeing big industrial vats and car batteries outside his farm – did they contain chemicals?

And he would've easily been able to find my mum's address in my phone's contacts app.

My gut lurches. Yes. He could've done it all.

But *why*? What motivation could he possibly have for doing this to me?

I sit back in my chair and look past my laptop. Why? As my eyes fall back down to the screen, I notice the little dot glowing at the top. My webcam is on.

As if electrified, I jolt back from my laptop. The dining chair scrapes the floor and tips over behind me with a thump. Is Rob watching me RIGHT NOW?

Why has this only just dawned on me?

The fury I felt when confronting Jenna returns. I got the truth from her and I'll get the truth from the IT guy. Internally, I shout: *I'm coming for you, Rob!*

Immediately I power down the laptop, switch off my phone and put them both in the fridge. I don't know why that comes to me, but I remember watching an Edward Snowden documentary and him asking visitors to do that.

Purpose surges through me. I'm going to get this sorted once and for all.

Jogging back through the house, I pick up my

dropped coat, scarf and car keys, find my handbag, and open the front door.

But the way is blocked.

A man in a big parka jacket with the hood up against the driving rain stands with his back to me on the front doorstep, his arm up as if talking on the phone.

He spins around before I can slam the door shut.

"Akshay?"

He looks as surprised as I feel. He lowers his mobile from his ear.

"Your phone's off," he says.

I nod.

"I've been stood here a while, wanting to knock, but then I thought I'd better try calling first..."

He trails off. And looks desperately forlorn. Rain splatters my face, and I gesture for him to come inside. He steps in and closes the door behind him. We look at each other.

For something to say, I point at his coat. "Is that new?"

"Yeah, got it in New York. I didn't realise how bloody cold it was going to be."

Every part of me longs to hug him, touch him, kiss his beautiful wonky lips. But I don't. He walked out on me, believed I was having an affair, told me he wanted to sell this house.

He looks at me quizzically. "Are you feeling okay? You look wired."

"A lot of shit has happened to me these past few days. Are you surprised?"

He nods sheepishly, realising that was a stupid question to ask. He changes the subject. "What happened to the front door?"

"An acid attack."

His eyes bulge out of his head in alarm. "What?"

"And there was a fire at my mum's apartment."

"Are you *kidding* me?"

But I have no time to explain. "What are you doing here?" I ask.

"I saw all that stuff on your Facebook page."

I go to protest that it wasn't me, but he holds up his palm.

He continues, "I know it wasn't you. That's not who you are, Lauren. I know that. And it got me thinking. And I've been so stupid. You told me that you didn't have an affair. You told me that someone must be targeting you. And I believe you."

I chew my lip.

He adds, "I'm so, so sorry. I made a huge mistake. Can you ever forgive me?"

His honest face is desperate, his eyes pleading.

I remember something. "Where have you been staying?"

"With my work colleague over from New York," he replies without hesitation.

"Maya?"

"Yes. She's here to finish that project, and work's paying for a two-bed city centre Airbnb for her. I didn't... couldn't... tell my family. They would've been devastated, and I was devastated. I wasn't ready to tell them..."

"You've been staying with another woman?" My voice increases, and realisation registers on Akshay's face.

"Oh, no. Goodness, no. It's not anything like that. She's married."

My mouth drops open.

"Here, look..." He pulls out his phone, opens Facebook and shows me photos from her profile. They're of

Maya's wedding... to a woman. They look blissfully happy.

He continues, "Lauren, I'd never do that to you. And I know now that you'd never do that to me. We were made for each other, and I'm a stupid idiot."

"What about all your stuff? And the expensive gifts you gave me and then took back?"

"I put everything in a storage unit. I know, I know, it was a ridiculous, kneejerk thing to do. Please forgive me. I'm so sorry."

I really, *really* want to be angry with him. But I just can't. He's admitted his mistake. And I have a tech stalker to deal with. My body reacts to my heart before my brain has a chance to kick in, and to his astonishment – and mine too – I hug him. I melt into him, and his steady, solid presence soothes me. I want to wrap us up in a cocoon and just pretend none of this ever happened, pretend that we're blissfully happy and that our lives are perfect and wonderful.

But that's a fantasy, and I need to deal with reality. I push away from him and say, "I know who's doing this."

"Who?"

"The IT guy at work."

"The one who was here when I got back from New York?"

"Yes. Him."

"Why?"

"I've got no idea. But I was on my way to find out. I know where he lives."

Akshay frowns. "Don't you think you should call the police?"

"I did. But they weren't really interested. They said they'd get back to me."

"Are you sure confronting him is a good idea? Maybe you should wait for the police."

I take a step towards the front door. I'm not waiting any longer. I need to get all that offensive content taken off my social media channels. I need to get back into my bank accounts. I need to fix things with Toby and Dad. I need to put Madeline straight. Yes, my fiancé has seen the light, but everything else is still in monumental chaos. "Akshay, I'm going now. So you can either come with me or stay here. Your choice."

He doesn't even hesitate. "I'm coming with you."

27

I drive like a maniac to Rob's farmhouse, remembering the way from my visit there on Friday.

Akshay and I don't speak. He's too busy clinging on for dear life as I tear across town, and stomping his foot in the footwell as if to hit the brake. If he talks to me, I think he thinks I'll lose concentration. He's possibly right. The rain is hammering down in sheets, and the windscreen wipers are on full speed but hardly doing their job, so I lean forward and peer through the smeary water on the glass.

My work laptop and phone are on the back seat. I retrieved them from the fridge before we left. Rob can flipping well delete all that crap off them in front of me and put this all right.

We leave the busy city suburbs and head into the remote countryside. It's dark and quiet, with not many others on the road, choosing to sit out the rain and shelter indoors.

"We're here," I say.

Akshay takes in the sprawling, isolated farm set a

little way back from the road as I slow the car. He looks at me in complete astonishment. "This place, seriously?"

"I know, not exactly where I thought he'd live either, but there you go."

I pull into the gravel driveway of the farm and notice all the windows of the farmhouse are dark. The rest of the farm and farm buildings seem deserted too. And, on a wet evening in November, the entire place is almost pitch-black, lit only by the moon and the occasional headlights of a passing car.

Akshay puts his hand on mine and gives me a look. "You're in charge here. I'm here for you."

I smile. I know this is a big deal for him. Akshay is a planner and likes to know every intricate detail of what is about to happen. I appreciate his trust in me. I appreciate him not asking me a million questions.

"When I was here before, Rob told me to go round the back to the back door. That's where his office is. He told me it was never locked," I say.

He nods.

I turn off the engine, put my hood up, stuff my laptop and phone under my coat, and climb out of the car. We jog around the back of the building, moving quickly to get out of the rain. I notice a faint glow coming from the window I assume is Rob's office. I push on the door; it opens easily.

Taking a deep breath, I step into the farmhouse and look around the dark kitchen. The *drip, drip* of our sodden coats on the tiled floor echoes in the space. I walk towards Rob's tech room.

The door is wide open, and I see a dwindling fire crackling and spitting in the fireplace. There are no other lights on, so the fire is what is giving off the glow. Has Rob gone out and left the fire to burn down? Is that not dangerous? But I'd never leave my house unlocked either, so perhaps that's just what's done in the country and on farms.

I step into the room, followed by Akshay, being careful to check behind the door to make sure Rob is not about to leap out at me.

But the place is empty.

The only thing that seems alive are the machines around and on Rob's desk that whir and flash.

"Perhaps he's gone out," I say to Akshay.

"Looks that way."

"I'm going to look around to see if there's any evidence."

Akshay looks out the window. "Shall I go and see if I can find Rob in any of the outbuildings?"

"Yes, good idea."

Akshay squeezes my forearm and then heads back out the way we came, turning on the flashlight app on his phone to see where he's going.

I'm not sure what I expect to find in this room, but there must be something that links Rob to all this. Doubt flashes across my mind – what if I got this wrong too? What if it's not Rob, like it wasn't Jenna or Imani. What if the person is still out there? I shake it off. Who else could it be? I go to Rob's swivel office chair, put my laptop and phone on the seat, and move the mouse that's sat on the desk.

The large screen sparks to life, asking for a password. Damn. I spot his MBW-branded notebook, which is given to staff when they first join. Mine is long-since used up, but Rob's looks untouched. I wonder if he's written his password in there? Unlikely – he strikes me as someone who is extremely online safety conscious, but I go to pick up the book anyway.

In the gloom, I didn't see it before, but there's a second notebook next to the branded one. In complete contrast, this one looks very well used with scuffed corners. It doesn't close fully, as loose papers have been stuffed between pages and corners have been folded over.

I pick it up and angle it towards the faint glow from the fire to read the scrawl on the front: *Lauren*.

My fingers fumble, and the notebook almost drops to the floor. My mouth drains of all fluid, and I dry-swallow, my throat scratchy and constricted.

I flick slowly through the pages. They are full of neatly written entries. I read one at random.

Wearing: blue wrapover dress and cream chunky knitted cardigan with black tights and heeled court shoes. Same pearl earrings. Hair in a low ponytail.
Mood: L sad today. Probs cos mother dying. L says she's being moved to a hospice.
Movements: Work, hospital to see mother for AM visiting hours, work, hospital to see mother for PM visiting hours, garage for petrol on way home, home.
Lights out 10.07.

I flick to another entry. It's about me. They're all about me: what I'm wearing, doing, saying. There are notes on my family and friends.

On one page is a printout of a photo. It's been sellotaped in the notebook. It's of me getting into my car outside my house and has been taken surveillance-style from a distance.

I find more photos: me coming out of the supermarket; outside the hospital devastated and clutching my auntie Joyce moments after Mum died; through the back window of my house on the day Akshay returned from New York – I'm wearing my loungewear set and opening the window while he cooks dinner in the background.

The last entry is from yesterday, and the final line reads: *Fire, fire, your mum's home is on fire.*

I skip to the first page. The date: 27 October. Rob has been watching me both online and offline for nearly five weeks.

This is seriously creepy. My heartbeat pounds in my ears. I need to find Akshay.

I turn to head out the door, but an excruciating pain blossoms across the back of my head, my vision goes black, and I slump, unconscious.

28

A throbbing pain in the back of my head rouses me. My scrunched eyes take a moment to adjust to the brightness.

What just happened? I feel disorientated, as if I'm on the waltzer at a fairground and the ride is now coming to an end but isn't quite stationary yet.

I reach a shaky hand up to touch the sore spot, except my hand doesn't move. I try again. And then I know. My hands are tied behind my back. No, not just behind my back but behind... the back of the chair too.

My eyelids snap open. I'm sitting on Rob's office chair, still in his office at the farmhouse. My coat has been removed, and the lights are on. I flick my gaze up, and he's right there, about two metres in front of me, leaning against the desk. His arms are folded, and he's staring at me.

This was not what I was expecting. I thought I'd confront him, and we'd talk; he'd apologise and put things right, and then I'd be on my way. Yes, I would've told Madeline and Ursula about it, and yes, he would've likely been sacked for creepy behaviour. But physical violence? And whatever this is... kidnapping? Being held against my will? This takes it to a whole other level.

He never struck me as the violent type. Not even in my darkest nightmares did I think he'd whack me so hard I'd pass out. I have no recollection of my coat being removed, or being propped on the chair, so I must've been out cold for a few minutes. I didn't think he'd have something like that in him.

I struggle against my binding and guess by the stickiness and squeaking that it's duct tape around my wrists. At the same time I glance around the room, but can't see Akshay. He must still be outside. Does Rob know he's here? My heart soars as I realise that Rob didn't know Akshay was coming with me. Akshay is safe and waiting for the right moment to take out Rob and set me free.

I immediately set my sights on Rob. I don't want him to twig that I'm looking for someone else.

Rob doesn't say anything, just watches me as I struggle with my bindings. After a while I give up and swear under my breath.

"Rob," I say cautiously, "let me go."

He doesn't reply. Just looks straight at me, his expression unreadable.

"Rob!" I try again, louder, in an attempt to wake him up to this situation – that he has a woman tied up at his house. "I know you've been stalking me online and offline. I know you put software on my laptop and phone."

No response.

I persevere. "I don't know what you're doing right now, but there's still time to make this right. Let me go, and we can put everything straight."

He blinks a couple of times, but still nothing. We eye

each other. The rain smatters against the windows, the tech hardware whirs, and the fire crackles. But Rob doesn't make a sound. He barely even looks as if he's breathing.

It's the most frightening staring contest I've ever been in. But I don't want to look away. I don't want him to think he's won. Perhaps that's it. The sicko is savouring this moment and the power he now has over me. He's trying to break me, like he's been trying to break me all along. Does he want me to cry?

My patience runs out, and my courage flares. "What the hell are you planning to do, hmm? You've got me tied up and now what? You're just going to look at me all night? Listen to me talk and try to convince you to let me go? Is that what you want – for me to beg or something?"

I glare at him. Rob looks on, in complete stillness, like an unsettling statue looming over me.

Then I think: what *is* his plan? A million terrible scenarios play on fast forward in my head, each worse than the one before.

Shit. Perhaps it's best to keep talking. To stay right here, tied up in this chair. I'm relatively unscathed apart from a bash on the head. If he can do that, what else is he capable of? One thing's for certain – I don't want to find out.

My tone softens, becomes pleading. "Why are you doing this to me? Did I offend you somehow?"

He remains impassive.

If begging is what Rob wants, then I'm not too proud to beg. I need to buy as much time as possible for Akshay to do whatever it is he has planned.

"Please tell me what I did, Rob. I'm sorry. Whatever it was, please accept my sincerest apologies. I try to be kind and patient with everyone, but sometimes I get stressed, and I get snappy. If I was short with you or in any way disrespected you, then please tell me. I can only learn if you make me aware of my errors. And I'll never, ever do it again. Rob? Please let me go."

Silence.

The begging has got me nowhere. I struggle, try to stand, but my arms keep me pinned to the chair, and the chair jerks with me, making it impossible.

I shout, "Aargh!" in frustration.

What is he waiting for? What game is he playing? What does he want? Perhaps he wants me to guess his motivation? I rack my brains for a plausible reason.

I run through every interaction I've ever had with him. There aren't that many. A couple of work social events where I said hello but nothing much else. A few emails back and forth about my laptop or phone and interactions purely about IT issues. A couple of times saying 'good morning' or 'hi' in passing in the hallway or in the car park. I recall one occasion where I'd said hello to him while we were both in the queue for a sandwich shop near work. Nothing, in my mind, that offended him or could've angered him. He wrote on my laptop: 'I know what you did'. *But what have I done?*

I need to look at this from another angle. Zoom out. See the bigger picture. Why do stalkers do what they do? Maybe I haven't pissed him off. Maybe it's the opposite...

"Was this all a sick way to get my attention? You're clearly obsessed with me. Did you think I'd come to you for help with all my tech issues? And fall into your arms in relief because I'm newly single? Did you plan to break me so thoroughly that I'd be more open to your sympathy and advances?"

Rob shifts ever so slightly, and I latch onto it.

"That's it, isn't it? Like the actress Jodie Foster's

stalker trying to assassinate the US president to get her attention. You think you're in love with me! This was all an attempt to woo me!"

Rob's eyes flick up and over my head. I hear a slow clapping from behind me.

I freeze.

Rob isn't alone. There's somebody else in this room.

The office chair is pushed, and I'm spun around to see the absolute last person I was expecting. My breath hitches in my chest as I stare.

29

S he grins triumphantly.

It takes my brain a moment to dredge up her name, as she's so out of place here. Her long hair, usually down, is tied up in a topknot, and she's not wearing a scrap of make-up. I've never seen her face without her trademark lipstick and eyeliner.

"Cleo?" I whisper in disbelief.

"In love with you." She laughs, then her face contorts, and she snarls, "As if, you fucking bitch."

My mouth drops so far open I have a struggle to move my jaws to close it. Cleo. My account manager at work. Here with Rob, the IT guy. I would never have put them together.

"What am I doing here, Cleo?" I stutter.

I felt more in control with Rob, the hapless IT guy with a freaky obsession. But Cleo? She's an unknown. I've worked with her for almost two years, but don't really know anything about her. However, I do know one thing, and it fills me with dread. I know she has a temper.

Cleo's face flits from anger to smugness. "Because

I've been planning this for weeks. You fell for our SPYR KEYLOGGR notification lure hook, line, and sinker. Bet you thought you were so clever, tracking it back to Rob? But no, it was all part of *my* plan. And you did exactly as I expected. So predictable. I've been following your juvenile detective work with Imani and Jenna with interest – and much hilarity. And I listened in to your call with the police. You think you're brave to come here. But you're really, *really* stupid."

She rolls her eyes at me. In her hands she's holding the journal, and I recall immediately where I've seen that neatly written handwriting before: at work, on Cleo's notes to me and other colleagues, and when she wrote on the whiteboard in the meeting room.

I walked right into her trap. I came here, a remote, isolated farmhouse, under my own steam. What an idiot. Except I wasn't alone. Akshay. He must've called the police by now. Perhaps he's in the kitchen, watching all this and planning how to disable not one but two people.

I need to keep her talking. To give the police the chance to arrive.

Menace sizzles off her like a glowing aura swirling with hate and the promise of violence, but there's one thing that I have to know. "What did I do to you?" I say quietly, not wanting to startle her.

But it's the wrong thing to say, and her face changes again. Her eyes narrow, and she takes a step towards me, raising her hand to strike. My body automatically reacts, and I flinch.

She steps back, satisfied. "You're really pathetic, you know that? Living your glossy, perfect life without a care in the world for those you trample on to maintain the illusion."

"I don't know what you're talking about."

"I ruined your life in exactly the same way you ruined mine. I worked so hard to crawl my way out of poverty, to get a decent career, to bag a rich fiancé, to live in a beautiful home and have nice things, and you – you fucked it all up for me!"

My face must show a blank because my head is a blank.

She continues, "I lost my job because of you. And I can't get another job *because of you.*"

"But... I thought you'd landed an incredible new job?"

She shakes her head. "There is no new job! Because *you* ruined my professional reputation, and no one will give me a chance. I read the email you sent to Lisa about that job she was going to offer me. And the one you sent Madeline."

My heart beats quicker. Lisa and I used to work together in my first PR job. We're still friends who go out for drinks every now and then. She emailed me off the record to ask about Cleo, as she'd applied for a job at Lisa's new agency. I'd been honest: I hadn't recommended Cleo. I didn't realise Lisa was ready to offer Cleo the job. And Madeline had asked me if she should let her 'network' know if Cleo was a safe bet or not. I'd told her it was entirely up to her, but it was a risk. Cleo could do what she had done at MBW somewhere else – lie.

Cleo's voice rises. "And because I lost my job, my temper flared. My fiancé dumped me after a blazing row, and then I lost my home because he booted me out of his house. And with no salary or job prospects, my finances are screwed, and I can't afford the repayments on my car or credit cards. I lost fucking everything! The only thing I didn't lose is my family – because I haven't spoken to those bastards for a very long time. But I wanted you to experience that pain, of having no one who believes you, no support network, no one to turn to, nothing left. And now you know how it feels. It hurts, doesn't it?"

Everything begins to slot into place, and I'm shocked. "So you've done all this because you're upset with me because *you* lied?"

Cleo explodes, her arms flailing, and yells, "You should've believed me, you should've had my back as my boss, my team leader. I slogged in that job for two years to keep you happy, and you betrayed me. You went snooping instead of leaving it be and found the CCTV. Yes, I know it was you. Madeline slipped up and accidentally told me."

Although I'm the one in the precarious position, I can't let this slide. I have to explain myself. "Cleo, you shouted at and shoved a client at a work event and told me the client had hit you. I believed you completely and confronted the client, who then told me her side of events – the two of you were having a talk in the hallway about how poorly the event was going, and you lost your shit, screamed at her, and shoved her."

Cleo sneers.

I continue, undeterred, "After hearing her story, I still believed *you*. But I know the manager of the hotel the event was in and asked her if there was any CCTV of that hallway – and there was. And it showed that *you lied to me*! You attacked the client. I couldn't believe it."

She shouts something over me, but I push on, "And I persuaded the client not to press charges or make a complaint, and I made sure you had the chance to hand your notice in before you got sacked – because that looked better for you. I did what I could for you even though *you're a liar*."

"Bullshit," Cleo screams. "That morning my fiancé

had falsely accused me of having an affair – I was stressed!"

"And you lost your temper. That has nothing to do with me."

"It has *everything* to do with you. I told you that morning I wasn't in the right frame of mind to manage that event on my own, and you told me it was just first-time nerves and, essentially, to get on with it."

This is true. I'd assumed that she was nervous managing her first client event without me there, but I also had full trust in her abilities that she could run it on her own. Up until that point she'd been an excellent account manager. I was trying to bolster her confidence; I didn't suspect that there was an issue in her personal life. I thought she'd needed to hear a pep talk from me, and that's what I'd given her. How wrong I'd been. How terribly I'd misjudged the situation.

"I believed in you. I was trying to help you in your career," I say.

She snorts and shakes her head. "You fucked me over, Lauren. So I've fucked you right back. And it's been a pleasure to watch. But I'm not done."

Cleo's entire demeanour flashes a fiery red, and I recoil from the rage in her eyes. What does she mean she's not done? She's so fixated on blaming me for her life falling apart that she could do anything. She's a loose cannon. And she's in control here. My guts churn.

"I'm sorry, Cleo. I'm so, so sorry."

"It's too late for your pathetic apologies. They don't mean anything, anyway. You can't turn back time and make things better, can you? No, the only way is forward."

Cleo looks over my head and says, "Rob, honey, come here."

Rob. I'd forgotten all about him. He appears from

behind me and goes to Cleo. She puts her arm around him and tenderly kisses his cheek, making eye contact with him for a beat too long and stroking his neck.

Oh, bollocks. Cleo is the girlfriend that Rob mentioned when I was last here. When I told him I could kiss him after he thought he'd found my presentation in the cloud. He looks at her doe-eyed and visibly melts at her touch and attention.

I force my face to remain still, not to grimace at this overt PDA.

Cleo keeps her arm around Rob's shoulders, anchoring him to her, and looks at me.

"Rob is very skilled at technology stuff," she says as she squeezes him into her, "but did you know he grew up on this farm? When his parents both died, it was left to him. Others run it for him now, but he's still a skilled butcher. You never forget the things you learn in childhood, do you?"

Butcher?

Cleo must see the horror in my face as she smirks.

She gestures vaguely outside. "This is a livestock farm, and there's lots of pigs. Pigs eat anything... including human remains."

She means to kill me. They mean to kill me. I squirm desperately, twisting and turning my hands in the duct tape, attempting to loosen and stretch it.

Akshay, I scream in my mind, *where the hell are you and the police? I need you to do whatever you're planning to do RIGHT NOW.*

Cleo turns back to Rob, stuffs the journal under her arm and cups his face with her palms. He beams at her in a dizzy love haze.

She kisses his lips and then the tip of his nose. "Honey, it's time to go to the meat-processing room."

Rob's face is one of bliss, but his mouth turns down at the edges.

Cleo plants a flurry of little kisses on his cheek. "I love you so much, Rob. And if you love me, you'll do this. It'll be just like we talked about. There are only a few more things I need you to do for me, okay? Then this'll all be over, and it'll just be the two of us, forever."

The creases across his brow ease, but not completely.

Cleo continues, "I love you so, so much, honey. We were meant to be together. I was meant to find you when I did. A work romance – who'da thought it. Our little secret. Madeline wouldn't have approved. But we're so happy, aren't we? I moved in here when Lawrence kicked me out, and it's been perfect. We're perfect."

While this little show of affection plays out, I desperately attempt to manoeuvre my wrists free of the duct tape without drawing their attention. It's stuck tight, but I have to get out of this chair. I have to escape.

Rob nods, his face a picture of contentment once again. Cleo faces me.

"You can't just murder me," I yell. "You'll be caught."

She rolls her eyes and puts on a mocking, babyish voice. "Lauren Cohen committed suicide. What a tragedy. She went to the farmhouse of her work IT guy to ask him to help her to access her social media and bank accounts. She still maintained that she hadn't posted any of that offensive content and that she'd been hacked. Rob was worried about her but told her he couldn't think of any way to help. Distraught, Lauren decided to drown herself in the nearby Manchester Ship Canal with her car, phone, and laptop found nearby. And the phone had a hastily written suicide note on it. Boohoo."

Cleo pretends to snivel and wipe away tears.

"The police will never believe it. They'll know it's a faked suicide. What about all the technology stuff?" But as soon as I say it, I know.

"Rob has already deleted most of the tech trail that leads back to us. We just need to wipe your phone and laptop, which you so conveniently brought here for us. We'll have a little bonfire of any remaining evidence in the fire pit out the back. Very normal for farms to have fires."

"But there'll be no body!"

"The ship canal is deep. Perhaps you weighed yourself down with rocks. Or, by the time they find your abandoned car, have already washed out to sea."

Petrified, I groan, redoubling my efforts to loosen my wrists.

This sound of my fear pleases Cleo, and she gloats, "You always underestimated me. Never again."

There's a noise from outside, and I stare at the door. Akshay! OMG, just in time.

But Cleo laughs. "Expecting someone to come and save you? I have to say, we weren't expecting the ex-fiancé to arrive with you. But he's not coming to rescue you. He's in the pigpen."

She pulls out a wallet from her pocket and holds it up to me. I recognise it immediately as Akshay's.

All hope drains from my being. *Akshay.*

"What have you done to him? Is he dead?"

Cleo taps the side of her nose.

My heart feels as if it's been punched out of my chest. Akshay... dead? "No. *No.* He's done nothing to you. Nothing. How could you? You'll pay for this. And you'll have to include his murder in your suicide story. The police will never believe it."

"Where there's a will, there's a way. Ha. I think you told me that. I'm quoting you."

She laughs, then quietens and rubs her chin, thinking, before continuing, "It'll be easy. Everyone knows your mental health has been unbalanced these past few days. And tonight, in a moment of blind, passionate rage, you kill the man you love by bashing him over the head and chucking his body in the river. Then you jump and kill yourself. Akshay's body is in the car when you come to visit Rob, but he doesn't see it, of course. I'll have to iron out the finer details, but that'll be the gist of it. Convincing, right?"

"You monster," I say as tears stream down my face. "You're insane."

Her face snarls up once again. "I'm sick of your irritating voice. Rob, put some tape over her mouth."

Rob flinches slightly at this direct command but heads towards the duct tape on the desk.

He's my only chance. And he might not see what she's doing, but I do. Loud and clear. "Rob! She's manipulating you. She doesn't love you! She's only with you to get to me – surely you must see that. She moved in here because she had nowhere else to go and is using you—"

But my words are cut short as he puts tape over my mouth. I attempt to make eye contact, to appeal to him, but he doesn't look at me. He snips the roll of duct tape with some scissors and puts both back on the desk.

"Bring those," Cleo says, and Rob picks up the tape and scissors again.

Cleo walks to the fire and throws her journal in it. She watches as the flames lick up its sides and then flare up to consume it. The dancing fire lights up her face with a demonic glow.

"Let's go," she says.

30

Rob moves towards me. I kick out at him, swivel the chair, and push it away with my feet – everything I can think of to prevent him getting near me.

Cleo tuts. She holds the back of the chair so I can't turn it while Rob shunts my arms over the top and lifts me off the chair. I struggle and try to catch his eye. But he's determined not to look at me and to carry out Cleo's wishes. He takes hold of my bicep and attempts to guide me towards the door. I let my legs go heavy and drop to the floor. There's no way I'm walking to my doom.

Cleo takes my other arm, and together they drag me across the floor of the office head first, my nose skimming the ground. At the doorway to the kitchen, I latch my feet behind the doorframe, and we lurch to a halt. Cleo drops my arm and kicks my shins while Rob pulls me past. I attempt the same trick at the back door, but Cleo is ready for it this time. They lug me through the gravel in the pouring rain – my toes leaving a trail through the stones – and towards an outbuilding.

To open the door, Cleo drops my arm. Now's my chance. I spring as quickly as possible to my feet, taking Rob by surprise, and make a run for it.

But Rob still has hold of my arm, and Cleo slices her leg out and under and trips me up. With my arms still tied behind my back, I overbalance immediately and fall heavily – and painfully – on my side. Sharp stones prick the skin on my face.

"Stop trying to fight this," Cleo says icily in my ear. "It's inevitable."

They haul me inside on my knees, and Cleo flicks on the light switch. The overhead light flickers a few times and then blinks on.

It's a small, white, sterile room with no windows. It smells of cheap cleaning products and pine-scented bleach – laced with the distinct whiff of raw meat, which turns my stomach. Along the sides are waist-high silver units, one with a big wooden chopping block on top. At the back, silver hooks hang from the ceiling. At one end there's a machine with a big round blade that I assume is for slicing big joints of meat. Opposite that is a deep sink. Near the door there's one floor-to-ceiling shelving unit full of cleaning items and other things to process and package meat. And along the wall on the right is a magnetic strip with an entire display of different kinds of knives, including a large meat cleaver.

Cleo pulls out a high stool from under one of the silver units and plonks it behind me. She nods to Rob, and they force me to sit.

"Tape her ankles to the stool," Cleo instructs while holding my shoulders down so I can't move.

I kick at him, but he's learnt that lesson and comes at me from the side. He follows her orders, and my ankles are taped to the bottom of the stool so I can't stand up. As he's finishing up, Cleo is distracted by the knives

and wanders dreamily over to them, running her fingertips along each, a look of awe on her face. While they're
not looking, I twist and yank at the duct tape around my
wrists.

I feel a give in the tightness, some slack in the tape. I
gasp – I can't help it. My eyes scan between them.
Neither seems to have noticed.

Cleo selects a knife and grabs it off the magnetic wall
rack, admiring the light glinting off the polished blade.
She turns back to me and beckons to Rob. He goes
obediently to her side.

She holds up the knife and points it at me. "I've
waited six weeks for this moment, and by god, I'm
going to savour it."

She takes a step towards me and then edges behind.
She grabs my hair to expose my throat. I struggle,
attempting to hit her with my arms, which are behind
my back, and jerk my body. I try to scream, but the tape
over my mouth holds it behind my lips, and it comes
out as a high-pitched whine.

Cleo wrenches my hair, and out of the corner of my
eye, I see the knife flash past.

"Cleo," Rob shouts and breaks her concentration.

Her clasp on my hair loosens. "What?" she says
impatiently.

He dips his head and looks up at her through his
eyelashes like a naughty child that knows they've done
something wrong.

"Do you… do you really love me?"

"Of course, my darling. With all my heart."

I mmmm through the tape and shake my head.

"And you're not just using me?"

Cleo tugs my hair to quieten me. "Don't listen to this
bitch. She's toxic. She lies. I've told you this."

Rob chews his lip.

She continues, "We're destined for each other. Can't you feel it? Everything between us is so real."

I continue to make as much noise as I can. I try to yell, *Wake up, Rob! Wake up!* But it comes out as incoherent mumbles.

He glances at me. He's heard me! He understands. But then his face melts into bliss. "I think it's real. That passion between us can't be made up, can it?"

"No." She blows him a kiss, and he blushes. "Now, shut up so I can finish the job."

But Rob fidgets and wrings his hands, clearly still agitated. "Umm..." Rob gulps as Cleo tsks but ploughs on. "It's just..." He gestures vaguely at Cleo holding the knife to my neck. "I don't think I can go through with it. I don't want to murder anyone."

"You won't do the actual murder, honey. I'll slit her throat, and you can catch the blood in that bucket there. Then you can tell me how to carve up her body if you don't want to do it. Then we'll feed her to the piggies. We've gone through all this."

Tears and snot stream down my face, and I mmmm through the tape, attempting to yell 'Rob, help me!'

Cleo jerks my head again, but I continue, louder.

Rob glances at me and back to Cleo. "I think we've scared her enough."

Although I can't see Cleo, I sense her entire body stiffening behind me. I nod desperately at Rob and plead with my eyes: *let me go, let me go, let me go.*

Rob raises his chin and stands up straighter. He takes a step towards Cleo. "If you love me, you'll let her go."

31

Cleo moves closer to Rob, and I see her face. All the warmth drains from it, and she turns as cold as ice, her stare carving shards off Rob's resolve.

It's obvious he's interrupting her meticulously designed plan, and it's obvious she's about to lose her temper. Rob wavers in the face of her simmering fury, but glances at me and doesn't back down. She erupts.

"Of course I don't fucking love you, IT freak!" Cleo spits in Rob's face.

He recoils as if stung. He clutches his chest, and the expression on his face indicates his heart is breaking. I can almost pinpoint the exact moment it shatters.

He looks at his feet as tears well and fall from his eyes, his shoulders slump, and his arms hang limply by his sides.

Dejected, he sniffs and mutters, "You were my first girlfriend. I did everything you asked of me. Everything... I thought I pleased you. I thought we were going to get married. Start a family. You said we'd be together forever."

Cleo's knife lowers as her attention turns to Rob. I desperately continue to loosen my hand bindings. The sticky side of the duct tape has rolled up, and I pull my hands apart with all my strength, stretching it a little further.

"You gullible fool," Cleo says viciously.

"So you *were* using me?" Rob asks, still unbelieving.

"Duh. I needed you to get close to her." She uses the tip of the knife to point at me.

As she indicates me, I stop wrestling with my bindings. I don't want her to see that they've loosened.

Rob stares at me, and I 'mmmm' again through the duct tape and lock eyes with him, appealing to him to help me.

But he looks at Cleo and sobs, wiping away tears with his sleeve.

"Go and get that bucket," Cleo orders.

Rob doesn't move. Slowly, defiantly, he shakes his head. "No."

"You're so bloody stupid. You have to help me finish this whether you want to or not. You're implicated in this whole thing. What do you think, we let her go, I go to jail, and your life goes back to normal? No fucking way. You're my accomplice, Rob. If I go down, you go down."

All Rob's emotions play out on his face: shock, confusion. He flicks his gaze from me to Cleo, me to Cleo, conflicted. And then his face settles into… realisation. He gawps at Cleo.

I shake my body, scream a muffled noise at the top of my lungs, and attempt to bang the stool legs against the floor. Anything to get Rob's attention back on me.

But I've lost him.

He steps back and picks up the bucket.

"Good boy," Cleo says as if praising a dog. "Now bring it here and get ready."

I yell his name from behind the tape, but it's no use. He moves nearer to me and holds the bucket close to my torso. A terrified growl rumbles from deep in my throat. This cannot be my end. I struggle frantically, but Cleo keeps a firm hold on my hair, holding my head in place.

"I'm going to enjoy this," she says and swipes the knife.

I clench my eyes shut as the edge of the blade makes contact with my neck. I shriek in pain as blood trickles to seep into the collar of my jumper.

But the knife doesn't slice. There's a pause. I dare to open my eyes.

In front of my face, the blade hovers just millimetres from my neck. Rob clutches Cleo's forearm, stopping her from drawing the knife across my throat. Her arm shakes as she uses all her strength against him. His arm also shakes.

He shouts, "I can't let you do this!" and whacks the bucket across Cleo's head, then shoves her away from me.

Behind me I hear a thump and assume that Cleo has fallen to the floor. Rob remains standing by my side, staring at Cleo, breathing as if he's about to have an asthma attack.

I crane my neck to try to see what's happening but can only see Cleo's foot.

A noise emanates from Cleo. As it grows, I realise that she's whimpering.

It turns into a full-blown wail, and Rob extends his hand to help Cleo up. She stands, and I can just about see her.

Fat tears stream down her cheeks, and she hangs her

head. "Oh god, what have I done?" Over and over she repeats, "What have I done?"

"It's okay, Cleo. We'll sort this all out," Rob says sympathetically.

"I've been so stupid," Cleo mumbles. "I can't believe I let it get this far. I can't believe I persuaded you to help me. Oh god."

"Murder is wrong," Rob says.

"I know. Of course I know. I don't understand what got into me. Oh god." Cleo's shoulders heave, and her entire body shakes with her wails.

Is this for real? Please tell me it's for real. But my gut klaxons in my mind: those tears aren't genuine. Oh, god, no. *No!* I attempt to warn Rob, but he's transfixed by Cleo's fake remorse.

He shifts awkwardly, not knowing what to do next. Then he opens his arms to Cleo. She sniffles and falls into them, and he hugs her tightly, patting her back in comfort.

I see a flash, and Cleo stabs the knife into Rob's side. His breath hitches just as her crying ceases.

Rob's eyes go wide as he releases his arms and looks at the knife in his side, the handle still clasped by Cleo.

Cleo glares at him and then grins as she twists the handle in his body. "I guess I'll have to stage it so Lauren kills you first, then her fiancé and then commits suicide. A right murder spree."

Rob swings a fast punch at Cleo. Surprise registers on her face as she only just ducks out of the way. She pulls out the knife and attempts to stab him again, but he grabs her wrist and lunges forward into her. They topple behind me.

I hear the fight – the grunts, the yelps, and heavy breathing. I wrench apart my wrists with a huge effort, and the tape stretches enough for me to twist out one wrist.

My hands come free. I lean forward off the stool to grab the meat cleaver from the rack. I hold my left leg as far away from the stool leg as possible and saw through the tape with the meat cleaver. My ankle pops away. I do the same with the right leg.

I move to stand, but my hair is viciously tugged back. The jerk makes me drop the meat cleaver.

"Where do you think you're going, bitch?" Cleo hisses in my ear.

The meat cleaver skids across the floor to a stop by Rob's ankle. He's face first on the floor, not moving. Blood pools out on the concrete around him. His head is turned away from me.

She's killed him. And I'm next.

I fight back with everything I have, twisting my body round to face Cleo, punching and kicking at her. She drops my hair and slices at me with the knife. I attempt to dodge the slashes, but she's fast and stabs me in the front of my shoulder.

My legs give way as pain shoots through me, and blood sprays out. I slump to the floor like a rag doll.

Cleo straddles me and attempts to grab the knife, which is still wedged in my body.

Rob's voice startles us both. He's shouting out his address, screaming for help, for police, that there's been a stabbing.

Cleo whirls on him.

Clutched to his ear in a blood-slick hand is his mobile phone.

She stamps on his hand and the phone. There's a sickening crunch, of his bones or the phone screen – I can't tell.

"You called 999? You fucking moron," Cleo screams.

She sees the meat cleaver by his foot and grabs it. She positions herself over his body and raises the cleaver to slice his head in two. With my last shred of energy, I stand and grab the big wooden chopping block off the top of a silver unit. And, ignoring the pain that explodes in my shoulder, I dive towards Cleo.

I smash the board into the side of her head as she slices down with the cleaver.

It knocks her off balance, and the knife flies from her hand, clattering on the floor inches from Rob's ear.

She trips on the tipped-over stool and smacks her forehead on the side of a metal unit. She drops to the concrete with a yelp. I stare at her for a long time, but she's silent and unmoving.

I collapse to the ground, dizzy from the blood loss. The pain in my shoulder is unbearable. I edge closer to Rob. I put my hand on his back and feel it rising and falling. He's barely conscious.

Akshay. I have to find him. I have to be with him. I crawl towards the door on my one good arm, clutching the other to me, careful not to knock the handle of the blade that sticks out of my shoulder. But as I inch closer, all my strength trickles away. I make one final attempt to move, but it's no good; my head drops to the floor.

The last thing my fuzzy brain registers is the sound of sirens.

32

S *ix months later.*
    Akshay kisses my cheek as he heads off to work in his cycling gear. He bikes into work now we've moved to Bristol. He's fully recovered from the vicious whack across the head from Cleo that left him unconscious. The police had arrived and found three barely conscious adults in an outbuilding and then, on a wider search of the property, discovered him. He'd woken up in hospital with no recollection of being tied up and locked in a pigpen.

I wave him off from the front door and then return to the sofa. I'm working from home today and am still in my pyjamas and have no immediate plans to change out of them.

I love my new job as the head of communications at a small cyberstalking charity. My boss is brilliant; there's a healthy work-life balance and a relaxed, friendly work environment – none of the stress or greed of MBW, the frowns if you – heaven forbid – actually left on time, or the culture of working yourself to the bone to line the agency's pockets.

No, I've left that well behind, as well as Manchester. I had my priorities all wrong. Work isn't everything. Akshay and I are trying for a baby now, even though the wedding is only two months away. I don't want to put it off any longer. The wedding will be spectacular – a wonderful mash-up of Christian and Hindu religions and traditions.

I was sad to leave our Chorlton house, but with the address having been shared widely online, I no longer felt safe there. Plus, the whole sordid tale was heavily reported in the media, and I became a minor celebrity. Especially since I used my skills to PR myself and put the record straight in numerous national newspaper, radio, and even local television interviews. The most hated woman in the world became the most interesting woman in the world for a little while.

Rob and Cleo are both behind bars, awaiting trial. Cleo is likely to get twenty years for three attempted murders – mine, Rob's and Akshay's – as well as numerous other charges, including arson. Rob will likely get a few years for his part in all of it. I supported his statement that he did all he could to save me, and he willingly agreed to testify against Cleo.

Naturally, it all came out about Cleo's history, with the media digging into her background. Clementine Flickinger, that posh name that I didn't think quite matched her, turned out to be false.

Chantelle Kershaw had a difficult background, growing up with an alcoholic mother, no father, and a string of her mother's abusive, often drunk or drug addict boyfriends in one of the roughest neighbourhoods in Manchester.

That nick out of her ear and ugly scarring came about when one of her mother's boyfriends beat Cleo, or Chantelle, senseless at fourteen and slashed her ear with a knife because she was starving and had asked for something to eat. Her mother hadn't believed that he'd done it and had refused to take Chantelle to hospital to get it stitched. Instead, they'd held her down and cauterised it with the same knife that had been used to slice it, heating the blade over a gas hob first.

Chantelle had developed anorexia after that and left home at sixteen, moving in with a much older man who worked as a mechanic. She left him at eighteen and went to university to do a PR degree, changing her name to Clementine Flickinger when she graduated.

The most shocking revelation was that the man who had slashed her ear died a little under a year later of an overdose in Chantelle and her mother's lounge. But there'd also been a small fire, thought to have been started by his lit cigarette, which had torched most of his body and the sofa he sat on. It was hinted that Chantelle might've had something to do with it, but never proven.

Either way, her traumatic childhood had scarred her, and she had worked tirelessly to move up the social class ladder from poverty to wealth by studying hard, pursuing rich men, and getting well-paid jobs in PR.

But when all her hard work started to crumble, she snapped, blamed me, and became obsessed with taking revenge.

Her ex-fiancé was quoted as saying: 'At first she was fun, charming, the life and soul of the party. But after I'd spent more time with her, I realised there was no depth. She was completely emotionally unavailable. I thought this was because she was having an affair. I've since learnt it was because she was manipulative, deceitful, and cold. She didn't know how to offer emotional support to others because she'd never had any emotional support growing up.'

According to the detective who managed the case, and who stays in close contact with me, Cleo/Chantelle has since been diagnosed with antisocial personality disorder and is receiving treatment. The detective told me that Rob hadn't had an easy time of it, either. He was orphaned at nineteen when his parents died in a horrific accident at the farm involving a tractor. Rob had found their bodies. As an only child, he inherited the farm. His relatives pressured him not to sell, as it had been in their family for generations. So he hired others to run it at the same time as pursuing his IT studies and subsequent career. A lot of burden to have been put on a young man's shoulders.

I turn on my work laptop. It's a bit old and creaky, the newest machine they had at the charity, but I don't mind. As it loads, I tap out a quick WhatsApp message on my new phone to Kemi to say I'm looking forward to seeing her later for some Friday drinks and a gossip.

Tomorrow, Dad, Diane, Toby, and his new boyfriend are coming down from Manchester to stay with us overnight. Akshay has booked the six of us into the best Thai restaurant in town – according to Kemi's wife – and we're all excited to catch up.

While the laptop slowly whirs to life, I touch the almost healed wound on my shoulder. It'll leave a big scar, a reminder of that brutal night. I google for the umpteenth time the name of the honeymoon hotel that we've booked for two weeks and scroll through image after image of pristine white sandy beaches and glistening crystal-clear sea. After all the drama, I can't wait for a holiday.

AUTHOR'S NOTE

Did you enjoy reading *Now You Know*? Please could you leave a review on Amazon. Your review will help other readers to discover the novel and I hugely appreciate your help in spreading the word.

Massive thanks to Brian and Garret at Inkubator Books. Brian is a brilliant editor and a lot of fun to work with.

As always, endless appreciation goes out to my folks, Ann and Brian, for all their support. And to my awesome sister, Kath, who always gives honest feedback.

I'd also like to say a huge thank you to my farm owner friend, Jo, and my firefighter friend, Amy. Both gave me really useful insight that I've included in this novel.

My gratitude to friends and family who have supported me unwaveringly and enthusiastically on my author journey.

And big-ups to all my readers – thank you for taking a chance on me and my novels. Thank you as well for taking the time to read *Now You Know* – I'm very grateful for your support.

Nora Valters
May 2021

ABOUT THE AUTHOR

Nora Valters grew up in the New Forest in the south of England and has lived in London, Manchester, Bournemouth, Oxford and Dubai.

She studied English Literature and Language at Oxford Brookes University before embarking on a career in marketing and copywriting.

Her debut psychological thriller *Her Biggest Fan* was published in October 2020. *Now You Know* came out in June 2021 and *Here For You* in January 2022. She's currently writing her fourth novel, which will be out soon.

Nora loves to travel and has journeyed around the world. She enjoys exploring new places, painting, hiking, and is an avid reader. She's also a bit obsessed with dogs…

Find Nora on her website www.noravalters.com or connect with her on her social media.

ALSO BY NORA VALTERS

Inkubator Books Titles

NOW YOU KNOW

HERE FOR YOU

Other Titles

HER BIGGEST FAN

Published by Inkubator Books
www.inkubatorbooks.com

Printed in Great Britain
by Amazon

81462846R00171